An excerpt from *Bound in Blue*

She rolled over and looked at him, but she didn't say anything, because she was afraid of the ridiculous, lovelorn things she'd say. He drew her into his arms, cradled her against his chest so her cuffed hands nestled between her breasts. She pressed her head against his shoulder, enjoying the comfort of his embrace. Ah, his hair was so soft, and it smelled so good. She sniffed it furtively, imprinting the scent of him in her memory.

"Struck speechless, are you? I guess that's a good thing."

"It was fun. Very fun." It hurt to belittle their incredible scene, their incredible connection, with an adjective like "fun," but it would hurt more to give voice to the depth of her feelings. He might see how infatuated she was, and how foolish. "Are you going to uncuff me?"

He drew back from her. "Not yet."

"I have to go."

"Not yet," he repeated. He helped her up and drew her over by the bed. He sat on the edge of it and tugged her forward until she was standing between his legs. He was dressed now. Well, half dressed. His chest and muscles still beckoned her. She could have traced them for hours, never tiring of exploring him. He looked bemused when she finally dragged her gaze up to his.

"Still set on one time? I'm not trying to talk you into anything, but…you're sure?"

She nodded, hardening her heart against him. He was *leaving*.

"I'll be here a few more days. I work for—"

Her cuffed hands flew to his mouth. "Don't. The more I know about you, the more difficult you'll be to forget."

Cover art by Adrienne Wilder
For Affordable Custom Cover Art visit
http://cityofdragons.daportfolio.com/about/

* * * * *

Bound in Blue

*

Annabel Joseph

Other erotic romance by Annabel Joseph

Mercy
Cait and the Devil
Firebird
Deep in the Woods
Fortune
Owning Wednesday
Lily Mine
Comfort Object
Caressa's Knees
Odalisque
Command Performance
Cirque de Minuit
Burn For You
Disciplining the Duchess
The Edge of the Earth (as Molly Joseph)
Waking Kiss
Fever Dream

Erotica by Annabel Joseph

Club Mephisto
Molly's Lips: Club Mephisto Retold

Chapter One:
Extra

Jason Beck braced in the back seat of the swerving taxi, tapping his fingers on his thigh. *Breathe in. Breathe out.* The smoke, crowds, and hectic commotion of Ulaanbaatar's downtown district were not things he could control.

As much as he liked control.

The cab dodged a drunken pedestrian and turned on a narrow street lit by neon signs, then glided to a stop beside a low building with a scarred, black door.

"This is it?" he asked the driver.

"This is it," the man replied with a knowing smirk. "I hope you have enjoy."

Jason made a conscious effort to return the man's good-natured grin. He knew people perceived him as rigid. Uptight. At Cirque du Monde, he was considered a workaholic in a company of workaholics. He preferred to think of himself as responsible, but at the end of the day he was mostly an out-and-out, three-alarm control freak. Maybe his boss was right. Maybe he needed to loosen up a bit, stop thinking about work so much, even if work had brought him to this far-flung place.

"You're strung so tight," Michel Lemaitre had chided as Jason prepared to leave on his scouting assignment. "I want you to take time to enjoy the local pleasures while you're in Mongolia. I'll be disappointed if you don't."

Jason knew Lemaitre wasn't talking about Mongolia's food or scenery when he talked about *local pleasures*. The man was a hedonist, a sex freak. Jason was pretty freaky too…when he wasn't burying himself in work.

He made excuses for all the time he spent at work, for his obsession with self-discipline and control. He was driven by the ideals of Cirque du Monde—that circus could be entertaining, even visionary, without the use and abuse of animals. The only animals at Cirque were its human artists and performers, many of whom Jason helped train. Michel Lemaitre, the CEO, had mounted productions in cities all over the globe, sixteen productions in all, and that only happened with a hell of a lot of self-discipline and control.

Jason's dedication to Cirque had him moving up the ranks, and he had no intention of backsliding. He'd recently been promoted from the coaching team to the Department of Artistic Development, a promotion that included longer days, a more intense workload, and greater involvement in Lemaitre's decisions. It was a dream come true for Jason, even if his personal and social life suffered. To see an act develop from a scattered hodgepodge of ideas into a polished show-stopper…that brought him more pleasure than he'd ever achieved from serial dating, or casual scening at BDSM clubs.

Then why are you sitting in a cab outside a Mongolian fetish club?

Because of Lemaitre's little lecture? Or because, somewhere deep inside, some part of him wanted *more*? More than Cirque, more than talent development, more than the euphoria of a successful opening night? More than a string of short, controlled relationships with women he barely bothered to know? Michel Lemaitre thought Jason needed to loosen up, work less and experience more pleasure, and maybe, just maybe, he was fucking right.

Jason shoved a hand in his pocket and paid the Mongolian cabbie, then emerged from the taxi onto a littered, cracked curb. He straightened the wrinkles in his charcoal suit jacket, adjusted his collar and tie, and ran a hand over his hair, tamed into a low ponytail. When he walked closer to the building's door, he noticed a hand-lettered sign to one side that read *BDSM Fun Club* in curly letters.

Maybe this would be stupid.

Maybe it would be sexy.

There was only one way to find out.

The burly men inside the door looked him up and down, assessing his suitability as a patron. Ulaanbaatar was Mongolia's largest city—nightclubs and bars abounded—but this club apparently strove for exclusivity. He tried to exude his most austere, exacting-dominant demeanor. Otherwise it was a night in a vanilla bar somewhere, or back to the hotel.

At last the head doorman nodded and motioned him forward. They probably gauged his monetary worth more than his fetish potential, but he was in and that was a good thing. He showed his American passport rather than his French one and forked over the exorbitant cover charge. Well, that was the same all over. Single men paid the most for their pleasures. That done, he was waved toward a pair of black curtains.

"No touch girls," the doorman warned. "Pay for private room, you like. Extra." He emphasized the *extra* with an arch of his brow.

Well, obviously the sex was extra, probably a lot extra for a foreigner with an American passport. It didn't matter, since prostitutes weren't covered under Cirque du Monde's travel budget, not even for a newly-promoted Director of Artistic Development. Jason might hit up his boss for the cover charge, though. Michel Lemaitre loved fetish and owned his own network of BDSM clubs, all called *le Citadel*, one in every city where Cirque had a show. Lemaitre would have visited this club if he'd come to Mongolia, and probably would have taken over the whole damn thing by the end of the night.

Jason entered the main bar and sat at a table near the back, taking in the familiar trappings of the fetish world. Low lights, dark, soundproofed walls, pretty girls writhing in cages in the corners, some nude, some wearing black, strappy lingerie. Others were cuffed to posts or racks, waiting to be played with—for a price. Every woman in the club wore a thick, black collar, even the waitresses weaving between the tables. Most of the patrons sat alone, although a few sat in larger groups, joking and talking.

At the front of the room, a spotlight illuminated a raised platform with a BDSM scene in progress. A short, pudgy man and a very tiny woman were performing some mash up of an English schoolmaster and French maid theme. The woman was cute, if a little shrill for his tastes. Her dominant glowered, brandishing a cane and scolding her in the local tongue. Jason figured he'd do that for a while, talk and lecture and threaten. Titillate the audience to frothing needfulness so by the time the "headmaster" actually started playing with his victim, half the men would be in the back, in the private rooms. Paying extra.

"Good evening, Master."

Jason turned at the soft greeting. A slender, skimpily-attired waitress placed a napkin on his table, her gaze cast down in true submissive style. "May I get you something to drink?"

She spoke English, sweet, slightly-clipped English with a British lilt. He stared for a moment at the delicate flare of her hips above the band of her lace garter skirt, then raised his eyes to her breasts, perfect in her low-cut bra, and then to her slave collar and the sweep of her shiny black hair. Her high, broad cheekbones gave her an elegant prettiness. She was gorgeous. Exotic.

Young.

"How old are you?" he asked. He had standards. He wasn't going to slaver over her unless she was at least eighteen.

Her pale blue eyes met his. *Blue eyes*? Mongolians didn't have eyes like that. Contacts, most likely. It made a pretty effect, although the blue darkened slightly around the iris, revealing her true color. Blue-eyed or dark-eyed, he found her magnificent. Her bronze skin looked so smooth and soft.

"I'm twenty-two," she said. "Old enough." She leaned closer, so her breasts lifted a little from the cups of her bra. She was delicious, so tentative and shy. There was naked flesh all around him, bold, seductive women, but all he could think was, *I want this waitress. I want her tied up. I want her in a cage, peeking out at me in dread.* "Please, Master," she said, interrupting his thoughts. "I'm here to serve you. A drink," she added, lest he misunderstand.

He looked at the laminated page of squiggles she handed him. "Do you have any menus in English?"

"If you need help making a choice, Master—"

"Why are you calling me Master?" It irritated him, because he wouldn't be allowed to master this girl. He couldn't even touch her without getting thrown out. Bouncers massed in the back, watching all the activity in the room.

She looked away, focusing on the couple interacting on the stage. "We're supposed to call our visitors 'Master.' If you don't like it..." She blinked mournfully and looked down again.

"I don't mind it," he heard himself say. Snort. Guh. Wow, she was beautiful. He swallowed hard, fighting uncontrolled arousal. Maybe...*extra*...

No. He'd never paid for sex in his life and he wasn't going to start now. "Can you get me a drink, little slave girl? Something cultural? Local? I've never been to Mongolia before."

"Yes, Master."

She hurried off. He wondered if all these hot little sex workers spoke English, or whether she got his table because she was the only one. He watched the sway of her hips as she headed for the bar, the curve of her ass cheeks barely showing beneath her tight-fitting skirt. The sight of her walking away was worth the cover charge he'd paid.

Okay, enough gawking. She was a cute young woman in a short skirt. No need to be creepy. There were plenty of other women to look at. The dancers in the cages grew more suggestive as men milled around, checking them out, and the girl onstage was finally getting her palms whacked by the schoolmaster.

Her palms? Yawn.

Jason wanted to see her ass played with and punished, her cheeks scarlet with cane stripes. Breasts bared and tortured with tit clamps. In his mind's eye, he pictured his pretty waitress bent over, crying out as he caned her. He pictured his hands on her delicate hips, grasping tight as he plunged inside her pussy...

"Here you go, Master."

Her melodic voice arrested him mid-fantasy-thrust. For a moment he said nothing, because everything that came to mind was inappropriate. *Kneel down. Take out my cock. Suck it.* "Thank you," he finally said in a tight voice. "What is it?"

"It's a Mongolian sort of vodka. It's called *har.*" She bit her lip. "It's very strong."

Good. He needed something to take the edge off his rising desire. He lifted the glass to her in tribute. "To—what's your name?"

She shook her head, tracing the rough edge of her collar. "We aren't supposed to tell our names. You can call me girl if you like, or slave."

"I don't want to call you girl or slave."

"Please, it's not allowed. I need my job here and if I break the rules..." She glanced over her shoulder at the stone-faced bouncers lining the walls. "We're not supposed to talk to any customer too long, unless you pay."

"Fine. Go. I don't want to get you in trouble."

Jason watched her move to another table, wondering if the *extra* also applied to her. Was she one of the girls who worked in the back rooms? He didn't want her to be, because that seemed dangerous and depressing, but at the same time...

Extra. Just a bit extra. Let go of control and do something reckless, just this once. Had she looked hopeful, then disappointed when he sent her away? Was he only imagining it?

He sipped his drink, wincing at the sharp, dry taste. It was like vodka, but stronger, more viscous. He couldn't decide if he liked it or not. As he nursed the clear, cold *har,* the audience grew more vocal around him. Everyone was drinking, and some yelled comments at the couple onstage.

Jason didn't say anything. His mouth felt cottony, and God, a little numb. He was a big guy, and usually had a pretty high tolerance for alcohol, but a few sips of the *har* had his skin flushing and his head whirling. The alcohol hit him so hard, he wondered if he'd been drugged. He stared at the couple onstage, irritated to find them going in and out of focus. The cages in the corners were blurs, the voices around him blathering away in a sing-song language.

He'd only had a few sips…hadn't he? Where was his slave girl? He needed her. If he passed out here, alone, what would happen to him? Just as he reached the edge of panic, she was there, touching his elbow.

"Master? I brought you this."

She held out another drink. He eyed it suspiciously. "Is that soda water?"

"Yes, Master. Mongolian spirits are very strong. Perhaps that drink does not agree with you?"

She leaned down and peered into his eyes. He subdued the urge to grab her, his lifeline to the world. "You drugged me."

"No, Master. I swear, it's the *bar*. They told me to give you full strength but this will be better." She looked around, a furtive glance. "Please. Just wait a few moments and the effects will pass."

He hoped to God she was right, because he wasn't feeling so hot at the moment. He took the drink and gave her the other one. "Thank you."

"Yes, Master."

He stayed upright long enough for her to leave, then leaned on his elbows and sipped the sparkling water. When he finished, she brought him another. He drank all of it, feeling his vision, his thoughts and most importantly, his control, return in slow degrees. Through all of this, the waitress hovered and flitted, watching him. A half hour later, he was almost himself again.

"Thank you for saving me," he said the next time she came to his table. "If I'd drunk much more of that, I'd have been under the table."

She wouldn't meet his eyes. "In Mongolia, alcoholism is a serious problem. The liquors are...what's the term...very high proof?"

"Yes, proof. Alcohol content. At any rate, thank you for protecting me from myself."

"You're welcome. Would you like some other cocktail? Something less potent?"

"I think I'm off alcohol for the night." But he didn't want her to leave. He didn't want her to go off and ignore him. "More sparkling water would be great."

Up on stage, the maid was forced onto a spanking bench, her skirt tossed up and over her back. When his waitress turned to go, he stopped her with a sound.

"Are you ever in the shows?"

She turned back. "No, Master."

"But you wear a collar."

"I have to."

He felt disappointment. "You don't do this in real life? Fetish? BDSM?"

"I am submissive, yes." She glanced at the stage, where the French maid was finally getting her ass beaten by the schoolmaster. "Just not like this."

"Hm. That's an intriguing comment."

He heard her soft intake of breath. She stared into his eyes and he saw something that pleased him. Interest. Maybe even longing. Just as quickly, the revelation was shuttered. "I'm sorry, I have to keep moving. You're certain you are better from the drink?"

Yes, he was better. Too much better. He was sober enough to want her with a needling ache. "I'm totally better." He lowered his voice. "I wish you'd tell me your name."

She wanted to. He could tell she wanted to. He wasn't misreading her longing looks, her attraction. She fluttered her eyes closed. "I can't. I'm not allowed. I'll get you another sparkling water."

She moved away just as a customer across the room stood and beckoned her with a sharp voice. Even when she went to him, the older man shook his finger and scolded her.

Jason didn't know what the man said to her, but heads turned toward them—and toward him. His waitress bowed and apologized to the customer. Soon, two of the suited bouncers approached, trying to smooth things over. As Jason watched, they nodded to the complaining man and yanked his girl toward the back.

His girl. Why did he think of her that way? Because she'd been calling him Master for the last hour? Or because of something else?

It didn't matter. Either way, he wasn't letting them manhandle her like that. He was on his feet, heading for the corner where the three heavies surrounded her. They barked at her in a rough stream of foreign syllables, and she yelled back, gesturing toward the tables and then toward the place he'd sat.

"What's going on?" he asked.

She turned to him, her face tense with anger. "They're angry because they wanted me to serve you strong alcohol. They wanted to get you drunk, take advantage of you and get your money, because you're American—"

One of the men pressed a palm over her mouth to muffle her words. No, that wasn't okay with Jason, not at all. He knocked the guy's hand away from her face, and then they were scuffling, pushing at each other.

"Don't touch her," Jason said, even though he doubted the guy could understand him. "Don't fucking touch her like that."

The bouncer tried to knock him back but Jason was bigger and stronger. And angry. But before he could give the guy the beating he deserved, an army of bouncers convened on him, hauling him toward the door. Okay, he was getting thrown out. That was fair, but he wasn't leaving until he knew she'd be all right. He cast a wild look over his shoulder, but she was gone. Where had they taken her? "Let go of me," he yelled. "Where is she?" Everyone stared as he struggled to free himself. Even the scene onstage had stopped.

Then she was there, storming along beside him, a bag slung over her shoulder. She took off her collar and flung it at the biggest man's face, along with a stream of furious words. The man yelled back at her, a heated exchange that probably included both the words "I quit" and "You're fired." After the doormen extracted payment for Jason's drinks, he and his waitress were forced out the door.

Fucking hell. It was cold outside, and she stood in nothing but a bra, garter skirt, and stockings. He took off his suit jacket and wrapped it around her until she could pull some jeans and a sweater from her bag. People hurried by, minding their own business. *Nothing to see here. Just got kicked out of a fetish club.*

"That was fucking ridiculous." Jason fumed when she handed his jacket back. "Is that true what you said? That they were trying to get me drunk?"

"They do it all the time, to all the tourists who wander in there."

She'd almost said *stupid tourists.* He was glad she stopped herself, because he already felt humiliated enough. "We should go to the police."

"The police won't do anything." Her gaze darkened, her blue eyes snapping in anger. "And I won't get my money. All that work, three weeks, for nothing."

"I'm sorry. I guess that was my fault."

She gave him a look of exasperation and walked away.

"Hey." He shrugged into his jacket and followed her. "Let me make it up to you. How much money were you due?"

She put her head down, walking faster. "I don't want your money. It wasn't your fault, not really. And I hated that job."

"I owe you. You saved my ass in there with that *horror* or whatever it was called."

"*Har.*"

"Will you stop a minute?"

She halted and turned to him, her arms crossed tight over her chest. Inside, he'd sensed some chemistry between them, but now…

He broke out his most charming, seductive smile. "You can tell me your name now, can't you?"

"I'd rather not."

"Would you like to get something to eat? I want to make this up to you but I don't know how." *I'd like to fuck you too, and explore your beautiful body, and kiss those pouting lips.* "There's a place at my hotel, a restaurant with a bar. It's not too far from here." He was propositioning her. They both knew it.

She studied him in silence. What did she see? A stupid American? Some businessman looking for a one-night stand? "I'm not hungry," she said in a flat voice.

"How about some coffee then? We should hang out for a while."

"Why?"

"Because…" *Because my boss told me I had to sample the pleasures of Mongolia.* But that wasn't why. There was something else in play here, some weird, aching attraction that wouldn't go away. "Because you helped me," he finally said. "Because I'm a flailing, clueless American in Ulaanbaatar and I just got you fired, and I'd like to make it up to you, if there's any way."

"There's no way. You can't make it up to me."

She took off again. He lunged and grabbed her elbow. "Please, wait."

She angled herself away from him, but she didn't go. He stared down at her, wondering why he was doing this hard sell. He didn't usually have to. Women threw themselves at him in Paris, due to his reputation as a skilled Dom. Women liked his body, his build. He was tall and muscular, and exceptionally fit from his background in acrobatics. How long since he'd petitioned a woman like this, begged for sex? He hadn't begged yet, but he might if it came to that, if that's what it took to possess this lovely creature *just once*. One time, that was all he needed, or he'd spend his whole life wishing she hadn't gotten away.

"Do you have to leave right now?" he asked. "Where are you going?"

"Home. It's late."

"It's not that late."

"It's cold and I just got fired."

"I can warm you up." He didn't mean the words to sound sleazy. Oh wait, yes, he did.

She shook her head. "You're a tourist. You're going to leave. I don't have time for this."

She set her jaw, her lips pursed into a heart shape he wanted to kiss. She wanted him. He knew it, but she wouldn't have him. She was too angry, too conflicted. And he would leave in a few days, as she said. She didn't want a hook-up, and that was all he could offer her.

"Okay then." He gave up, because he believed in control, even control of his own passionate urges. "Let me give you some money and find you a cab."

"No."

He let out a huff of frustration. "Tell me your name, at least."

"No."

"You're full of *no*s. To be honest, I preferred the *Yes, Master*s. They were pretty great." He put a thumb under her chin and tilted her face to his. "Are you okay? Have those guys roughed you up before? Was it a…a bad place to work?"

She swallowed hard, her gaze flitting away. "It was an awful place to work. This is an awful place to live. You're lucky you get to leave."

Surely she would fit in his suitcase. He could take her home, put a collar around her neck. "My name's Jason," he said, taking out his wallet for a business card. "Jason Beck. If you ever need anything, I live in Pari—"

She pushed his hand down before he could give it to her. "Please, don't tell me. I don't want to know."

* * * * *

For a moment, he looked so angry she thought he might slap her. But no, he wasn't that type of man. He was civilized, disciplined. Controlled. He returned the card to his wallet as she saved his name in her memory. *Jason. Jason Beck.*

When things got bleak—and they were always bleak—she would repeat it to herself and remember there were men like Jason Beck in the world, men with big, graceful bodies and kind eyes.

But to go with him to his hotel, to accept the one-night stand he was offering, that would only bring regret.

Push and pull. She'd always liked that English phrase, and now she understood it. Jason Beck was like some physical force of nature. The harder she pushed him away, the more she felt pulled to him. He had pushed and pulled at the club, pushed away Tomor when he tried to silence her. He'd tried to protect her.

That was an entirely new thing.

"If you're going to leave me with nothing," he said, pocketing his wallet, "at least give me a name. Any name. Otherwise I'll make up something ridiculous to remember you by, like Fantasia Dee-lite, or Cinnamon Buns."

A sense of humor too. She let out a sigh. "I suppose you could call me...Sara."

"Sara? That's an English name."

"If you wish."

His eyes narrowed and his lips turned down at the corners, not in a scary way, but enough to see the dominant personality there. She was certain he was dominant. His posture, his questions, the way he'd defended her at the club, even his persistence in the face of her refusals, all of it communicated dominance and power. This man was used to being obeyed. She wondered what it would be like to do a BDSM scene with him. She could find out if she wanted to, if she wasn't so tired of loss, of hurting.

"Silly Sara," he said. He slid a hand across her cheek, then cupped her face. She studied his Western features in the dim glow of the surrounding shop lights. Wide-set, long-lashed blue eyes, a straight, handsome nose, and full lips that curved in the most seductive way. His shoulder-length brown hair was pulled back, but some stray strands escaped. Under the streetlight she could see other colors reflected in them. Gold, mahogany, brass.

"Why did you call me silly?" she asked.

"Because you won't come to the hotel with me. You want to. You just won't."

"I can't." A stupid, vague excuse, but she couldn't be more specific. She couldn't confess that one night with him would probably destroy her, because nothing afterward could ever live up to it. She hated this sexy, powerful, enthralling, foreign man. She also wanted him more than she'd ever wanted anything in her life.

"I'm very kinky," he said. "You would have a lot of fun with me, because I think you're very kinky too."

She looked around self-consciously. There were people everywhere, coming and going from the clubs. "That's good to know. Let go of me, please."

He didn't let go of her. "Do you have a lover here, Sara? Someone who satisfies your needs? I hope so. I hope that's why you're turning me down."

"I'm turning you down because you're leaving." To her horror, she felt tears glossing over her eyes. That was all she needed, to start bawling in front of him.

"I'm not leaving yet." His fingers trailed over her jaw line. "I have three days. Maybe four."

"One night," she heard herself say. "One time."

Really, Sara? After all that, she was going to give in? But the pull…the pull was so strong.

He let go of her face and touched her arm. "If you like, it can just be a scene. No sex. It can be anything you want it to be."

She gave a short, fluttery laugh. "No sex?"

"Or sex. Lots of sex. Either way."

She hugged her bag closer. "This is a horrible idea."

"We'll probably have a horrible time, but as you said, it's just one night."

She ignored his teasing, his beguiling smile, and spoke with intensity. "I meant what I said. One night, because you're leaving and I don't want to get attached to you only to say goodbye. I don't want you trying to talk me into anything else. Not two nights. Not three nights. One night together. That's all."

"Okay. One night."

"You promise? Say it to me. '*I won't try to talk you into anything else*.'" She stared at him so he would understand how serious she was.

"One night," he said after a moment. "I won't try to talk you into anything else." Again, the teasing edges of his mouth turned up. "You're awfully demanding for a slave type."

"I'm not making demands. I'm negotiating."

He threw his head back and laughed. It was such a rich, surprising sound that she couldn't hold back an answering smile. She hadn't smiled in so long.

One night. She'd earned it this last couple years. She would deal with the loss of him later. She told herself it was better than dealing with the loss of him now.

He slid a hand around her waist and placed another on her neck. He squeezed, not hard, but hard enough to make her tremble. "Do you like it rough or gentle, Sara? Playful or intense?"

She should lie and say gentle. Playful. He was a stranger, someone she hadn't known a couple hours ago.

But he would know if she lied. He stared at her as if he was analyzing every feature, every whisper of emotion on her face. In the end she gave him truth, because they only had this one time. "I like it intense, Master. I like it to hurt." His fingers tightened against her pulse, prompting deeper confessions. "I like it to feel real."

His lips closed a moment, then opened. She could feel his cock against her front, a large, hard warning of things to come. *What are you getting yourself into? He's a huge guy. He could take you somewhere and beat you to death.*

But he wouldn't. She knew with some inborn, animal sense that this man preferred to nurture, not destroy. She could see in his eyes that he understood her—and even better, that he knew how to meet her needs. "Where can I get something hurty in this city?" he asked. "A whip? A cane? I find myself suddenly in need of one."

She shivered, holding his gaze for long seconds. "There's a shop around the corner."

What are you doing, Sara?

But it was out of her hands now. It was force, magnetism drawing them together. Push and pull.

Chapter Two:
Eternal Eyes

At the sex shop, Jason selected a slim rattan cane from a corner case, and a pair of wide leather cuffs. With Sara there to haggle for him, he avoided paying a tourist tax. Even better, he found the items to be of exceptional quality. The cuffs weren't pleather, but real, fur-lined leather in caramel brown. As for the cane, rattan was rattan, but it was finely turned and polished. Sara swallowed hard when he picked it out. The shopkeeper slid the items into a discreet black bag Jason carried under his arm until they could hail a cab.

Now he faced her across a quiet, dim hotel room, raging with lust for her. What had become of his self-discipline? His control? *One night.* He had one night and he wanted to make it good for her, make it a night she'd remember her entire life.

"Undress," he said, pitching his voice low and firm.

She complied at once, slipping gracefully into her role. No bratting, thank God. No nonsense, no games. She stopped when she stood in her lingerie from the club, her pretty bra and garter skirt. "Do you want me to leave these on?" she asked.

"What did I tell you?"

Jason wasn't a yeller. He wasn't a scolder. He said it to her matter-of-factly. It was his gaze that made her cringe and blush.

"You said to undress, Master," she said, bowing her head.

"Did I instruct you to leave anything on?"

"No, Master."

"Does that answer your question?"

There, that was a good beginning. Establish authority and strict boundaries. Instill a little fear. It was his own playbook, one he'd developed over years in the lifestyle. He was a hardass. She might as well know.

She peeled off her lingerie, eyeing the cane as he tested it in his hands. The hotel room was large but austere. Not very classy, but his soft-voiced slave girl lent a sensual beauty to the stark space. When she stood before him, vulnerable and naked, he laid the cane on the bed and approached her. He loved being clothed when his slaves were naked…a delicious imbalance of power. He stroked her cheek, brushed a hand over her soft black locks. Only then did he shed his suit jacket, tossing it over the back of a chair. His tie came next, then he started flicking open buttons.

"I want to touch you," she said in the barest whisper as he shrugged off his shirt.

He didn't answer, only pulled her close against his front, so he could feel the press of her firm breasts and the hardness of her nipples. As he did so, he drew her hands behind her back and held them there for ten seconds. Fifteen maybe. Just enough to make her shake, and then he let them go. "You can touch me if you like. For a moment. Then I'm going to be doing the touching."

She reached out to him, gingerly at first. She stroked his chest and shoulders, and his abs, down to the waistband of his jeans. She wasn't only touching him, although that would have been stimulant enough. She was *admiring* him. His cock pulsed and his muscles jumped to life under her hands. He was stiff and sore from a fourteen-hour plane trip, so her squeezing, massaging exploration felt like heaven. He groaned and flexed as she applied pressure in all the right spots. Every so often she made little approving sounds, as she outlined his abs or measured the width of his shoulders with her palms.

When she caressed lower, holding his gaze, he let her undo his belt, flick open the button of his pants and draw down the zipper. She slipped a hand inside his boxer briefs, peeking up at him from beneath her lashes. His cock bucked against her fingers and his whole body tensed. The way she explored him, like he was some wonderland she'd discovered…

Next thing he knew, she was falling to her knees, tugging down his waistband. He arrested her wrists with a sharp sound. "Naughty girl. Slaves don't take whatever they want. Not my slaves, anyway."

She stared at him a moment, then crumpled into a ball, pressing her forehead to the back of his hand. "Master, I'm so sorry. I beg your forgiveness. How forward I've been!"

Jason loved begging, especially from naked, pretty girls. He let her go on for a while, about what a shamed, worthless slave she was, about how she ought to be punished, and then he grasped a handful of her hair. She looked up at him, real anguish in her features. Ah, she was so good at this. His fist tightened and curled into the silken strands.

"Of course I'll punish you. That's how you learn, yes?"

"Yes, Master."

He heard true submission, true feeling in her response, even though they both knew he wasn't really her Master. She was trying so hard to make this good for him, and he was bound and determined to do the same. He went for the cuffs, buckling them around her wrists with a grim, stern expression.

"You need control, yes?" he asked. "You need to be put in your place."

"Yes, Master."

He clipped the cuffs together in front of her, then held them in one hand. "You're very quick with the *Yes, Masters*. I hope you mean them."

"I do," she cried. "I want to serve you."

Goddamn her, his cock was about to explode. His fingers tightened around her bound wrists. "Let's see if that's really true."

He guided her, face down, to the carpeted floor, until she was propped on her elbows and knees, then he placed a hand between her shoulder blades and pushed her lower. He said "Stay," and then he grasped and lifted her hips.

What a view. This was worth it, all that begging, all that pleading and fighting for his needs. She was smooth all over, delicate and feminine. He couldn't resist assessing her as a scout, a coach. She had a beautiful, proportionate body and long smooth muscles that hinted at hidden strength. At his lightest guiding touch, she arched her back and pressed her knees together, her forehead resting on the floor and her bound hands curled into fists above her head.

"I want you to stay this way," he warned. "No matter what I do to you."

In answer, she uncurled her fists and spread her fingers wide against the rough carpet. Lovely, obedient girl. He went to the bed to pick up the cane, letting her worry and shake for a bit. They'd done no bargaining, no real negotiating aside from her insistence that they play only this one night. How trusting she was to follow him here and let him bind her hands. To let him use a cane on her. He wanted to punish her for her recklessness more than anything.

"Please, Master," she said in a trembling voice as he took up a position behind her. Did she mean *Please, Master, don't hurt me*? Or *Please, Master, just get it over with*? Or did she really love the cane?

"Did you mean what you said earlier, slave girl? About liking pain?" He asked not only for safety's sake, but because she fascinated him and he wanted to know.

She didn't even hesitate. "If you wish to punish me, Master, then I wish to be hurt."

He traced the tip of the cane up one quivering thigh and down the other. "Stop with the role-playing for a second. Answer me honestly. How hard can I go?"

She turned her head back toward him, thinking a moment. "Hard enough to make it feel real."

His already-engorged cock swelled even hotter with pleasure. "Eyes down then. Be still. I'm going to make it feel real for you."

"Thank you, Master," he heard her whisper as he drew back his arm to land the first stroke. He loved these kinds of games, loved to see her body jolt and the pink cane stripe bloom and deepen on her skin. He hadn't started with an awful stroke, no, but it wasn't a warm-up either. She yelped and squeezed her legs together, her little ass cheeks clenching and unclenching. It made a lovely target for the second stroke. Jason was an experienced D-type—he knew canes hurt like hell—but he'd also come to understand that some women needed pain to arouse them, to open them up.

He watched his reckless slave girl, looking for signs that the pain was right. On the third stroke she made a pleading sound and drew her spread fingers into fists. On the fourth stroke she cried out, but then she arched her back higher, as if to offer herself for more. Oh, beautiful. So beautiful. He gave her one more stroke in that graceful position and then paused.

"Spread your legs."

She looked back at him, blinking. He wouldn't repeat himself, because he knew she'd heard him the first time. "Are we a naughty slave girl or a good slave girl?" he asked. "Show me."

Slowly, she lowered her head and inched her legs apart.

"Wider. I want your knees two feet apart and I want your ass in the air. I want to see everything, clit, pussy lips, asshole."

He was mindfucking her a little. Trying to scare her. Trying to make it feel *real*. She complied with a lovely mien of dread, offering her body to him in the requested explicit pose. He took a moment to sit on the bed and admire the picture. Her bare pussy glistened, her engorged clit peeking from between the folds. Her little asshole spasmed with fear or nervousness. Caning a woman wasn't strenuous but she was putting a huge strain on his cock. He stood and moved behind her. Again, her fingers curled into fists above her head, but she didn't cringe, didn't cower. Maybe she whimpered, just a little bit.

Music to his ears.

He enjoyed playing like this, pushing her boundaries, keeping her in the dark about how many strokes she'd get, or how hard they'd become. Right now, she was scared of getting caned on her sensitive center. The prospect was tempting. He slid the tip of the cane along her labia to tease over the bud of her clit. She made a sound somewhere between terror and bliss, lifting her hips for more at the same time she shuddered with misery.

It was so hard not to drop to his knees and thrust into her and fuck her across the floor, but it wasn't time for that yet, not for either of them. Again, he slid the cane over her gleaming slit until she dipped and danced to feel the pleasure of its touch.

"Keep your legs open," he said. "Arch that back and offer yourself to me like a good slave."

She complied with another nut-clenching whimper. Blood swarmed in his pelvis, arousal building to a fever pitch. He drew back his arm and saw her tensing. Waiting.

Yes, this one enjoyed pain.

* * * * *

Sara drew in a deep breath and held it, bracing for God knew what. That was the scary thing about giving a complete stranger control over your body. She'd never done anything like this before, but then, she'd never met a man like Jason before, who was kind and protective and stern, and breathtakingly handsome all at once.

"Oh, Master," she cried out as the cane landed in a line of stinging fire.

It hurt so badly, but it felt perfect. For her, perfect meant terribly painful, but not so painful that she couldn't bear it. She could even feel a whisper of the cane against her clit, a bit of sting but no injury. What a controlled touch. She'd assumed he was experienced at exchanging power, just from the way he talked and the effortless way he took control of her. Even his physique spoke of authority and power. This guy worked out and took care of his body. He was perfectly made, from the top of his broad shoulders to his cut abs to his sculpted thighs and calves. His skin was golden and flawless, his complexion marred only by a bronze scruff of stubble she'd explored with light fingers.

Her boss had taken one look at the well-dressed, towering *Amerik* and told her to get him plastered, so they could lure him into one of the private rooms. In the three weeks she'd worked at the club, she'd seen it done seven times...hapless, passed-out tourists charged an exorbitant amount of money for sexual favors they didn't even receive. But she could tell right away that Jason Beck was a kind man, that he was noble. She hadn't been able to do what her boss asked.

And now here she was. Unemployed and sprawled on his hotel room floor with her ass in the air.

"*Owww.*" The next cane stroke caught her by surprise. Her body surged with adrenaline and her pussy grew even wetter. She ached for him to take her. Big muscles, big body, big cock. She wanted him to push it inside her while her ass cheeks still smarted from his punishment. He was the first dominant man to arouse her to such a fever pitch. And how? A few curt orders, a bit of pain.

More than a bit. He gave her another fiery stroke, then tapped her on the small of her back. "Don't tense up. Spread for me. Open yourself to it."

"Yes, Master," she whispered. She wanted to be open for him. She *wanted him.* She looked back over her shoulder, a look meant to entice, even though she knew it might anger him.

He made a low sound in his throat. "You're a greedy little slave, aren't you? You want my cock? You want to be fucked?" She shuddered as he stroked her clit again with the tip of the implement.

"Oh, please, Master," she begged. She wanted to grab the cane and masturbate against it, slide along its length as her bottom throbbed. He was so good at this...

"Aren't you being punished for lack of self-control? If you want my cock, you need to learn your lesson first, don't you?"

"Yes, Master."

But she couldn't control herself, not when he tapped just so at her clit, just enough to hurt her and tease her and make her ache in the exact, perfect way. She arched against the cane with a sob. She heard his tsk just before she felt the white-hot pain of the next stroke.

"Master, I'm sorry. Please!"

"Please? There's only one person here who needs to please, and that's you. Be a good slave. Be still and let me touch you as I want to. Control yourself."

Sara squeezed her eyes shut, feeling close to tears as the cane's tip molested her most sensitive parts. She truly felt he was her Master and she wanted to please him, even though all of this was a game. She gritted her teeth and steeled herself not to arch and press against the blessed relief of the implement's caress.

"That's right. Still and docile. Fulfilling my pleasure, not yours." His low voice thrilled her, gave her the fortitude to hold motionless as he teased her, on and on and on. It was maybe a minute, but it felt like an hour that he toyed with her clit. She heard him laugh, felt the cane disappear and then felt a light tap across the soles of her feet. "Uncurl your toes, good girl. That's over. The teasing anyway."

But not the—*oww*! He gave her a solid, burning stroke, so she howled and twisted out of her required pose.

"No," he said. "Try again. I thought we were getting somewhere. Kneel straight and open yourself for Master. For Master's will and Master's punishment."

Something about his voice hypnotized her, or bespelled her. Something about him touched her so deeply that she resumed her position, even knowing the pain to come. She'd never cried during any scene in her past, but her eyes felt hot and prickly. She felt a few tears squeeze through her tightly-shut lids.

How much more would he give her? How much more could she take? Her ass felt huge and hot, each stripe of the cane a throbbing weal. What she wanted more than anything was to be joined to him physically, to take his power and mastery into her body in the ultimate surrender. She wanted the memory of his possession, a memory she could treasure forever. She wanted to cry, "When will you fuck me?" but he didn't want that. She understood that he didn't want her demands and greediness, her horny weakness. He wanted her submission. He wanted her to be a pleasing, well-behaved slave.

So she gave him well-behaved. She groveled on the ground, ass up, hands still, his name on her lips. *Master, Master, Master...* He gave her five more strokes, solid, burning ones, and she accepted each one of them with a dignity that came from within, that she never really knew she had.

"My God," he murmured when he was done, and she echoed him silently. *My God, I never knew I had that in me. I never felt enslaved by someone until now.* She'd scened with a few local men in the lifestyle, submitted to their barrage of toys and playthings, clamps and whips and handcuffs and ball gags, but it had never felt *real.* This man had brought out her deepest submission with one rattan cane. He lowered it beside her head and tapped at her cheek.

"You made a mess of this. Clean it up."

Oh...wow. She opened her mouth and he inserted the tip, watching her lick and suck it in a shameless dramatization of what she wanted to do to his cock. Meanwhile, he placed a hand over her spread, exposed pussy. She almost bit off a piece of the cane when he thrust a finger deep in her cleft. His hand was so big, his finger so thick and long. She squeezed on it but she didn't dare hump it the way she wanted to.

Then the finger was gone. She saw his boxer briefs hit the floor, and she heard him putting on a condom. She turned to see his thick cock jutting out from a thatch of dark hair. Her breath caught in anticipation.

"Are you done cleaning that off?" he asked, inspecting the cane. "Good. Now hold it between your teeth, to remind you about the perils of being greedy with Master's cock."

He drew her head back by her hair and made her open wide, and set the cane far back in her teeth so it acted as both gag and reminder. *Don't be greedy. Don't do anything. Let him manipulate you.*

He rearranged her on her hands and knees, still holding her hair so her chest was lifted off the floor. "Now, stay," he said. "My pretty little plaything."

And then he played with her, until her teeth ground against the rattan barrier in her mouth. He traced her sore cane marks, taking his time to study every one, then slid two fingers into her pussy. Then three. It wasn't only the fullness that aroused her, but the aggressive, careless way he did it. She truly was his plaything, his toy to poke and explore at will. He didn't touch her clit, which was certainly on purpose. "You're so wet, little slave. So tight and hot and wet down there. What about here?"

He withdrew from her pussy and pressed a finger against the tight ring of her ass. She tensed but he drove it in anyway, using the copious wetness of her pussy to ease the way. She squirmed and twisted as he pressed deeper. "Enough," he said sharply. "Whose pleasure do you serve?"

"Yours, Master," Sara whimpered, going still. But oh...*wow.* He resumed his "pleasure" while she shook and accepted it. "Very, very tight," he said in an approving voice, when she was fully impaled.

"Nice and tight for Master. I wonder if you could handle two fingers?"

She waited in a silent panic as he withdrew the first finger and added another. She felt discomfort, stretching. A bit of fear. What if he tried to put his cock in there? She'd done anal before, but not with any guy as big as him. He slid his fingers out a bit and then thrust them back in, mimicking anal intercourse. She took quick breaths, biting on the cane. She was still trying to accustom herself to the invasion when she felt his cock at the entrance to her pussy.

Yes, yes, please take me. He eased forward, his cock stretching her pussy just as his fingers stretched her asshole. She felt so full, so controlled. She couldn't cry or beg, or say anything, only make shuddering gasps past the implement in her mouth. He pressed all the way in, until she felt his thighs against the back of her legs. At the same time, he teased her asshole with his fingers, driving them in and out.

It was shameful, raunchy. And it was *him*, which made it wonderful beyond belief. The gorgeous, commanding *Amerik* was joined with her, something she'd wanted since she first gazed into his eyes. She tensed her ass cheeks, keening behind the cane. The stripes on her ass tightened and ached with the movement of her muscles. She turned to watch him fuck her, his rippling torso tapering to sculpted hips that banged against her cheeks.

Now that his cock and his fingers were both comfortably buried inside her, he fucked her faster, harder, so she never had any relief from the fullness of his possession. She braced her tethered hands against the floor and bit down on her gag. She wanted to stroke her clit but she didn't dare, not without his permission. In some way it was the frustration and discomfort that fanned her arousal so high. She was a masochist. She got off on this.

"Please, Master," she cried, her words distorted by the cane between her teeth.

"If you're begging me for anything, you're welcome to continue. But I'll do exactly as I like, and I'll let you come when I like. *If* I like."

She danced on his hand, on his cock, his erotic puppet, and yes, it seemed he held everything in his hands, her desire, her will, and definitely her ability to orgasm. "That's a good girl," he said as she shuddered with the knowledge. He reached around and caught one of her nipples with his free hand, and squeezed it hard, twisting it. She threw back her head in agony, but her pussy clenched at the same time. He pinched the other nipple, brutally hard, brutally uncaring.

"You like that, don't you? Being hurt? Being used for Master's pleasure?" he asked. "I can feel you squeezing my cock. I want you to come hard enough for me to feel it. I want to feel your ass clamping down on my fingers too."

All she could do was groan and obey him. He held her completely in his hands. One hand tortured her nipples as the other frigged her asshole. He pounded her pussy with his huge cock, pounded her so hard she had to brace against the floor. *Master, Master, Master...that hurts. Please, hurt me.*

Her submission and his mastery meshed together into one consuming flame and her orgasm arrived, torment and pleasure melting together. The cane clattered to the floor as she cried out at the power of her climax. This was worth it, surely, the loss to follow. Behind her, her Master reached his own completion, driving deep inside with shattering thrusts. She felt so much joy at satisfying him that she paid no attention to how rough he was.

It was pain. It was pleasure. It was service...and it had never felt quite like this before.

For a while they were still, shuddering together, gasping for breath. Then he ran a hand up her back and eased out of her, first the fingers in her asshole and then the thickness of his cock. She sank down to her stomach on the scratchy carpet, feeling empty. She heard him behind her in the bathroom, washing up.

She didn't want to move, because then this would be over. She was the one who had insisted, *one night, one time.* She hated herself for that, but it was self-preservation. She heard him pulling on his boxer briefs and then his pants. *Goodbye, beautiful cock. It was nice knowing you.* He came to her, sat beside her and stroked her hair.

"So," he said in a low, warm voice. "Real enough? How did you like that?" When she didn't answer, his voice took on a note of concern. "Was I too rough?"

She rolled over and looked at him, but she didn't say anything, because she was afraid of the ridiculous, lovelorn things she'd say. He drew her into his arms, cradled her against his chest so her cuffed hands nestled between her breasts. She pressed her head against his shoulder, enjoying the comfort of his embrace. Ah, his hair was so soft, and it smelled so good. She sniffed it furtively, imprinting the scent of him in her memory.

"Struck speechless, are you? I guess that's a good thing."

"It was fun. Very fun." It hurt to belittle their incredible scene, their incredible connection, with an adjective like "fun," but it would hurt more to give voice to the depth of her feelings. He might see how infatuated she was, and how foolish. "Are you going to uncuff me?"

He drew back from her. "Not yet."

"I have to go."

"Not yet," he repeated. He helped her up and drew her over by the bed. He sat on the edge of it and tugged her forward until she was standing between his legs. He was dressed now. Well, half dressed. His chest and muscles still beckoned her. She could have traced them for hours, never tiring of exploring him. He looked bemused when she finally dragged her gaze up to his.

"Still set on one time? I'm not trying to talk you into anything, but...you're sure?"

She nodded, hardening her heart against him. He was *leaving*.

"I'll be here a few more days. I work for—"

Her cuffed hands flew to his mouth. "Don't. The more I know about you, the more difficult you'll be to forget."

The twinkle left his eyes, replaced by resignation. He drew down her hands and worked at the clasp between the cuffs. "Would you like to keep these? Or will they also make me too difficult to forget?"

"You have to keep everything."

He unbuckled the first cuff, setting it on the bed. "That's fine. I won't mind remembering this. Remembering you." He unbuckled the other one and paused. "You're a very memorable person. A Mongolian woman who speaks English like a proper British person."

"Do I?"

"Almost. It's very charming. I like your contacts too."

"My contacts?"

He pointed. "Yes, the blue contacts. For your eyes." He leaned closer at her expression of confusion. "Or are those your real eyes?"

She gave a nervous laugh. "What else would they be?"

"Some people wear contacts to change their eye color. I thought... Well, I hadn't seen anyone else here with eyes that color."

She lowered her lids, the way she always did when people noticed her eyes. Sometimes people teased her about them, a mean kind of teasing that said *you don't really belong here*. But she'd been born in Mongolia, to Mongolian parents. People whispered that she wasn't her father's daughter, that her blue eyes had come from someone else. She'd have to find out about these contacts, so she could make her eyes gold, or brown.

She looked back up at him and shrugged. "My mother used to say they were blue because I was born outside, and I looked up at the sky, and so my eyes stayed blue. In Ulaanbaatar, it's dirty and polluted, but in the north and the west, the blue sky stretches as far as you can see. Do you know they call Mongolia 'the land of eternal blue sky'?"

"No, I didn't know, but now I do." He squeezed her hands, then inspected her cuffless wrists. "I want to give you some money."

"No. Absolutely no. This wasn't a transaction."

"Of course it wasn't. Sara, I don't want to cheapen what we just experienced. Because we just experienced something. Something you're going to remember every bit as vividly as me."

Exactly. That's why I have to get out of here. She didn't know if it was the kindness in his voice, or the wistfulness, or the beauty of his words, or his insistence on intimacy even as she shied away from it. Whatever it was, it brought tears to her eyes.

"Please," she said. "I have to go."

He hugged her again, tightening his knees around her so she felt enveloped by him. By the time he drew away, she'd mastered herself.

"If you want to give me money," she said, "I would appreciate cab fare, so I don't have to walk home alone."

"I'll take you home."

"No. Please. I'm sorry. I'm thankful for tonight, but—"

"Let me help you."

"I don't need help."

"Your job—"

"I'll find another job. I have another job. The club was for extra money. So…I'll be okay. I don't want you to worry about me."

"But you won't take my money."

"I don't need it." *I don't need you.* She was trying to convince herself. And failing.

He stared at her a long time, though his expression was cloaked. She preferred that. She didn't want to know his thoughts. It would be hard enough to let him go without knowing the real man, the sober, concerned, slightly heartbroken man looking at her right now.

"You'll be my best memory of Mongolia," he said at last. "My eternal girl with the eternal eyes." It was his goodbye, a very poetic one. He released her and she went into the bathroom, cleaned up as best she could, and dressed to go.

Jason walked with her down to the lobby of the hotel and out into the smog and noise of nighttime Ulaanbaatar. He stood out among her fellow Mongolians, with his unusual height and his tousled, brown-golden hair. Even the way he hailed a cab was gorgeous…the raise of his hand, the intent expression on his face. He held the door as she climbed in, giving her money for the driver. "You better bargain the fare," he said. "He'll cheat me."

I'm sorry, she wanted to cry. *I'm sorry this is a dirty, corrupt city that takes advantage of foreigners. I'm sorry I'm leaving you alone. I'm sorry I have to protect myself from you.*

"Thank you," she said instead. "For making it so real."

"You're welcome. Please take care of yourself. My last orders," he said, waving a finger at her. Then her beautiful Master kissed her on the forehead, closed the cab door, and stood watching from the road side as she disappeared from his life.

It was only later, when she went to pay the driver, that she realized Jason had pressed an entire month's salary worth of money into her hand.

Chapter Three: Sara

Jason moved carefully through the second-world circus tent, stepping over rough benches and dodging unrecognizable puddles of matter on the floor. His Mongolian translator pulled her scarf more tightly around her neck and gave him an encouraging smile. He had no idea of her age. She might have been thirty or sixty, with her smooth, broad cheekbones and wide-set, smoky-rimmed eyes.

She was pretty, but nowhere near as pretty as Sara.

She'd been gone one day. Not even one whole day, but he still felt her loss like a hole inside him. He wished he'd never gone to the BDSM Fun Club. If only he'd stayed at the hotel and worked. If he hadn't traipsed off to that damn club like some sex tourist, he wouldn't have met her and he wouldn't have gotten her fired. *And you wouldn't have had a night with her either. You wouldn't have known her submission, or enjoyed that longing in her gaze.* The way she'd touched him, the way she'd responded to him…

Now he was suffering. Sex hangover. He'd spent all morning and a good part of the afternoon fondling her cuffs and masturbating to the scent of her on the cane. No matter how many he rubbed out, he couldn't stop craving her. He couldn't get her out of his mind.

Had she gotten home safely the night before? Would she find another job? A better one this time? He'd given her all the money he could while she was too upset and distracted to notice. Did she have regrets this morning? Was she missing him too?

Jason was supposed to be focused on work, focused on this act Lemaitre was so interested in. Before his promotion Jason had been an acrobatics coach, but now he scouted all kinds of acts in search of undiscovered talent. That was why he was here, not to get torn up over a cocktail waitress he'd met at a kink bar. She'd told him straight out, *one night.* Now he had to get over her. Jason hoped this trapeze act was good enough to warrant all the drama of this journey.

He and the translator finally settled on a bench halfway up the stands. She left an appropriate amount of space between them, causing Jason to suffer repeated bumps from the brawny man on his other side. He sucked air through his mouth rather than his nose. These folks obviously weren't into showers. With the cool temperatures outside, Jason wasn't sure he blamed them. Even in spring, Mongolia was chilly, sometimes snowy. The stands were soon full to bursting with an exuberant Saturday night crowd.

The show started late, without any intro or fanfare. Jason knew within minutes that he'd been sent on a wild goose chase. It might be Mongolia's largest circus, but it had no production values, no polish. It was only a series of acts performed by people who looked every bit as rough as those in the seats. Juggling, a little tightrope, but not very high off the ground. There were muscle men lifting things like oil drums and tires, and a smiling trio of contortionists who balanced bowls on their heads. These acts were interspersed with comedic bits that his translator tittered at but didn't bother to translate.

This ragtag revue brought to mind circuses of the past, before innovators like Michel Lemaitre arrived with glossy lights and special effects and a million-dollar infrastructure whose sole purpose was to create theatrical art. He looked around at the smiling, clapping spectators. What would they think of a Cirque du Monde show? They were so appreciative of this low-level nonsense. A show like *Cirque Brillante* or *Cirque Vivide* would probably cause a riot.

The entire program lasted a little over an hour. The crowd grew restless, and Jason worried that the trapeze act he'd been sent to scout wasn't even going to perform. Then a great cheer went up, pounding and yelling. The children rose to their feet and bounced up and down as a beat-up trapeze dropped almost to the ground, then was ratcheted skyward in uneven tugs. Jason looked up and saw men winching the ropes to the rigging. It didn't look safe, not by Cirque du Monde standards. Not by any standards.

Jason took a deep breath as the trapezists, a man and a woman, took the stage. The man was compactly built, typically Mongolian, with a broad, attractive face. His partner stood with her back to the audience, her dark hair styled in a tight ponytail. She had a gymnast's body, lithe and muscular, beautifully proportioned. Her red leotard was plain in design, but it brightened up the dreary circus tent.

"These performers are well known, very popular," the translator said over the din of the crowd. "The woman's parents also did trapeze, but they died in an accident."

He grimaced, watching them raise and lower the off-kilter bar. "A trapeze accident?"

"A car accident."

Jason glanced down at the note in his hand. The performer's names were miles long, indecipherable. At last the apparatus was ready to go, and the man leaped up and caught a rope affixed to the bar. He used it to haul himself up, and then hung by his knees, extending his arms for his partner. The woman climbed the rope next and he grabbed her by her arms. A warbling soundtrack whirred to life over static-y loudspeakers. At the resounding approval of the audience, the woman looked over her shoulder and smiled.

Jason froze. He knew that smile. He realized now that he knew that body too, that perfect, proportionate body. He looked back down at the note. The man was *Baatarsaikhan*, the woman, *Sarantsatsral.*

I suppose you could call me...Sara.

Just like that, his heart was in his throat. He looked up into the rigging, hoping the trapeze was truly secure. There was no cushion or safety net underneath, no space-age crash mat like they used at the Cirque. He'd been worried before, but now it was his Sara performing. His Sara?

One night, he reminded himself. *You spent one night with her. She's not yours.*

Even so, he didn't want to watch her plummet to her death. He hunched over, biting his nails as the act unfolded. The duo was fast and reckless, doing releases that made his mouth drop open. She did somersaults, flips, and even handstands on the narrow bar. Then she did them on her partner's shoulders while the bar shimmied under them, and he wanted to scream at her, *stop that. Get down! It's not safe.* It wasn't even really a trapeze act. It was aerial acrobatics, with a little suicidal crazysauce mixed in.

So many goddamn releases, so many skills in the air... *Sara, what are you doing to me?* But her partner always caught her, always propelled her into the next move. His strength was amazing, her acrobatics were amazing, but the timing was the awe-inspiring thing. So many opportunities to drop her, but the man caught her every time in smooth, perfect coordination. The translator clasped her hands to her chest and took sharp breaths at each risky stunt. She was enjoying this. Jason was on the verge of a meltdown.

Then the man let go of one of her hands. The audience cried out and Jason tensed, but it became apparent it was part of the act, as Sara rolled into a ball and twisted around in a circle, supported only by one hand. The man's fingers were miraculous, and she moved like water, fluid and sinuous. A flex of arms and legs and she was airborne again, then caught and swung, each muscle in perfect alignment.

The act concluded with a lightning-fast barrage of risky catch-and-release maneuvers, shock and awe as the music rose to a fever pitch. If Jason had her back in his hotel room, he would have caned her to shreds for what she put him through, but she didn't make one mistake. Finally, Sara shimmied back down the rope and her partner followed, and they took a bow for the cheering audience. The translator turned to Jason, her eyes alight in wonder, and she didn't even understand the important things, like how strong the man was, whatever his name was, or the precision of Sara's performance. They had so much potential, so much to offer Cirque du Monde.

He couldn't wait to get her there. She'd have no more worries about a second job, or about money. What would Sara think of the sprawling Paris headquarters, with its luxurious practice studios and cutting-edge training equipment? What would she think of the costumes, the makeup, the flashy sets? He had to get both of them there right away, her and her partner. They didn't belong in this marginal circus, in their plain red leotards, climbing a rope to their trapeze in a rickety tent.

But after last night, how could Jason approach her, professionally, as a talent scout?

After ten solid minutes of applause the program ended and the audience filed out, chattering happily. Jason looked over at his translator. "I need to talk to them. Can you introduce me?"

They made their way behind the curtain, to the dank, windowless staging area. Jason clutched his notes, his Cirque papers that gave him an official, legitimate reason to be here, even though he'd caned and fucked the shit out of Sara last night. Never doing the local-pleasures thing again, no, because Sara with the eternal blue eyes was part of the goddamn act he'd come here to recruit.

The translator led him to the man first. Baat-something-or-other. She pitched into a lengthy introduction, and was midway through it when Sara turned from her gym bag and saw him. Her eyes went wide and immediately flew to her partner. She gave the barest shake of her head. Jason understood the message. *Pretend we've never met.*

It was difficult but he managed as best he could. The translator was still prattling on in Mongolian to the man, gesturing, her voice rising and falling. Jason didn't have the first idea what the woman said about him. "*Cirque du Monde*," he heard in the midst of it. "*Paris*."

"Tell them the offer is immediate," he said, cutting in. "They could come right away, train at headquarters, and be placed in a show after the Exhibition in a couple months."

The translator only spoke to the man, and he didn't seem impressed with what he was hearing. Sara stood behind him, off to the side. She looked shell-shocked. Traumatized. Jason stared at her, trying to express without words that everything would be okay. He assumed from her behavior that this partner must be her lover, maybe even her husband. He wouldn't judge and he wouldn't get her in any more trouble than he already had. He wished he could touch her again, though, fuck her, give her pain, give her joy. They'd had such a wonderful scene together, such a connection. At least now he understood why she'd been so insistent about leaving. *One time. One night.*

The translator prodded him. He'd been so lost in memories that he'd missed her comment. Sara's partner glowered at him.

"They do not wish to come to Paris," the translator repeated in her clipped voice. "They prefer to perform here."

What? They didn't wish to come to Paris? The man hadn't even asked Sara, and anyway, no wasn't an option. They had to come. "Did you explain about the state-of-the-art facilities?" he asked. "About the excellent benefits and salaries? About the beautiful theaters?" He cast a pointed look around the sagging tent.

With a terse smile, the translator addressed the man again. He shook his head and went off on a long spiel that didn't need translating. He wasn't feeling the whole Cirque du Monde thing.

Jason met Sara's eyes. He couldn't understand why she wouldn't speak up. Was she afraid of her partner? Or afraid that Jason would expose what they'd done together?

With one last scowl at Jason, the man took Sara's arm and led her away into the night. Halfway across the dirty, graveled lot, she tried to turn around, but he nudged her forward with a sharp word. Jason almost lost his shit. If they were in Paris he would have said something, or done something, but this rough-edged town probably wasn't the place to start an international incident.

He wanted to, though. He wanted to beat Baat-de-baklava or whatever into the ground and kidnap Sara and put her on a plane. He wanted to rescue her from her lug of a partner and take her to the Cirque, and make her the star she was born to be. They could find her a new act, a new partner. Michel Lemaitre would take care of everything.

Jason wanted to do that, but he could only stand, powerless, as Sara and the other man walked away.

Back at his hotel room, Jason paced and fumed, and sulked over the previously-arousing leather cuffs. Stupid. He was so *stupid.* Of course a gorgeous woman like Sara would already be in a relationship. He didn't know why it bothered him so much, that she could be so open and submissive to him when she was already with someone else.

Well, he knew why it bothered him. Because he was strung too tight. Because he liked the people in his life to be well-behaved and perfect. He wanted Sara to be well-behaved and perfect because some part of him still thought she was his slave.

But she wasn't his slave—she never had been—and he didn't even know if he could get her to Paris now. What a clusterfuck. It was nearly eleven, with a long, cold Mongolian night staring him in the face. He spent a half hour trying to get onto the hotel Wi-Fi so he could bring Michel Lemaitre up to date.

Michel,

The trapeze act was spectacular. Unfortunately, they didn't want to come. Or rather, he didn't want to come. I'm still hoping to speak to the woman again, because I think she might be convinced. She's talented, real Cirque material.

Also, I may have accidentally done a BDSM scene with her and fucked her to pieces. Do you think this will be a problem?

He deleted the last part and sent it, and then collapsed on the bed. At some point, he drifted off, because he woke to a tapping on the door.

He flew to unlock it, his fingers fumbling with the unfamiliar deadbolt. *Please be Sara.* "Hold on a second," he said. "Don't go."

He glanced at the clock. It was almost two in the morning. He opened the door and there she was, his beautiful slave girl. His trapezist with the eternal eyes, now red from crying. He almost kissed her, almost pulled her into a crushing hug, but then he remembered he had to work with her now. Professionally.

"Thank God you're here," he said instead, drawing her inside. "Thank God you came." Then, "Does he know you're here?"

Her face crumpled and she covered her eyes. "No. And I don't know if I should be here."

"It's okay, Sara," Jason said, pushing her hair back from her face. "It's really okay."

"Last night...when me and you..." She cried harder. "I didn't know you were here to see the act, and to offer us the job. When I saw you backstage, I felt so embarrassed. I'm sorry I went with you last night. That I slept with you and left you."

She shrank away from him every time he reached out, or he would have taken her in his arms. "Please stop apologizing," he said. "I wish you weren't in a relationship, but I wouldn't give last night back for anything. Really, there are no hard feelings. I'm more worried about you and your lover. What will he do if he finds out about…you and me?"

She sniffled and swiped at her cheeks. "My lover?"

"Your partner? What's his name?" He made a pitiful stab at the conglomeration of syllables, but Sara cut him off before he could finish.

"Baat? Baat isn't my lover." She made a disgusted sound. "He's just my trapeze partner. We've known each other a long time, and we live together to save money. So he'll know if I leave and he'll try to stop me. I only need to get there, you see? And then he'll probably come."

Now it was Jason shaking his head in confusion. "What? Get where?"

"To Paris," she cried. "To Cirque du Monde. Baat won't come, but I want to go." Her voice shook with emotion, or perhaps fear. "Is it possible for me to come without him? Do you still want me after…after what went on last night?"

Jason fell silent, confused by the idea of how he could possibly not want her. Especially now that he really couldn't have her again.

"The past is the past," he made himself say. "See, if you'd only let me finish when I started to tell you where I worked."

"I'm sorry."

"Don't apologize again. I mean it. Let's start over, okay? So, you want to come to Paris?"

"Yes! If I go, perhaps he'll come too. Otherwise we'll both stay here forever, and this isn't the life I want."

Her gaze pleaded with him to understand, but he understood completely. She'd learned flawless English. She'd taken a job at a sex club to raise extra money. She'd had a plan to escape her current situation, and thank God, he could help her with that.

"I have the money you gave me," she said, reaching in her bag. "And my passport. Is it enough to get there? I can pay the rest back later, out of my earnings."

Jason tucked the currency back in her bag, and trapped her shaking hand. "Cirque du Monde will pay for everything. They'll handle the visas and work permits, all that. If you're anxious to go, we can swing by your place and get your things, and leave as soon as tomorrow."

She shook her head, bursting into tears again. "No, see? We can't get my things. Baat won't let me go. I had to sneak away."

Jason stared at her. Again, the words "international incident" pinged in his brain. But she was a grown woman with money and a passport, and a job offer. Well, presumably she had a job offer, even if Baat wasn't coming. Jason would pay to keep her in Paris himself, if it came to that. But he didn't think it would come to that.

"Are there any legal reasons you can't go? A contract with Baat, or Circus Mongolia?"

She shook her head. "No, there's nothing."

"So it's the whole lure-your-partner-to-Paris-by-stealing-away-in-the-night gambit?" he asked. "You're sure about this? It's a long trip."

She nodded, touching her lips. "I'm sure I want to go."

Jason thought she looked awfully conflicted for someone whose mind was made up. "What about tonight? Where will you stay?" He couldn't hold back the words, although he tried to. "Would you like to stay here? As my guest, of course. We don't have to..." *Attack each other. Fuck each other to pieces. Fall into our true roles—Master and slave.* Her hair was still damp from a shower, her face free of the vampy makeup she'd worn at the sex club. She smelled like flowers and looked like innocence.

Oh God. As much as he wanted to, he couldn't play with her again. Professionalism. Boundaries. They'd be working together in Paris since he was in charge of new act development. Even as a coach, he'd never slept with his charges.

"You look exhausted," he said, getting up to cross to his suitcase. "Why don't we finalize our plans in the morning when you're rested?" He handed her a bottle of water. "Drink at least half of this, then lie down on the bed and close your eyes."

Damn it, that was his Dom voice. He didn't know how else to behave around her, but he had to figure it out. *Professionalism. Boundaries.*

She gave a little sigh, a shiver revealing just how exhausted she was. She drank the water as he'd told her, then recapped the bottle, kicked off her shoes, and went into the bathroom. When she returned, she stopped by the narrow bed. "I don't want to take up your space. Maybe I should just—"

"What did I tell you to do?"

She blinked at him, then answered quietly, "You told me to lie down on the bed."

She's not your slave. You shouldn't do this to her. But in his heart she was his. She cried out for his control with her eyes, her body language. The air between them changed, vibrated with longing and emotional resonance. Slowly, with the grace of a slave, she climbed onto the bed and lay back. Blood filled his cock even though this wasn't a sexual moment. Her obedience alone aroused him.

He pulled the blankets up to cover her. "Close your eyes."

She did as he asked, but her whole body was tense. Jason left her and went to his computer, because if he touched her, if he went anywhere near her, he'd lay waste to her body.

Instead he composed another note.

Michel,

Sara (trapezist) is coming. She's going to need shelter, clothing, and money right away. Please have H.R. purchase another ticket for the flight 23 May.

He knew the ticket would be in his inbox in the morning, that Lemaitre would never fail an artist in need. His boss might be angry the partner wasn't coming, he might demand explanations, but he'd let Sara come and prove herself.

And if she woke in the morning and changed her mind? He'd have to convince her to go, explain that her destiny lay elsewhere.

She was an artist with great potential. She had no business waitressing at a sex club for extra money, in a noisy, dirty city in Mongolia. She belonged in Paris, under Michel Lemaitre's wing.

He turned back to the bed to catch her watching him. He made a soft, chiding sound. "Why are you still awake?"

She wrenched her eyes shut. Adorable, obedient slave.

No, not your slave.

He crossed to the bed and shed his shirt, but left his jeans on. *Professionalism. Self-control.*

"Is it okay if I sleep next to you?" he asked, sliding under the covers. "I won't do anything, I promise."

Her eyes were still shut tight. "It's okay if you want to," she said in a quivery voice. "If you want to do something, because..."

"Because what?" he asked when she didn't finish her thought. *Boundaries, motherfucker!* "Come here."

She turned and pressed against his front, and held onto his shoulders. It was like she was trying to burrow inside his chest. "I can't say it. I can't explain."

Both hunger and understanding surged within him. Somehow, they were connected this way. "You don't have to explain. I feel it too. However, we're going to be working together in Paris. It would be better if we...if we..." He lost his train of thought tracing the slender column of her neck.

She sighed and looked up into his eyes. Blue, such a crazy, pale blue. "Better if we what?" she asked.

"Better if we keep a professional distance."

She was plastered against his front, every inch of her pressed to every inch of him. When she moved her hips, his cock ached in response. He tightened his fingers around her neck. She could still breathe, but only because he let her.

"Oh, please," she whispered. "Please, Master."

Fuck boundaries. They were obviously incapable of boundaries. "Naughty girl," he said, nudging her legs open. "What did I tell you to do?"

"You said to lie down and...and close my eyes."

He kissed her hard, a first kiss, a demanding kiss as he stroked her pussy through the barrier of her jeans. No, it wouldn't do. He needed more. He needed all of her, right now. He yanked at his button and zipper, pushing off his pants. He turned to her next, stripping her naked. She was as beautiful as he remembered. Even more beautiful, because this time he wouldn't have to let her go. "Close your eyes," he said when their gazes locked. "Be a good slave."

He got up and crossed to his luggage for a condom. He wanted her mouth, had dreamed of her Cupid's-bow mouth since the moment he met her. He needed that mouth, and now seemed like a good time to take it. Her chest rose and fell as he rolled on the condom. He grabbed the headboard and knelt over her, trapping her shoulders between his knees. "Eyes closed, mouth open, little slave. Open wide."

She obeyed with a sob, and stuck out her sweet pink tongue. He almost came right then, because she was so eager, so willing. He shoved himself between her lips, not politely or tentatively, but with the authority of an owner. He owned this mouth. She offered it to him with no compunction. He didn't stop sliding forward until she gagged. Her hands flew up and he grabbed them.

"Okay. I know." He eased back and then forward again, penetrating her slowly, watching her lips stretch wide to accommodate him. He wanted to bury himself in her throat, but he controlled himself. Time for that later. Time for so many things. She moaned as she took him as deep as she could, then he pushed himself a little deeper. She gagged again, tears squeezing from beneath her closed eyes.

"What a good girl," he gasped. "Jesus fucking God." He pulled out of her mouth because he'd come in five seconds if he didn't. He slid down her body, tugging at his cock, anxious to be inside her. He grabbed her hands and held them above her head, and pressed inside her tight pussy, inch by inch.

He belonged there. She was his. He fucked her with quick, hard strokes, bearing her body down into the bed. "You see, you don't have to explain anything. It's because of this, yes?"

"Yes, Master," she gasped.

"Because your body was made for me. Because your pussy is mine, and that beautiful little mouth. Every part of you, all made for Master's cock. Lie down and close your eyes, and be mine, little girl."

"Yes, Master, I'm yours. I want to be yours."

There was no wanting about it. She just was. He kissed her again, thrusting inside her, controlling the movements of her hips. Within seconds he could feel her coming, her pussy clamping hard and rhythmically around his length. He emptied himself inside her, letting her orgasm milk him dry. As he came back to earth from wherever he'd gone, he could feel her fingernails embedded in the backs of his hands. Slowly, as they rested together, her fingers opened.

He subdued the urge to make some crack, to diffuse the frightening power between them. *Jesus, that was crazy. What the hell was that? What's going on?* At some point they'd figure out what was going on, but he knew that no woman, no submissive, had ever affected him like she did. In the end, all he said was, "Are you okay?"

She didn't answer. Her breathing was light and slow. "Yes, you should rest," he whispered. "Tomorrow will be a busy day."

He covered her with the blankets and brushed a kiss across her forehead, and let his exhausted slave sleep.

Chapter Four: Flight

Sara woke in the dim hotel room and looked across at an empty pillow. She bolted up in the bed, holding the sheets to her chest. Where was he? Had he left her?

No, Jason Beck was there, near the window, at a small table. He smiled at her and she felt sheepish for her panic, then a flush burned over her face as she remembered the heated intimacy of the night before. *Eyes closed, mouth open, little slave…*

"Good morning, Sara." His intent expression told her that he remembered too. He gestured to the paper bag in front of him. "I ordered some breakfast, if you'd like to get up and eat something. We should probably leave for the airport by noon."

She didn't know what was in the bag, only knew she was starved. She pushed her hair back, wincing as tangles caught on her fingers. She must look like hell. "I'm sorry I fell asleep."

His laugh was low and rumbling. "You needed sleep. I'm jetlagged, so I've been up for a while."

He looked fresh and groomed, from his damp, shoulder-length hair all the way down to his weathered boots. He wore dark jeans and a beige, marled sweater that complemented the earth tones of his hair. She used to think Baat was tall, but Jason was taller. Even sitting in the chair, he looked rugged and long-limbed. He stuck his legs out and flexed them, then crossed them at the ankle.

She felt suddenly, inexplicably shy. He'd fucked her now—twice. Not just fucked her but broken her down into a quivering pile of slave girl, and now he sat across from her with such casual ease while she was freaking out inside.

She went into the shabby hotel bathroom and did her best to fix her appearance. She brushed her teeth and showered, but she had to put on the same clothes she'd worn the day before. Baat would have suspected if she'd packed a suitcase. How had it come to this? She'd been living like a vagabond ever since her parents died, ever since her safety net disappeared. She wanted security and safety more than anything in the world. Jason said the Cirque would take care of her, that they'd take care of everything.

She hoped it was true.

When she came out of the bathroom, he crossed to her and put his hands on her shoulders. "How are you feeling this morning? Okay?"

"Yes, okay." She nodded, searching his eyes. What would happen now? What would happen when they got to Paris? Would he be her lover? Her Master?

"This is all pretty crazy, huh?" he asked.

She swallowed and nodded her head. "Crazy in a good way."

The corners of his mouth turned up, then his lips were on hers. Warm, soft, encompassing. His hands traveled over her, tracing her hips, her ass, before wandering up to clasp her shoulders. His kiss felt rough but gentle, the experience punctuated by occasional tugs of her hair. This meant something, surely, this heated embrace, this kiss. He wouldn't do this if he meant to dump her once they got to Paris. They had something more going on. Didn't they?

He pulled away, but she still clung to him, unbalanced. His sweater felt soft under her fingers. "I like you," she whispered in the understatement of the year.

"I like you too," he said, smoothing back her hair. "I'm excited you're coming to Paris. I hope, when we're there..."

He left the suggestion trailing and she picked it up with an avid nod. "I would love to spend more time with you. We can do whatever you like."

He made a teasing, warning sound. "You should probably figure out what I like before you offer me whatever I like."

"I only meant that I was open to exploring…you know…some kind of relationship between us." She didn't know if she'd said too much, or not enough. Her English was pretty good, but she'd never engaged in these kinds of negotiations.

To her relief, Jason smiled and kissed her again. "There will definitely be 'some kind of relationship' between you and me. But for a while...in the beginning..." He paused, his smile fading. "In the beginning, we'll need to be discreet. My behavior toward you would be considered unprofessional by the people I work with. Inappropriate, really. It's best if you don't tell anyone how we met."

"I understand. The sex club, the BDSM."

"Oh, you don't have to hide that. At the Cirque..." He paused. "Well, I'll explain later. It's not the BDSM that's inappropriate. It's that I came here to scout you as an act, so if we return as Master and slave, with you wearing my collar, some eyebrows are gonna go up."

Sara touched her neck. "I don't like collars anyway. They remind me of work."

He traced over her fingers, trapping them in his hand. "No collars then. Just you and me, and this connection we share. When the time's right, if everything works out, we can be more public about our feelings." He squeezed her hand and let it go. "We'll figure things out. For now, sit and eat something so we can get to the airport with plenty of time to catch our flight."

While she was in the shower, Jason had laid out fried bread, millet and yogurt, and milk tea. She was so hungry it tasted like heaven, even cold and slightly congealed. Halfway through, she slowed down and made herself savor it. She wouldn't have these familiar foods in Paris. Everything would be different, and she'd probably feel homesick.

While she ate, Jason moved around the room, collecting his clothes and toiletries and shutting down his computer. She was so infatuated, it was a pleasure just to watch him pack. "What is Paris like?" she asked.

He turned to her with a bemused expression. "What *isn't* Paris like? It's a big city. You can find almost anything and do almost anything there."

She traced the rim of her cup. "What do they drink at breakfast?"

"Coffee. Tea. Somewhere in Paris, I'm sure you could find milk tea and Mongolian bread, and *tarag*."

He said the word for yogurt with a stilted accent. It touched her, that he tried to speak her language. She blinked down at the last of her meal.

A moment later, he stopped packing and came to sit with her. "It's normal to feel scared. But I promise, you won't be alone. I'll be there, and you'll have a coach and a physical therapist, a whole team of folks who'll want you to be successful. If Baat doesn't come, they'll find you a new partner, a good match, so the two of you can start working on an act together. There are always new shows in the works, and older shows that need new material, like you. You're something fresh that no one's ever seen. When someone's talented, when they have vision and skill and drive, Michel Lemaitre takes care of them. He'll take you as far as you can go." He shook his head, letting out a soft laugh. "Trust me, he's going to love you."

"Who? Mee-shell Le-May...?"

"Michel Lemaitre," he said, writing the name on a piece of hotel stationary. "Your soon-to-be boss. He lives for performers like you, the ones who have that fire in them."

There was some shadow, some hardness in his expression that made Sara think he didn't completely approve of Michel Lemaitre. She chewed at the corner of a nail, a horrible habit, although short nails were necessary in trapeze. Would Michel Lemaitre approve of her?

She stood and started to clean up her breakfast things. They were going to leave for the airport soon, and once they were there, she couldn't come back. She was abandoning her homeland—and her long-time trapeze partner—to follow her dreams. Was it worth it? She had a paralyzing moment of doubt.

Jason took her in his arms, speaking to her in an achingly tender voice. "Everything's going to be great, Sara. But if you're not ready to make this decision, that's okay too. If you want to stay, you can stay."

"I don't want to stay," she said against his shoulder, and she realized she meant it. "I want to go."

"Let's go then. If you get to Paris and you don't like it, you can always come back."

But she couldn't come back. That's what he didn't understand. Baat would never forgive her for doing this selfish thing. Even if he gave in and came to the Cirque, he would never forgive her.

Oh, but Jason's arms were so strong around her, and her dreams were so close. A fourteen-hour flight, and her life could start over. She'd be part of the world's most famous circus.

And this strong, kind, masterful man would be with her. That would be the most wonderful thing.

* * * * *

Sara was quiet during the cab ride to the airport. Jason couldn't blame her for feeling pensive. For doubting. She had nothing with her, only her dreams and convictions. She'd put her life in the hands of a stranger she'd just met. She was either very brave or very stupid, and he didn't usually go for stupid women, so he had to bank on brave.

As for him…he fought his own doubts. Perhaps he should have delayed this abrupt departure, asked her to mull over her choices a little longer. Perhaps he shouldn't have slept with her again last night. Impulsive, unprofessional behavior, but what could he do? She had a way of stripping his self-control. Him, Jason Beck, the most controlled, by-the-rules guy at the Cirque. Even now, he was aware of her every movement, every sigh and every shift.

About halfway there, she sat up straighter in her seat. She spoke to the taxi driver in Mongolian and he eased to the side of the road, stopping on a corner. She turned to Jason. "This will only take a minute." She spoke again to the driver and got out of the car.

Jason followed, afraid to let her out of his sight, but she only went a short distance, to an alley beside a soot-blackened cement building. A small, circular heap of rocks nestled just inside the corner, against the wall.

"My parents died here," she said, turning to him. "Almost two years ago now. A drunk driving accident." She knelt down and replaced a few stones that had come dislodged from the cairn. "Baat helped me build this to remember them."

Yes, the accident. The reason she had no money, the reason she had to make her way alone. Jason looked back toward the cab, then leaned to help her. "Did they catch the person at fault?"

"The person at fault was my father. He drank a lot. Alcoholism is a—"

"Serious problem in Mongolia. Yes, you told me, that first night." When they stood, he took her hand, wanting to comfort her. "I'm sorry you lost your parents."

She didn't seem to want comfort. She pocketed one of the smallest stones and looked up at the sky. It wasn't very blue in Ulaanbaatar. It was smoggy and cold.

"Last chance," he said quietly. "Last chance to stay."

She shook her head. "I've been leaving for a long time. There's nothing for me here."

They rode the rest of the way in somber silence, then the bustle and confusion of the airport swallowed them up. He kept hold of her hand, like a father corralling a child, until they found the correct gate and boarded. Since they'd bought Sara's ticket at the last minute, they couldn't sit together on the plane. She sat two rows in front of Jason, on the aisle, so at least he could watch her. From time to time she turned to look at him, as if he might disappear.

He wasn't going anywhere.

Not now, but she might have to leave him at some point. There was only one Cirque show in Paris. The rest of them were spread all over the globe. Some were touring shows that moved from city to city, pulling up roots every six or eight weeks. He hadn't warned her about that, hadn't explained that Paris would only be her temporary home. If she was placed in Stockholm or Berlin or Rome he'd have to let her go, or leave his job in Paris and go with her, doing whatever was available at her new show. If they didn't need acrobatics help, he might have to move into physical therapy, or nutrition. Or costuming.

He shuddered. Costuming? Maybe, if it meant staying close to her. Even two rows away in an airplane felt too far.

Fortunately, they'd have time before they had to make hard decisions. The Exhibition wasn't until August. Anything could happen. Maybe things would burn out between them. Maybe she'd fall for someone else. There were plenty of compelling Doms at Cirque, not counting the Uber-Master himself, Michel Lemaitre. Lemaitre would notice Sara right away. He'd sense the purity of her submissive nature and he'd want her. If he made a move on her, Jason would have to publicly claim her as his own or else release her, because Lemaitre wouldn't accept anything else.

Damn Lemaitre. He hoped Sara didn't fall under his spell. Lemaitre wasn't a nurturer. He was a gauntlet, a survival course. Jason didn't want that for her. He wanted to challenge and control her, but he wanted to take care of her too.

She'll get to decide what type of mastery she wants. Not you.

It was a bittersweet arrival in Paris, because he had to give up his guardianship of her. She belonged to Cirque du Monde now, and even at three in the morning, representatives were there to greet them and help with Sara's paperwork. One of them, motherly Meg, took charge of Sara, clucking over the dark circles under her eyes. She assured Jason she'd get Sara settled in the dormitory apartments. It wouldn't have been appropriate for Jason to invite himself along, although he wanted to.

Instead he hugged Sara and pressed his cheek to hers. "You'll be fine," he said in her ear. "As soon as you feel ready, you can check out the practice facility and meet your new coach." Whoever that was. All the coaches were good, but he hoped she got the best one, one who would appreciate her unique qualities.

Meg cleared her throat, staring at him, and Jason released Sara. "My number's in the Cirque directory," he said, trying to sound casual. "If you need anything."

Jason needed something. He needed to take Sara to his BDSM-equipped bedroom and lose himself between her thighs, but that wasn't happening. Sara deserved to start her Cirque career on her own merits, not as a Director of Artistic Development's fuck toy. They exchanged a brief, secret smile, then Jason left her in the capable hands of Cirque's relocation specialists.

His capable hands would have to wait.

* * * * *

Jason reported to Lemaitre's office the following afternoon as requested. Over the past five years, he'd managed to earn some measure of respect from the man, but one never really felt comfortable in Lemaitre's presence. *Le Maître*, they called him at his clubs. The Master. With his black hair, carved features, imposing build, and piercing blue eyes, he lived up to his name.

Lemaitre glanced up from a file on his desk when Jason knocked. "*Viens*," he said. "You have returned from the Asian steppes."

"Yes, from my first and last trip to Mongolia. Next time you're pissed at me, dock my pay instead."

"I sent you because I trust you, not because I was angry at you. Although..." He snapped the file shut. "I am somewhat upset. You only brought me half the act."

Jason slid into the seat across from Lemaitre's desk. "I brought as much of the act as I could."

"You brought her, or you smuggled her out?" he asked in his clipped accent. "I hear she arrived with nothing but the clothes on her back."

How to explain it? Her desperation and his impatience to get her out of the country? "It was a rushed acquisition, yes. But clothes are cheap. Things are cheap." Lemaitre's steady gaze dragged the rest out of him. "I didn't want to leave her there."

His regard sharpened. "Why? What was her situation? Your note explained nothing. Why didn't her partner come?"

"Her partner wasn't Cirque material. No artistry, no imagination. Believe me, you got the better half."

Jason fell silent, unsure of Lemaitre's mood. After a tense pause, the man leaned back in his chair and flicked the edge of the file.

"Perhaps you have brought us a treasure," he said. "I hear she's already on the practice floor, anxious to begin. You are well?"

"I'll be well if I never have to go back to Mongolia. How about that?"

"No sense of adventure." Lemaitre shook his head and rose to his full height. "Come. Introduce me to this new trapezist."

The men left the office complex and headed out into the larger facility, toward the soaring aerial arts space. While they walked, Jason talked to Lemaitre about Sara, trying not to betray his feelings for her. He definitely left out the fact that he'd slept with her—twice. He also shared his impressions of the Mongolian circus, from the Soviet-era facilities to the lack of production values. Lemaitre nodded, as if he knew all of it already. He made it his business to know everything about everything, especially in the circus world.

"So, where are you thinking about using her?" Jason asked. "Which show?"

"Do I have to decide that now? *Brillante* perhaps."

"Vegas?" Jason choked on the word. He couldn't see Sara in Las Vegas. It was too crazy and hectic, and it would place her so far away. "I didn't realize *Brillante* needed a new act."

"We always need new acts. People have children, family emergencies, injuries, and they must leave for some period of time. You remember Kelsey Martin?"

"Yes, I remember her." Jason had trained her a couple years ago, until a man named Theo Zamora had commandeered her for an aerial silks piece in the Marseille show, *Cirque de Minuit.* "Something happened to Kelsey?"

"Nothing major. A shoulder injury that needed surgery and a few weeks' rest."

"So Sara might go to Marseille?"

Lemaitre waved a hand. "That temporary act is already in place. As I said, I don't know yet where I'll send her. Or why you're so wrought up about it," he added with an assessing lilt to his voice.

Jason looked at the floor, avoiding his gaze. "I scouted her. Why shouldn't I be concerned about her future?" He quickly changed the subject. "Do you have someone in mind for her new partner? If the old guy doesn't come?"

"I'm going to get the old guy to come."

"You won't be able to."

Lemaitre shrugged. "I have a way of getting what I want. In the meantime I've found her the perfect coach. Trapeze expert." Michel pushed open the door. Jason saw Sara first, sleek and slender in her Cirque du Monde training uniform. Then he noticed the dark-haired man hanging by his knees above her, offering French-inflected directions.

Jason turned to Lemaitre. "Theo? Seriously?"

"He knows trapeze better than anyone. He's done aerial work all his life."

"He's a performer. He and Kelsey have an act."

"He'll be a coach for the next couple months, while Kelsey rests her shoulder. Until the Exhibition, at least. It's perfect timing, no?" Lemaitre watched as Sara tucked into a tight somersault, then caught Theo's hands on the downswing. "You see? Timing is everything in trapeze."

Jason pursed his lips, declining to comment. He respected Theo, but the aerialist had a complicated past. Back in the day, before he'd married Kelsey, Theo had been Lemaitre's right-hand man at the Citadel in Paris. He'd partied and drank and slept around a whole fucking lot.

He's changed, Jason thought to himself. *Kelsey's reformed him. It'll be okay.* Sara watched her new coach as he spoke to her upside down, indicating a change in position. When she did what he wanted, he praised her effusively, so her face lit up in a smile. Now Jason remembered why he didn't like Theo. The ladies always melted for his accent and his dark, brooding eyes.

Theo noticed them then, and lowered Sara to the mat before he flipped down off the trapeze. The two of them walked over, and Theo extended his hand.

"Jason Beck. Long time, no see."

"Hi, Theo. How's Kelsey?"

"Ah." Theo shrugged. "She's enjoying a little rest. You know, she needed her arm fixed. It's still tricky, from that one time she—"

Fell. Almost fell. All three men looked at Sara and decided not to continue that line of conversation. Jason greeted Sara next, trying not to be inappropriately familiar. A handshake, a professional nod. The lights and blue mats made her eyes even prettier. She blinked at him. This was awkward, so awkward. *I wish I was fucking you right now, Sara. God help me.*

"What did I tell you?" he said to her instead, waving an arm around the facility. "Better than Mongolia?"

"It's amazing."

He turned to introduce her to his boss. "Sara, this is Michel Lemaitre, Cirque's owner and director. I suppose you might say all of this is his."

Lemaitre shook his head. "It's not mine. It belongs to my performers. *Mademoiselle Sarantsatsral.*" He said the rush of foreign syllables without a hiccup. "I'm so pleased you're here."

"You can call me Sara," she said when he took her hand.

"Sara, then. All is well? You're getting along with Theo? We thought you might rest a few days before your training began in earnest. And we must lure your partner here, no? We need both of you together, making your magic."

As Sara and Lemaitre spoke, Theo leaned toward Jason and raised a brow. "Where did you find this one? Good raw material."

Jason scowled, recalling Kelsey when she'd arrived at Cirque du Monde. Jason knew too well what Theo had done with *that* raw material.

"Oh, these frowns," Theo sniped in French. "You always think the worst of me. I am very much in love with my wife. I won't pervert your sweet little muffin."

"She's not my sweet little muffin," Jason muttered under his breath.

While he and Theo batted at each other, Lemaitre had drawn Sara away for a more private conference. There was something in the way he studied her, some heightened interest. Just as Jason suspected, she'd caught Lemaitre's eye. Sara stared at the Cirque boss, blinking, nodding to whatever he was saying. Probably something along the lines of "*Would you like to be my sex slave? The position comes with a lot of perks.*"

Theo followed his gaze. "It's not me you have to worry about, eh?"

"She's too young for him."

Theo burst into laughter. "They're never too young for him. As long as they're legal."

Jason didn't find the situation funny. "I don't want him messing with her. How did you keep him away from Kelsey?"

"Kelsey was mine and I let him know it. If you want to keep him away from Sara, let him know she's yours."

"She's not mine," Jason said, feeling heat creep along his hairline.

Theo looked at him sideways. "*Non?* Well. She's a smart girl. I'm sure she can handle herself with Lemaitre." He jerked a chin in their direction. "He likes her. It assures her career."

"Her talent assures her career."

Theo smirked. "As you say." He thought a moment. "Now that we're back in Paris, you'll have to stop by *Rue des Jours* and see Kelsey. She's going out of her mind with nothing to do."

He said it in such a way that Jason understood she had plenty to do, all of it involving Theo, sex, and their Master/slave relationship. Lemaitre's beckoning finger rescued Jason from further conversation. Both men joined him at Sara's side.

"We were speaking about the act," said Lemaitre. "Jason, you'll supervise with Theo? Help develop the performance? Handle the Exhibition side of things?"

His boss wasn't really asking. He was telling him to do these things. "Of course," Jason answered. "Maybe Cameron for her partner? He's done aerial before."

"But not trapeze." Lemaitre thought hard a moment, then turned to Sara. "For now, you can train with Theo as a partner. Until I convince your young man to join us here."

"Do you think you can?" she asked, clasping her hands. "Baat's very good. He's only wary of leaving Mongolia. He doesn't speak French, or English, and he's never traveled. But if he understood the opportunity here..."

"I'll do my best," Lemaitre promised. "But if he won't come, we'll find you another partner. We want you to reach your full potential. In the meantime..." He gestured toward her new coach. "You'll be in excellent hands."

"I'll try really hard to live up to your standards, Mr. Lemaitre." Good God, she meant it. She was so adorably earnest.

Lemaitre stared at her a moment, then turned to Jason and Theo. "I'd like to see preliminary development in two weeks. *Ça va?*"

"*Oui,*" Theo drawled. "No problem."

A few more clipped instructions and Lemaitre walked away. Sara's eyes followed him, not with lust, but with respect and admiration. Maybe her sweetness would be her shield. Jason could tell Lemaitre didn't know what to make of her.

After that, Sara and Theo returned to the trapeze. Jason had to admit the man was a skilled coach. Under the guise of playing around, Theo was figuring out what she could do and what she hadn't mastered yet. They practiced a whole repertoire of trapeze skills, both of them speaking a specialized language Jason didn't know. He sat on the edge of the crash mat, trying not to be jealous. When the training session was up, Sara walked over and flopped beside him. She was all smiles, her face glistening with a sheen of sweat.

"Good day?" he asked, offering resistance to help her stretch her legs. "Is it what you'd hoped?"

"It's beyond anything I dreamed of. The lights, the big windows, the beautiful equipment."

Sad, to find standard equipment "beautiful," but Jason supposed it was, if you weren't used to having it. To her, it was luxurious, a miracle. He realized how spoiled all of them had become.

"Wait until you're performing in a show," he said, pushing back her other leg. "With the costumes and makeup, and the special effects, and the cool props." He studied her as she relaxed into her stretch. Her muscles were strong, slender. Perfect. He wanted to rip off her clothes and thrust inside her, gripping her neck, whispering in her ear. He tried to refocus his thoughts to the conversation. "You're with Cirque du Monde now. We're state-of-the-art. And Lemaitre's taken a shine to you." At her confused look, he clarified. "That means he likes you. He thinks you're good. Sara...just...be careful."

She gazed at him, guileless as a baby deer. "Careful of what?"

Careful of Lemaitre. Careful of your beautiful spirit. Don't be too brave. "Just...be careful of everything," he said. "Until you're settled in."

"Mr. Lemaitre said he would get Baat to come."

He could see the tension beneath the hopeful expression on her face. "Mr. Lemaitre has a talent for persuasion, so your partner should arrive shortly. In the meantime, Theo will keep you on your toes."

"On my toes?" Her brow wrinkled in confusion again.

"It's an expression, to keep someone sharp, on their toes. Your English sounds so natural, I forget it's not your first language."

"My mother used to help me before she died. She spoke English and a little French. Before me, she traveled with her family's act all over the world." She hugged her knees to her chest. "Of course, in those days, there was no Cirque du Monde."

"She would have been proud of you."

Sara didn't answer. She looked a little peaked. He wanted to take her in his arms, comfort her, but he didn't dare do it in front of everyone. "Do you like your new place? Your new apartment?"

"It's wonderful. But I miss you," she said softly.

He slid a look at Theo, who was eavesdropping on their conversation with a bemused grin. "Do you want to see a show tonight?" he asked, angling away from him. "A Cirque du Monde show? There's one here in Paris."

All her sadness fled, chased away by an excited smile. "Of course I want to see it." She turned to Theo. "Will you come too? So I can meet your wife?"

"Not tonight, *ma brillante.*" With those words, he nodded to both of them and walked off.

Sara turned to Jason with a questioning gaze. "What did he call me? *Mob-bree-yawn*?"

"*Ma brillante.* Do you know the English word, 'brilliant'?" Jason shrugged. "Take it as a compliment."

"He looked upset."

"He doesn't care for *Cirque Tsilaosa.*" Jason couldn't tell her why. He couldn't tell Sara that Theo had dropped his trapeze partner in that show a couple years ago and that she'd died, because Theo was Sara's coach now and she needed to have faith in him. Theo hadn't really dropped Minya anyway, only lost her. It happened. What had Lemaitre said? *Timing is everything in trapeze.*

"Don't worry about Theo," he said, standing and taking her hand. "He doesn't like *Tsilaosa*, but I'm sure you will."

Chapter Five: Dream

Sara sat across the table from Jason, in a beautiful bar on a beautiful Parisian street, in a beautiful dress she'd borrowed from her neighbor at the dorm. She barely sipped the *Kir Royale* he'd ordered her. It was bubbly and sweet, but she was too excited to drink.

She'd just watched her first ever Cirque du Monde show, and she had no words to describe the magic. This was what she'd ached for all those years in her dreary circus tent, even though she never realized until now that it existed.

"Don't you like it?" Jason asked, pointing to her drink. "I can get you something else."

"It's good. I'm just...still..." She shook her head, at a loss for words.

"It's okay to be overwhelmed," he said in his deep, soothing voice. Then he fell silent, studying her. She felt hot all over when he looked at her that way. She was falling so hard for him, but then, that was only natural, wasn't it? If not for Jason, she wouldn't be sitting here. She'd be back in Mongolia serving drinks at a sex club and waiting to do another pathetically amateur show. She didn't realize back then how awful their show was. Her face burned, remembering

Jason's praise backstage, his excitement, when in his head he must have been comparing their circus to the splendor of a production like *Tsilaosa*.

"I owe you so much." It was all she could think to say.

"You don't owe me anything." He took a sip of his drink and pushed back his hair. Sometimes he wore it in a ponytail but mostly it was loose. It made him look wild and a little dangerous.

"We need to talk," he said abruptly. "About us. About our thing together, about what happens now."

"I want to be your slave." The words came out before she even thought them.

"I know." She felt his hand under the table, tracing her knee and then closing on her thigh in a tight grip. "I want that too. I've had lovers, little one. A fair amount. I'm thirty-four, twelve years older than you. I've been around, played in vanilla relationships and Dom/sub relationships and Master/slave relationships. None of them have ever made me feel the way you do."

He meant what he said, she could see it in his eyes, feel it in the tightening of his fingers on the sensitive skin of her inner thigh.

"But..."

There was a but. Sara didn't want a but.

"But you and I have known each other less than a week. And in that week, everything in your life has turned upside down. You should take some time to get your bearings, to be sure. Because once you're mine..."

"I'm already yours."

His eyes bored into her, hard ocean blue. She put her hand over his and traced the tops of his fingers. "When I'm near you, I want to be yours," she said. "When I see you, I'm overcome with...with this feeling of need, of desire. I've never felt that with anyone else."

His fingers slid up, farther along her thigh. She tensed and drew in a shuddering breath.

"Don't react to what I'm doing," he said. "People will notice."

She tried to maintain a neutral expression as his fingertips inched to the gusset of her panties. The café tablecloth hid his actions but she had much more trouble hiding her reactions, especially when his fingers slipped under the material and caressed her smooth pussy lips.

"Open your legs."

She did, and then he said, "Wider," so she had to shift on the seat to comply. Her whole body trembled from the effort of keeping still. She wanted to moan and whisper to him, *I'm yours, I'm yours. Take me.* But she didn't have to say anything. She was wet for him, so wet that his fingers slid inside without the least resistance. She brought her hand to her mouth and bit down on a nail so she wouldn't cry out.

"You see?" she said. "How I feel for you?"

"Yes, I see."

"Please...Master," she whispered.

His fingers moved in her, forward and back, a pulse of possession. "Here's the thing. I've played before, done this for fun, but you don't inspire playfulness in me. This could be risky for both of us. You know what I mean?"

"I do trapeze for a living. I'm not afraid of anything."

His eyes burned, they were so intent. "You should be, little girl. If we do this, it's you and me. Master and slave. Your abject submission whenever we're together. I like control. I also like to hurt my slaves."

"I like to be controlled, and hurt."

"I might ask for things you don't want, things you don't like. I'll expect you to do them anyway. Those are my terms." He withdrew his fingers and wiped them on her leg, and squeezed her thigh. "Think for a minute before you say yes, because none of this is a joke."

Sara paused. *What if he asks me to do something I don't like?* But she liked everything about Jason. Everything about his body, his words, his expressions, even the fact that he enjoyed giving pain. Ever since she'd met him, some peace had settled over her, some knowledge that he was her perfect complement and that they belonged together. He knew exactly what to do with her. How much to hurt her, how much to soothe her. How to bring out the strange creature inside her that didn't respond to normal love and sex. She wanted to give all of herself to him because he understood her as no one else had ever understood her.

"I want to serve you," she said, because it was the simplest expression of her feelings. "I want to be yours. Even if we have to hide."

"And none of this is because you feel you owe me? Because I brought you here and showed you this new life? Because you'll have a whole new life in Paris. Are you sure you want to spend it tangled up with me?"

"Why are you warning me so hard? Don't you want me? If you don't want to be my Master—"

"You know I want you," he interrupted in a quiet but sharp voice. "I want you more than I should. I'm warning you 'so hard' because I scene hard. In public, we'll have to keep up appearances, play happy supervisor and artist. In private, I'm going to turn you inside out. Are you sure that's what you want?"

She stared at him, at the warning in his eyes. He could warn all he liked. In her heart, she was already his. "Yes, Master. I'm sure it's what I want."

He let out a breath and she did too, the wrought-up breaths they'd been holding. Around them, people continued chatting and drinking, living their normal lives. Life had just turned over—inside out—for Sara. She'd officially agreed to a Master/slave relationship with the beautiful man sitting across from her. She had no anxious feelings, no second thoughts.

He touched her fingers where she clung to her drink. "Come. Now. Leave that. I'm taking you home."

He swept her jacket off the back of her chair and wrapped it around her shoulders, and then downed the rest of his drink in one great swallow. When he finished, he put the glass on the table with a bang. To Sara, it sounded like the door of her past slamming shut. He took her hand, wrapped it tight in his fingers, and led her from the bar.

On the street he let her go. They were close to the theater, close to the Cirque dorms and headquarters. Their co-workers were all around them, people Sara could recognize as performers and athletes even without their costumes. A few times Jason greeted people, but it wasn't the type of greeting that invited them to stop and talk. She was glad because she felt anxious to be alone with him. Her desire must have been written all over her face, clear as day for people to read.

Finally, he led her to a stoop and through a door to a narrow stairwell. She followed him up two flights of stairs to a burnished mahogany door. It was an old building, a style she'd come to recognize as classic Parisian. He fumbled for keys and undid the lock, and only then did their eyes meet.

Had there ever been such an intense shade of blue? He said her eyes were pretty but his own were much more beautiful. He grasped her shoulder and then her neck, and practically dragged her inside. He trapped her against the entryway wall, his great body looming over her.

"Master," she whispered.

"Oh God." On the heels of that prayer, his lips descended over hers. She'd thought herself prepared but she wasn't really prepared for the intensity of his kiss, his rough embrace. His thumb stroked over the racing pulse at her throat, while his other hand yanked up her skirt. She responded clumsily, trying to match the passion and skill of his lips. This wasn't sweet or romantic. This was possession.

"Open wider," he said in his Master voice. Or maybe it was just Jason's voice, demanding and firm. She obeyed and he slid his tongue between her teeth, over her tongue. She felt a delirious, warm ache in her center and she wiggled closer against him, right against the thick, upstanding shaft outlined by his pants. His hands were all over her, pulling, twisting, trying to find the fastenings of her dress. He slid fingers beneath the neckline as if to tear it open.

"Please," she squeaked. "This dress isn't mine."

He slowed, letting out a breath. "Tomorrow, then, we'll go shopping for dresses I can rip off you."

She showed him the hidden zipper on the side and he helped her shimmy out of it. The bra and panties came next, pretty but practical undergarments that had been waiting in her room the night she arrived at Cirque. "If they're not what you like, I'll get others," she said. "Whatever pleases you."

He silenced her with a fingertip to her lips. "I like nakedness. I want nothing between you and me. I like naked slaves."

Naked *slaves*. Plural. She wouldn't be his first slave, nor probably his last. He might have other slaves here in Paris, women he used for his pleasure. She couldn't be upset about that. He hadn't known she existed a month ago. A week ago. She shook her head, willing those thoughts away. She had to stay in the moment, available to serve her Master. He twisted his fingers in her hair and wrenched her head back. She shuddered, staring up into his burning gaze.

"Undress me," he said through bared teeth.

It was an order, taut and firm. Her fingers trembled as she hurried to obey. She pulled off his sweater, revealing a finely tailored, expertly starched button-up shirt. Oh no, buttons. She undid them as best she could while he kissed her and pinched her nipples. Beneath the fabric of his shirt lay an undershirt, and beneath that, a sculpted wall of abs that bunched as she touched them.

"Keep going," he said. "Naughty, distractible girl."

He pushed her hands down to his belt and she unclasped the woven leather. It was supple and soft, and it gave her feelings only a slave-type person would understand. How old had she been when she started reacting to things like belts and canes inappropriately? When she dawdled over it, daydreaming, Jason drew it from the loops himself and doubled it over in his hand. "You really are distractible. Keep going."

He did the slightest flick of the belt against his thigh and her heart rate doubled. She started on his pants, undoing the button and easing down the zipper. "Do you want me to hang them up?" she asked.

"I want you to fucking take them off."

He was getting impatient. When she slid them down he kicked them away and she was left with the mouth-watering sight of his hard cock outlined by his tight boxer briefs. The sight of his huge manhood created powerful feelings of submission inside her. She wanted to touch it, lick it, worship it on her knees.

"Be careful," he said with a knowing glint in his eyes. "You got in trouble for taking without asking before."

Sara licked her lips. Maybe not the best time to remind her of their first sizzling encounter. She was dying of arousal. Was that possible? She was pretty sure it was. She slipped her fingers beneath the waistband of his boxer briefs and removed them carefully, respectfully, so she couldn't be accused of "taking without asking." She placed them by his pants, and then sat back on her ankles and went still, because she wouldn't do anything without his permission. He'd told her he liked control, and she really, really liked to be controlled.

"Look at me." She felt the belt nudge under her chin and she tilted her head up to see all six-feet-plus of her lover towering over her, strong and tan, as finely wrought as a statue. "Open your legs," he said. "Straighten your back."

She obeyed, trying not to flinch as he traced her shoulders and breasts with his doubled-over belt. Oh, those fingers. They were wrapped around the buckle, clenching it, beautiful and broad knuckled. She had a thing for hands and fingers, maybe because she was a trapezist and locating and grabbing fingers was integral to her continued existence.

"Focus," he said, tapping lightly at one of her nipples. "Eyes on Master."

Her gaze flew to his and he nodded in approval. "Listen, little girl. This is an old building with very thin walls. No matter what we do, you have to be quiet. Do you understand?"

"Yes, Master."

"Now, I want you to go to my bedroom. I want you to crawl there on your hands and knees."

She started to obey, then realized she had no idea where his bedroom was. "Which way, Master?"

"You have to find it."

Ohhh. A game. She could crawl around on her knees for an eternity if he enjoyed it. But then, she'd forgotten about the belt.

Whack!

It caught her right under her ass cheeks, a hot slap of fire. She cried out more from the surprise than the pain of it, and he whacked her again. This time it was painful.

"Hush," he said. "I told you to be quiet. Be a good slave girl and go to my bedroom."

She set off in the crawling version of a run. It would be a lot easier to be a "good slave girl" if she knew where she was going, and if he wasn't following her around with a whippy belt. His place was huge, unfamiliar, and there seemed to be doors looming in every direction. She didn't think his bedroom would be near the kitchen, so she went toward the other side of the house. She found a coat room first, and received a resounding smack for her trouble. She swallowed her yelp of pain and shut the door and went to the next one. A bedroom, but it was sparsely furnished, with a small bed. Definitely not his. But she was in the location of the bedrooms, thank God. The belt kept falling, hard smacks interspersed with lighter ones, her burning ass a moving target for his game.

A bathroom, another bedroom. "Keep going," he said. "You'll know my room when you find it."

She gave a little sob and scurried back out to the main room. A door beside the kitchen opened into a hall and mudroom which led to the back door. She tried to think about architecture and where his bedroom might be hiding, since all the ground floor space seemed accounted for. She scurried down the hall—*spank, spank, spank!*—to find a narrow door tucked in the back. She opened it and found an equally narrow flight of stairs.

She sat back on her heels and gave him a pleading look. If she crawled all the way up those stairs, getting whacked the whole way, and didn't find his bedroom at the top, she couldn't handle it.

"What did I tell you? I said to crawl, not sit." He pushed down her shoulders with one hand, and lifted her ass with the other. "I said to find my bedroom." He punctuated every other word with a crisp stroke of the belt. Sara cringed, covering her mouth so she wouldn't cry out.

"I'm sorry, Master. Is it upstairs?"

"You'll have to crawl up and see."

She ducked her head and started up the stairs. Between her burning ass, the narrow walls, the darkness, and her clumsy cringing, she could barely crawl, but she couldn't stop because he was coming behind her. *Whack!* "Please," she cried halfway up. "Please, Master."

"Hush."

When she got to the top she let out another cry, this time a cry of relief. Jason flicked on a light and she crawled into the room that was unmistakably his. The bed was polished brass, a poster bed with countless attachment points hidden in the design. The headboard was padded with black leather, the footboard padded leather as well, perfect bending-over height. There was other furniture she took in with a glance. Chests, a desk, a sofa near the window that looked fortuitously padded as well. She waited on the floor at his feet, aware that she'd been too loud and too slow, and not very slavelike in her crawling. Her ass throbbed all over. She wanted to rub and soothe it but she kept her hands clenched beside her.

"Sit up. Arch your back. Spread your legs," he said, exasperated. "I shouldn't have to say it every time."

She quickly assumed the pose he'd prodded her into downstairs.

"Look at me."

Gah, yes, she was supposed to look at him. She wanted to look at him, but in some way she was afraid to, because he had so much power in these games, and she had none. Her ass ached, prickly warm against her feet. She spread her legs wide, knowing he'd see her wet pussy lips, her engorged clit.

"What did I tell you?" he asked, his hands on his hips. "What did I say about being quiet? Even up here, they can hear you through the air ducts."

She blinked up at him, trying not to fixate on his thrusting, bobbing cock. "I'm sorry, Master. It hurt."

"Yes, I intended it to hurt, and I intended you to be quiet. Maybe we need to put something in that mouth." He sauntered over to his nightstand. By the time he returned, he was wearing a rubber. "Kneel up and open your lips."

She did as he asked, but even full height, on her knees, he had to bend to her a little. "Shorty," he murmured, not unkindly, and then he put his thumbs in her mouth and opened her lips even wider, and thrust inside. He'd done this to her before, at the hotel. Like so many things he did, she found it both horrible and exciting. She choked, gagging on latex and solid flesh.

"I'm sorry, Master," she gasped, pulling back for air.

"No talking," he replied, and then he was moving inside her again, easing past her lips and prodding the back of her throat. She gagged again, but not so badly this time. *Be his slave. Bring him pleasure.* She tried to withstand his deepening thrusts but she couldn't breathe, and every other stroke, she gagged. She brought her hands up to stop him.

"No, don't do that." He took her hands and forced them behind her back. "Leave them there."

"Yes, Master," she sobbed past the massive erection in her mouth. But as soon as he started thrusting again she instinctively brought her hands up. If only he'd let her control the depth of his entry!

He made an angry sound and picked up the belt. She flinched as he gave her a couple good wallops on her sore backside, but somehow managed not to cry out. "Put your hands behind you," he ordered. She obeyed, shuddering as he wrapped the belt around her wrists and then around her waist. "That will hold them until you get better at self control. Or deep throating. Or both."

"I'll get better, Master. I promise."

Now that her hands were out of commission, she realized she was crying, really crying, and she had no way to wipe away her tears. Jason took her chin in his fingers and used his other hand to brush the head of his cock over her lips. She wished they didn't have to use condoms. She wished she could satisfy him the way he wanted. Someday she'd be able to.

"Calm down," he said, wiping away a tear. "Nothing good comes of panicking. You must know that from trapeze."

"Yes, Master. I just...I want to do it right. I want to please you."

"Then let's practice. But you have to stay calm. I won't hurt you and I won't kill you. I won't suffocate you. Your job is to open to me, to open your body for my cock, wherever I want to put it. You understand?"

"Yes, Master."

"And to never push me away. You don't decide where my cock goes, do you?"

"No, Master."

He let go of her face and she opened her mouth. "Calm, calm, calm," he said as he pressed between her lips. "Good girl."

She found it much easier to take him deep when she relaxed. When she gagged, he rubbed her shoulder until she composed herself, and then he pressed forward a bit more. And she *could* do it.

He was right, there wasn't any need to panic. He pressed into her five, six, seven more times and each time it was a little less scary, even if she coughed and drooled all over her chest.

"I know, baby, it's awful," he said as he swiped away her trails of saliva. He tipped her head back while his cock was buried deep, and asked, "Can you be quiet now?"

She nodded since she couldn't talk.

"We'll see," he replied, which sounded ominous. He withdrew from her mouth and she knelt where she was, gasping for breath, enjoying the feeling of having her airway back. Jason crossed the room and got something from a drawer, something jingly and metallic. Nipple clamps. Although she quailed inside, she resumed the position he preferred, legs spread, back arched.

He knelt down in front of her, a smile tugging at the corner of his lips. "Do you know, you arched your back more when you saw the clamps? I like that about you."

She stared into his gorgeous eyes. "I'm scared, though."

"You like being scared, don't you? Are you okay? Your wrists? Your arms going numb? You want a safe word?"

She swallowed hard and shook her head. "I trust you."

"Trapezists. Reckless to the core." He flicked the first clamp open and closed, then traced it around her nipple's taut point. "Remember. Silence."

"Yes, Master." She gritted her teeth and braced.

"Look at me while I put them on."

"Yes, Master." She studied his dusky eyelashes, his sculptured jaw line. When the pain bloomed, his gaze met hers and she could see him basking in her anguish.

"It hurts, doesn't it?" he asked. "I don't know why I like to hurt you so much. Perhaps because you bear it for me. For my pleasure."

Her eyes flickered with tears, not from the pain of the other clamp—although that hurt like crazy—but from the realization that he knew her so well. This odd connection between them, this understanding, it went deeper than she'd realized at first. When their eyes locked again, she could see he felt the same. How? Why? How long? She didn't know, but in this moment, she would have given him anything he asked.

"Come on," he said, twitching the chain between the clamps. "Over to the bed."

It was hard to rise with her nipples tugged painfully and her hands cinched behind her back, but she managed as best she could. He led her across the room as if the chain was a leash, and each time he tweaked it the pain in her nipples sharpened, but she didn't make a sound. He sat on the edge of the bed and lifted her astride his lap, his sheathed erection jutting up between the two of them. "Do you want my cock inside you, baby? Are you turned on?" He reached between her legs to grope her. She was so wet, she could hear the sound of his fingers parting her. She wanted him so badly, she would have fought through a dozen brick walls to get to him. But he was here, right here.

He eased back across the starched, down-filled white comforter, pulling her with him. His hair obscured his features as he leaned forward to grasp her hips, and then he lowered her onto his thick cock. As wet as she was, it was still a slow process to take him all the way inside. She felt impaled, helpless.

He jerked the nipple clamps. "What a view. Move on me. Ride me." He flicked the chain like it was a horse's reins and she rode him as best she could without her arms to help. His head fell back and he spread out his arms, flexing his muscles. He looked like an angel...and a devil. She squeezed on him and he bucked his hips up against her clit.

"Oh, God," he sighed. "You feel wonderful."

He started working her hips in a circle, manipulating her so that even though she was on top, she had no control. He filled her again and again, tweaking the nipple clamps when her moans got too loud. It was so hard to be quiet. With the pain she could concentrate, call on her self-discipline to help her, but in this pleasure, she was losing all control.

"Oh, it feels...so...good..."

Undressing him, scurrying to find his bedroom, taking his cock deep in her throat, all of that was foreplay, all of it culminating in this, the joining of their straining bodies. She wanted to come but she was afraid to come because she might turn inside out, just as he'd warned. She felt inside out already, like everything inside her was bared to his gaze.

Her cries got louder the closer she got to orgasm. If she could have, she would have muffled them with her hands, but they were trapped behind her back by his belt. She rode his cock faster and faster, seeking fulfillment or pain, whatever he wanted, because that's what she wanted. She arched toward him when he pulled the clamps, offering her torment for his pleasure.

With a rough movement, he tumbled her sideways, still fucking her. He hit her clit with every stroke then, excruciating pleasure building to a peak. "Oh God, oh God!" She was getting really loud now but she couldn't help it. She was too far gone to obey. He pressed a hand over her mouth, then took off the nipple clamps one after the other so sensation flooded back into her breasts.

That was the end of it for her. Every nerve in her body fired a delicious release. Her limbs trembled uncontrollably as she gasped against his palm. He pounded into her, driving her into the bed, filling her with his power and his raw sexuality. Her angel, her devil, her tormentor, her savior, her guide, her teacher. Her lover.

Her Master.

* * * * *

Jason drifted, basking in her, inhaling her flowery, feminine scent.

He moved his hand so she could draw breath again, and stared down at her flickering eyelids. She was either resting, sleeping, or passed out. "Sara," he whispered, and her eyes came open.

"Yes, Master?" she asked, even though she looked exhausted. So submissive, so willing. Such a treasure. There were two kinds of "slave" girls. The first only pretended to serve, while balking at anything they didn't want to do, anything that didn't bring them pleasure. The second kind truly believed in serving, in giving themselves up to Master's will. The first kind didn't last long in the kink scene at the Cirque, even the drop-dead gorgeous ones. The second kind...well. D-types fought over them.

No one's getting you, he thought, staring down at her. *No one but me.*

"Is everything okay?" she asked.

He chuckled, softening his expression, and got up to throw away his condom. "I was just thinking that I need a cage for you. Somewhere to keep you so you can never get away, and so no one else can ever steal you."

She laughed, a cute, nervous laugh that told him she wasn't entirely sure he was joking.

"I like cages," he clarified, returning to the bed, "but I won't ever put you in one without your permission. Well, without your consent."

"Aren't permission and consent the same thing?"

Jason sprawled beside her and unbuckled the belt binding her hands. "They're kind of the same thing, but kind of not. I don't like to ask women for permission to do the things I do to them, but I like to have their consent. Does that make sense?"

She stretched her arms and rubbed her wrists. Jason checked them to be sure there weren't any abrasions. When he finished he brought them to his lips. "Did you like what we just did, or was it too hard for you?"

She squirmed under his regard. "Well…did you like it?"

"I didn't ask if I liked it. I asked if you liked it. And tell the truth." He brushed a finger across her lips. "Never lie to Master."

She was quiet for a long time, so long he got nervous. Then she said, "I liked everything about today. Going to Cirque du Monde, meeting Theo and Mr. Lemaitre, going to the show, going for drinks with you. And coming here to your place...I liked that most of all. But I'm afraid." Her smile faded and her eyes went dark. "I'm afraid I'll wake up and find it's all been a dream."

"It's not a dream."

Tension wrinkled her brow. "If Mr. Lemaitre finds out we're doing this, will he fire me?"

Jason kissed the lines away and rolled onto his back. "No, he'll fire me. But if I begged hard enough he'd probably hire me back. Lemaitre understands passion, sweet pea. I'll give the man that."

"You'll give him...a sweet pea?"

"No, I called you a sweet pea. It's a kind of flower. And when I said *I'll give the man that...* Look, never mind. Don't worry about anything." He brushed back a lock of her dark hair. "You look tired. How about a shower?"

"Mm. Probably. I drooled on myself."

"Which was ball-numbingly hot."

"Ball-numbingly hot?"

"Very, very hot," he amended. "You'll never understand how hot. But it's late and you're probably still fighting jet lag."

They showered together in his chipped, claw-footed tub, and then he toweled her off, thinking how lovely she was. Lovely hips, lovely breasts, lovely exotic features and a stunning smile. Twenty-two. A mere baby. He was twelve years older. *Twelve* years older. He would master her as long as she wanted to be mastered, but if she decided she wanted someone younger, someone closer to her age, he'd let her go.

"What's wrong?" she asked, touching his face. "You're frowning."

He forced a smile. "Just afraid I'll wake up and find it's all been a dream." He took her to his bed, naked, the way a slave ought to be, and stayed up long after her eyes closed, watching her lashes flutter against her cheek.

Chapter Six: Stay

Jason woke in the morning to the sound of pounding. The front door? Sara sighed and stirred beside him.

"Don't get up," he said when her eyes blinked open. "Stay here."

He threw on sweats and a tee and padded down the stairs, wondering who'd be knocking at eight in the morning. He didn't have any work appointments until ten. When he flung open the door, Michel Lemaitre pushed Jason aside and strode into his living room. "Sara is missing," he said. "No one can find her. She hasn't been back to her dorm all night."

Well, this was a fucking situation. Lemaitre crossed to the window, his lips compressed in a line.

"She's not missing," said Jason. "She's asleep upstairs."

Lemaitre turned back to him and stared. He knew this house, because he'd sold it to Jason a few years ago. He knew "upstairs" meant Sara was in his bedroom.

"And why is Sara asleep upstairs?" he asked with a dangerous edge to his voice.

Because I got to her first, you horny lecher. Sara was twelve years younger than him; that meant she was twenty-two years younger than

Lemaitre. "Keep your voice down, okay? We were out late. I took her to see *Tsilaosa*."

"And then what?"

Jason headed to the kitchen. He needed coffee for this conversation. "Are you sure you want to know?"

"I'm sure I want to know." Lemaitre's voice sounded cold as ice. "I don't know what disturbs me more, that my most rigidly proper director is breaking the rules, or that he's breaking them with a woman who's been here for one day. *One day*, Jason."

Once Jason had the coffee brewing, he crossed to sit in the chair nearest Lemaitre, considering his options. He could lie to his boss, but lies were hard to keep track of. He could refuse to explain, which would probably cost him his job. Or he could tell the truth, which Lemaitre would eventually figure out anyway.

"Before I say anything, I want your word that you won't treat Sara any differently after you hear what I say."

Lemaitre narrowed his eyes. "*Dieu*, such drama."

"I want your word."

He threw up his hands. "Yes, you have my word, although I doubt this is her doing."

Jason paused, sinking back in his chair. "My first night in Ulaanbaatar, I went downtown to check out a BDSM club. That's where Sara and I met."

Lemaitre's eyes went from narrow to wide. "There's a BDSM club in Mongolia?"

"Yes, they have them everywhere. You of all people should know," Jason replied with an edge of sarcasm. "And it wasn't so much a club as a brothel. You know, girls dancing in cages, and private rooms available for the right price."

The older man's jaw worked. "What was Sara doing there?"

"Waiting tables in skimpy lingerie, serving drinks to horny, kinky men."

"Horny, kinky men like you."

Jason pursed his lips. "I only went there to relax, to *loosen up* as you told me to, but then shit started happening. They tried to get me drunk, tried to take advantage of the stupid American, but Sara wouldn't let them. To make a long story short, I got kicked out and she got fired."

"Then what?" Lemaitre asked.

Jason held up a hand. "Look, I swear to God. I didn't know she was part of the act I was scouting, and she didn't know I was with Cirque du Monde."

His voice turned a shade icier. "You slept with her."

"We were both freaked out by what happened. She was upset."

"So you lured her back to your hotel room and soothed her, is that it? Such a heroic, selfless act."

"You told me I worked too hard, remember? You told me to 'enjoy the local pleasures.'"

"I didn't mean her!"

Jason paused, grasping for calm. "You know I wouldn't have done it if knew who she was. We didn't find out any of that until the next day. Then her partner shut down the pitch about Cirque and wouldn't let her speak, so she came to my hotel again. Only to talk with me about coming to Paris."

"So you didn't sleep with her the second night?"

Jason pressed his fingers against his eyes. "I tried not to."

"But you did," Lemaitre snapped.

"Is it your business? It was private. Consensual."

"It's my business because she's my performer now. She shouldn't have been compelled—"

"I did not compel her. It happened."

"And it seems to keep happening, considering the fact that she's upstairs."

Jason sensed great fury beneath his boss's bitten-off words. Which made no sense, because Lemaitre slept with the talent all the time. He made them into his devoted sex slaves, for God's sake. Perhaps he was angry to learn that Sara had to support herself in Mongolia waitressing at a sex club, but circus wasn't always a lucrative career.

"You can't blame her," Jason said, heading back to the kitchen. "You can't hold it against her. She's here now, ready to work. That should be all that matters."

"Do you think I'd hold it against her? Really, do you?" He followed that question with a string of French expletives that made Jason's ears burn.

"She's sleeping," he reminded him. "Keep it down. Do you want some coffee?"

"I want to speak to her."

"No, you'll embarrass her. You'll scare her. If you don't trust everything I've said, then fire me. I don't want to work for someone who thinks I'm a liar."

"I don't think you're a liar. But I find you something of an opportunist."

Jason ground his teeth at that dig. "There was a mutual attraction."

"Imagine her being attracted to an important, attractive Cirque du Monde director who's offering her a new career."

"It wasn't like that."

"How was it, Jason?" He leaned forward, wagging a finger. "Once you knew she was a talent prospect, you should have gone out of your way to re-orient your relationship into a professional one."

"I tried. Honestly, I tried but—"

"But you preferred to keep fucking her."

"Everything between us has involved mutual consent."

"Jason?" The soft question arrested their rising voices. Sara stood by the door to the back hallway, clad in a blanket and his wrinkled button-up shirt. So much for his obedient slave.

"Sara, go back upstairs," he said in a firm voice.

She turned to Lemaitre. "You can't fire him. This isn't his fault. Last night he told me that we should take things slow, but I didn't want to."

Jason rubbed his forehead, stifling a groan. The last thing he wanted was for Sara to debase herself pleading on his behalf. Lemaitre turned to face her, his expression one of uncharacteristic gravity. "My deepest concern is for your well-being. While you're with the Cirque, you're under my protection."

Sara blinked at him. "You don't have to protect me from Jason. I want to be with him. I promise we'll be…discreet."

Lemaitre gave her one of his patented glowering looks. "This isn't a matter of discretion, my dear. It's a matter of professional behavior. Jason was sent to Mongolia to scout you, not seduce you."

"He didn't seduce me. It wasn't like that. Things just happened."

"*Things just happened* doesn't make it right," he said, his voice sharpening.

Jason made a low warning sound. Lemaitre could rail at him all day, but he wouldn't let him chew out Sara.

Lemaitre's scowl deepened as he lounged back on the couch. "You and Jason will be working together as part of a professional team. Whether 'things happened' or not, you both have an obligation to focus on the development of your act. Let me put it this way: I brought you here to grace the stages of Cirque du Monde, not the bedroom of Mr. Beck."

Sara straightened her shoulders and stared her imposing boss in the face. "You should have some respect for me as an artist. Do you think I won't give my all for Cirque du Monde? For my performance? Whether Jason's in charge of my act, or you, or someone else, it doesn't matter. I'm going to do my best work, regardless of my personal life."

She lifted her chin, as if daring Lemaitre to defy her. She didn't realize it, but with that brave outburst, she'd earned her boss's respect. Jason knew him well enough to see the approval in the twitch of his lips, the softening of his stare. "Very well," he said in a gruff voice. "Your best work? I'm going to hold you to that." He picked at the tailored cuff of his sleeve. "I apologize for waking you, *mademoiselle*. It is early. Perhaps you should retire again upstairs."

It was an order, not a suggestion, and it meant he wasn't done hammering Jason yet. Jason walked to Sara and pressed a kiss to her forehead. "Bad girl," he whispered, pulling her close. "I told you to stay in bed."

She gave him a look, that look slaves had when they knew they'd fucked up and were very sorry for it. If Lemaitre hadn't understood how serious their thing was before, he'd know now from the expression on Sara's face.

"It's okay," he said, tracing a thumb down the curve of her cheek. "We'll talk about it later. For now, you really need to go upstairs."

"Yes, M—" She slid a look at Lemaitre. "Yes, Jason."

Sweet, clueless Sara, hiding their dynamic from the outsider. She didn't realize yet that Lemaitre was the Master of them all. He'd have to explain it soon, so she'd understand the world she'd entered. He turned back to his boss, who regarded him with a shuttered expression.

"Very nice," was all he said.

Jason went on the defensive. "It is very nice. It happened naturally for both of us. You know how rare and special that is."

"'Rare' and 'special.' What a glowing way to look at it."

"I'm telling you, from the start, we knew. We sensed this thing between us. Even the first night, we knew something was going on. You don't understand the pull we feel to each other."

Lemaitre stood and stalked to the window, then turned back to him with a scathing look. "No, I don't understand, because I control my 'pulls' when they're inappropriate. It's called restraint."

"Are you lecturing me about restraint, Michel? Because I don't think you have any moral high ground to stand on. You sleep with your subordinates all the time."

"Perhaps, but it doesn't 'just happen.' I choose my partners with great care. I groom them for weeks, months, years sometimes. You've known Sara for what? Three days all together?"

"Almost a week."

Lemaitre's phone buzzed and he looked down at it. He glanced back at Jason, then out the window again. Struggling. Lemaitre was struggling with something, which almost never happened. Jealousy?

Michel Lemaitre wanted Sara for himself.

Jason suspected it, dreaded it, and now it seemed obvious. "I won't say I love her yet," Jason declared, "because as you said, I just met her. But I'm on the way to loving her. I'd appreciate it if you would respect that."

Lemaitre turned to him, stroking his chin. Jason endured his assessing stare, shored up by his convictions. He cared about Sara.

He would have lost his job for her. He still might lose his job over her, if Lemaitre couldn't let the jealousy go.

"You're off her act," Lemaitre finally said. "I'll oversee it myself with Theo's help. As for the other, I wish you both the best." He looked back down at his phone. "A few minutes ago, Sara's partner arrived at Cirque du Monde headquarters. I see no point in telling her until I've met with the young man and learned his intentions."

Jason's head spun from the sudden change of subject. "Baat's in Paris?"

"He's waiting at my office. Keep Sara away from headquarters until I call with news." He strode to the door, then turned back with his hand on the knob. "Don't be too hard on her. She only disobeyed out of concern for you."

"You know how this works. If we start letting little things go..."

Lemaitre waved a hand. "Yes. Unhappy slaves. Okay then, give her hell. But remember why she did what she did."

Jason saluted his boss and locked the door after he left. What a morning. Baat was here, Jason was no longer working with Sara, and Lemaitre had wished them "the best" in their relationship. Jason needed food, and coffee. Maybe a drink.

But first he had to discipline a naughty slave who'd really only had his best interests at heart.

* * * * *

Sara heard his feet on the stairs. Her heart pounded as she pulled up the covers and feigned sleep. Maybe if he thought she was tired...if she looked especially exhausted...

She shut her eyes and lay very still. She heard him cross the room, heard the rustle of him taking off his clothes and then his sigh as he walked to her side of the bed.

I'm sleeping, see? Poor, tired Sara.

But it was a lie, cowardly avoidance. A good slave owned up to her mistakes. She opened her eyes to find his face inches from hers. She blinked and scooted back as he crawled onto the bed after her. Within seconds, she was pinned underneath him, staring up into his steady gaze.

"I'm sorry," she whispered. "You told me to stay upstairs."

"Yes I did. Very simple directions. It seems you need to be reminded who's in charge."

She didn't really need to be reminded. He was making it obvious, with his dominant position and his threatening stare.

"I was afraid," she said. "I heard Mr. Lemaitre's voice and I worried he'd fire you."

"Those are excuses. I appreciate your concern, but you still disobeyed. Masters like submission and trust, and obedience. Do you know what they don't like?"

Sara took a stab at it. "Naughty slaves?"

He took one of her nipples between thumb and forefinger, pinching in a sharp, burning twist. "Naughty slaves who don't trust their Masters to handle their own business. My job isn't your concern. And for the record, I would have given it up for you. If it came to that."

"That would have been sad."

"You're about to be sad." He released her aching nipple. "But that's how naughty slaves learn."

Her heart had been pounding earlier but now it banged in her chest like a fire alarm. Punishments weren't sexy and fun. Whatever he did was going to hurt, and she suspected someone as meticulous as Jason would make it hurt worse than most.

"Master...please..."

"Hush. Turn on your tummy."

With a helpless whimper, she complied. She watched with her face half-mashed into the comforter as he crossed to a chest and hauled open a drawer. He took out a thin braided whip, about two feet long, and flexed it between his fingers. Oh, no. Narrow, whippy implements hurt the worst.

"Reach above you and touch the headboard," he said as he returned. "Scoot up if you have to. You're not to move your hands."

"Yes, Master." She trembled, wondering how many strokes he'd give her. Five? Ten? Twenty? *Please, not twenty.* Well, this is what she got for going downstairs and butting into his business with Mr. Lemaitre. "I'm sorry," she whispered as he pulled cuffs from beneath the padded footboard and buckled them around her ankles. His bed was so big, she had to spread her legs wide.

"I know you're sorry," he said, checking the tension. "This is to remind you who's the Master and who's the slave."

He walked around the bed and drew back his arm. She squeezed her eyes shut and waited in dread for the punishment she'd earned. The first slice of the whip was horrible, because there was no warm up, no exciting foreplay to make her want it. Her legs jerked but they couldn't move more than an inch or two. She clutched at the sheets, then returned her hands to the headboard as he'd instructed her. The next stroke tore a shriek from her throat.

"Be quiet or I'll gag you," he warned. "We talked about the air ducts. I don't want the police showing up."

She buried her face in the sheets, biting down on them to keep from wailing at the next stroke. The pain was fiery, impossibly sharp. Punishing. It was all she could do not to throw her hands back to cover herself. Five, six, seven. Eight. He paused, and Sara felt eight separate, throbbing welts on her ass, laid over the lingering bruises from his belt the night before. She braced for more, but then he moved away, put the whip aside. *Thank you, Master.*

"Reach back and part your ass cheeks. Yes, you can let go of the headboard. Reach back and spread them open."

Sara hesitated, reluctant and humiliated, and shy.

"You have three seconds to obey me before I pick up the whip again."

She reached back and yanked her ass cheeks apart, wincing as her nails accidentally raked one of the whip marks. She wanted to beg for mercy but she felt too punished and shamed to say anything. And too terrified of what was coming next.

She felt his weight on the bed beside her. He had a condom and a bottle of lube, and a grim expression on his face. "Do you like anal sex, Sara?"

She couldn't process his words for a moment. "Wha— What?"

"Anal sex. Do you like having your ass fucked? I know you like having it played with," he said with a ghost of a smile. Yes, he'd played with it that first time, but it had only been his fingers, not his huge cock. "Answer me," he prompted, "and keep those ass cheeks spread."

She stammered as he dripped cold lube into her crack. "I— I like it sometimes. But it usually hurts."

"I imagine it does." He pushed a finger into her, smoothing the lube around her sphincter. She felt close to panic, even though the pain hadn't started yet. She heard the rattle of the condom wrapper, and felt him shift as he put it on. "Sometimes I'll make you come when I fuck your ass, but this isn't one of those times. You understand why."

"Yes, Master." Tears filled her eyes. Fearful tears, penitent tears, maybe even thankful tears. She was too scared to know at the moment.

He paused with the head of his cock against her tensing hole. Her legs were still bound to the bed, her hands still holding herself open. "Lift your ass up. Offer it to me. My pleasure for your punishment."

It was too humiliating to bear, but she did it, and when he pressed the head in she sobbed into the pillow. It *hurt.* His cock stretched her, unfamiliar fullness that brought a frightening ache. If she'd screamed "Get it out!" the way she wanted to, she knew he would have done it, but she kept the words inside because he was her Master and this was how their world worked. *My pleasure for your punishment.* She arched her bottom even more. *Hurt me, take me, use me. As long as you forgive me afterward and tell me everything's okay.*

"Good girl," he sighed as she relaxed into the pain. It hurt the most at the beginning. She knew that. Now he was in and it was only a matter of enduring the fucking part. He held himself above her, thrusting steadily in and out, deeper and deeper each time. From the noises he was making, it felt extremely good on his end. Because of the lubricant, it didn't feel so bad for her. It was only that it was punishment.

"Who's the Master in this relationship?" he asked a few minutes in.

"You are. *Mmph.*" He did an especially deep thrust and she bit her lip to keep from crying.

"And who are you?"

"I'm your slave, Master. I'm sorry I disobeyed you."

"Your disobedience is why you have nine fat inches of cock buried in your asshole, isn't it?"

"Yes, Master."

"Are you enjoying this?"

"No, Master," she said truthfully. She had no doubt he could make it feel good if he wanted to, but her ass was already sore from the whip and he was fucking her like he was teaching her a lesson, not trying to make her come.

"Next time Master tells you to stay somewhere, what are you going to do?"

"I'm going to stay," she sobbed. "I'm going to listen to you, I promise."

"I hope so. I hope you've learned a lesson."

He punctuated each word with a hard thrust and then he jerked his cock out of her. A moment later she felt hot spurts of cum on her back, and on her ass cheeks where she held them open. It seemed like the worst punishment of all, that he didn't deign to come inside her, but this was one more display of who was the Master and who was the subordinate.

"Rub it in like a good girl."

She didn't question, just obeyed, releasing her ass cheeks to massage her Master's cum into her skin. She felt wrung out, exhausted, and yes, punished. Jason got up to throw away the condom, then uncuffed her legs.

"Don't move. Just lay there."

She rested her hands on the bed and lay very still, and submitted to Jason's inspection of her body. When he finished, he drew her into his arms and she sobbed against his chest, babbling a mish-mash of apologies. He stroked her hair and wiped away her tears, and then he told her she was forgiven.

It felt good to be forgiven, but she wasn't totally at peace. She clung to him, thinking she would never, ever disobey him again, or injure his pride, or overstep her boundaries.

There was no need, anyway. This morning he'd proved he could handle Mr. Lemaitre—and her—just fine.

*****

An hour later, Jason got the call from Lemaitre to bring Sara to practice. Baat was on board. Lemaitre had all but promised him *Cirque Brillante* in Vegas to get him to stay.

When Jason told Theo during practice, the other man shrugged. "I always assumed she would go to *Brillante*. They'll love her there." He gave Jason a searching look. "Will you go when she goes?"

Jason watched Sara and Baat working through intricate tricks on the trapeze, as if they'd never been apart. He wanted to be happy for her, but he felt unsettled. Anxious. "I don't know. It's early to think about it."

"Michel told me you're no longer on the act."

"I'm not."

"He also warned me to be careful with Sara's ass this morning," Theo added under his breath.

Jason wasn't in the mood to be drawn into this conversation. "She'd probably appreciate it if you were. Not that it's any of your business, or Michel's."

"She's my artist, my business." With that remark, he approached the trapezists to give directions and request improvements. Sara relayed his suggestions to Baat in Mongolian. He acknowledged them with a sullen expression.

Theo wasn't cowed. One thing about Theo, he didn't give a shit what anyone thought about him and he wasn't afraid to piss people off. At one point he made Baat get down so he could show what he meant, and partnered Sara through some moves they'd practiced while Baat was still in Mongolia. *Now you see how I feel*, thought Jason as Baat frowned from the sidelines. *How it feels to deal with an interloper.*

Jealousy. Jason had never experienced jealousy like this before, never fallen so hard and fast for a girl. He hadn't been joking about wanting to keep her in a cage. But he couldn't and he wouldn't, because she had crazy potential and a hard-earned career to pursue. He had a career too, artists to train, acts to develop. It wouldn't be healthy for either of them to get too lost in their dynamic.

Eventually Theo returned to his side, irritation tightening his features.

"What do you think of Baat?" Jason asked.

He waited a moment to answer. "I think he likes to do things his way. He likes her to do things his way. But this is the challenge of coaching, no? To get past the personalities to the talent beneath."

"Some personalities are worse than others," Jason joked, giving him the side eye.

Theo grinned. "My diva days are done. Kelsey made me grow up. It's good. Now maybe this is karma, that I have to work with this jackass."

"Karma's a bitch."

Theo nodded, but his gaze remained on Baat and Sara. "It's strange," he said after a moment. "They don't like each other. It's very bizarre, for trapeze. They work together, but it's very strained."

"Up until now, they probably had no choice but to work together. Mongolia's not a hotbed of circus schools."

"But if they don't have fun working together?"

"From what I understand, they grew up together. It tore her apart, leaving Mongolia without him. She wept from the guilt of it, and when I told her he'd come..."

She'd cried then too, great happy tears that he couldn't understand, except that Baat was her partner, and partners, especially trapeze partners, developed an iron bond.

"It's a Mongolian trait, this fidelity," said Theo in a pedantic tone. "Because their people's history is so steeped in communal herding. The interdependence of nomadic groups."

Jason snorted as Theo laced his fingers together, demonstrating his comment. "Since when do you know so much about Mongolian interdependence?"

"I make it my business to know, so I understand them better," he said, flicking a finger at the dark-haired couple on the trapeze.

Jason watched Sara, feeling chastened. He hadn't done any research on Mongolia beyond plane schedules and finding the BDSM club. All he'd researched about Sara were her pleasure points and her pain tolerance, and that she was amazingly good at the Master/slave thing.

He silently vowed to spend the next few weeks learning everything he could about her, not just what turned her on in bed.

She was his slave, but more than that, she was a fascinating, complex woman. Before the end of summer, before they had to make a decision about Vegas, he needed to know her inside and out.

Chapter Seven: Stress

Sara heard the tap on the door, saw Baat stick his head in.

"Sarantsat?" he said, his own nickname for her. He refused to use the English derivative.

She considered not answering. She'd taken to hiding from Baat during breaks, hiding in the locker room or empty conference spaces. They'd been here four weeks now, and he'd spent all four of them behaving like an ass. She was so tired of his complaining and negativity. She was tired of dealing with his unhappiness. Baat hated Jason, he hated Theo, he hated everyone he met, even Mr. Lemaitre. He claimed to hate everything about the Cirque. He cycled between wanting to go to Las Vegas and wanting to leave, in between blaming Sara for all his unhappiness. He spoke often about abandoning all their work to go home.

Because at home he could drink. At home there were no trainers, no artist dorms, no Cirque personnel checking on his well-being. Everyone in Mongolia drank, and so Baat drank, but here heavy drinking was frowned upon, and his habit was ballooning out of control. He knew it, she knew it. When she asked him to get help, he turned it back on her. *This is your fault. It's your fault I'm drinking, because I'm so miserable here.*

"Baat," she said. "*Sain uu.*"

He located her in the corner of the room and flicked on the lights, and returned her greeting. At one time it was a pleasure to speak to Baat because they both spoke Mongolian, but now all she ever heard were gruff, complaining words. "Why are you hiding here?" he asked.

There was accusation in his tone. *You,* Sara thought. *I'm hiding from you.* It was frowned upon to hide away, to be anti-social in their culture. *European manners*, he groused, angered by the hours she spent closeted at Jason's house. If he knew what they were doing there...

But it was none of his business, and the only way to spend time with Baat was to drink and complain, and Sara didn't enjoy either activity.

"Stupid Theo," he said, coming to flop in a nearby chair. "He treats me like an idiot."

"He treats you like a coach. He's trying to help. He's trying to make us better."

"I've been doing trapeze fifteen years now."

"He's been doing it longer." She'd anger him if she kept up. Then he'd start cursing at her and verbally abusing her, and he'd threaten to leave for the millionth time.

"Of course you defend him," Baat said, gazing at her through slitted eyes. "You've become such a slut. Are you sleeping with him too?"

Sleeping with Theo? Was Baat drinking during the day now? He usually saved the slut accusations for his drunken night time phone calls. "Don't say such things," she muttered. "It's not appropriate. Theo is very nice, and so is Kelsey, his wife. I've talked to her a few times after practice. You should chat with them too, get to know them better."

"How would I do that? I don't speak English or French or whatever they speak."

"Human Resources hired a translator for you," she pointed out. "You sent him back."

"Because he was a spy, not a translator. I didn't like him following me around."

"Then you should learn some other way to communicate. You can learn any language you want here. The Cirque has tutors who'll teach you for free."

"The Cirque this, the Cirque that." He wrinkled his nose in disgust. "You're obsessed with the Cirque, with your *success* and your *artistry*." He punctuated the words with effeminate flips of his hand. "You think any of these people care about you?"

"They care more than you."

"Because they chat with you after practice? I'd love to talk to you. Why don't you ever come to my place?"

"And watch you sit on your couch getting drunk and playing video games?"

He scowled at her. "I don't get drunk."

"You get drunk all the time."

"Never when I'm working. When I work, I work hard. What I do on my own time is my own business."

Except that his drinking would affect his fitness and eventually his ability to do their act. "I'm cooking for Jason tonight," she said. "Lamb and dumplings. Do you want to come?"

"And be a third wheel?"

"It's just dinner at his place. You never come out and do anything with us, or with Theo and Kelsey. Why don't you be social for once?"

He gave a huge sigh. "When are we going home?"

"As soon as dinner's over, I guess."

"No, not home here. Home to Mongolia. How long are you going to keep this up? Do you realize how unhappy I am here? Do you even care? Do you care about anything but your handsome American? I want to go home. I'll do this for a year, no more."

Sara stared at him. "You signed a three-year contract, Baat."

He kicked the table leg. "I can leave any time, so can you. The contract is a joke. This is circus."

"It's not just circus. It's Cirque du Monde. Why are you doing this? Whining and acting stupid, when we found a place with the best circus in the world?"

"The best circus in this part of the world," he snapped back at her. "What about our circus back home? You left, turned your back on everyone for this fancy, convoluted nonsense. Because of your blue eyes and your hunger for European men. The circus in Ulaanbaatar will fail by winter. Chuluun told me."

Sara wondered if that was true. "If it does, it's not my fault."

"How will they pay their bills? Pay for food for their families? Do you enjoy being the cause of starving children?"

"Shut up." Her voice rang out in the echoing room. When she made him angry, he got really mean. It seemed like she made him angry all the time now.

Or maybe he was just really mean.

"I'm tired of performing here," he said. "I'm tired of performing with you."

"Then go somewhere else." Her temper snapped, unleashed in a tirade. "Go back to Mongolia and drink away your life. Here, we're at the top of the heap. Cirque du Monde is professional, artistic. The circus in Mongolia was a joke."

"Perhaps, but here, you're a cog in the wheel," he yelled back. "You dream of grandeur. You're just a little dark-skinned, slanty-eyed trapezist. An exotic monkey for the owner to show off."

She gritted her teeth. She wanted to scream at him to shut up, to stop drinking and pull his shit together. She needed Baat with the same intensity that she hated him. She wished she could shout at him to fuck off, but without him she didn't have an act.

"They won't want you without me, you know," he said, reading her thoughts. "You can't do any of those tricks without me."

"And you can't do any tricks without me," she shot back. "So go back to Mongolia. The reason you're here is because you're nothing without me. Just like I'm nothing without you. It goes both ways."

"I'd be fine without you."

She stuck out her chin and crossed her arms over her chest. "Who would you perform with back in Ulaanbaatar?"

"Anyone. You think you're so special? There are gymnasts everywhere, trapezists lighter and stronger than you. You aren't indispensable. You're not even pretty. So I wouldn't count on a career at Cirque du Monde without me."

His words fell on her, piling up and piling up, until she felt like she was suffocating. It had gotten to the point where she didn't even like the sound of his voice. "Please go," she cried. "I'm taking a break. I need quiet. I want you to stay away from me while we're not working."

"I won't, if I don't want to." He scoffed, spitting on the carpeted floor.

"This isn't a yurt, Baat. It's a conference room. Don't be disgusting."

He turned on his heel and left, muttering derogatory things about her under his breath. It would probably be better for her sanity if he went back to Mongolia, taking his dark glares, his harsh words, and his emotional blackmail with him. But if he left, where did that leave her? There was a lot of competition at Cirque. Without an act, what would she be worth?

"I hate you," she whispered in the silence of the room. "I wish you'd stop being an asshole. I wish you'd be the Baat you used to be." She loved the old Baat, who'd been a mentor and a brother to her. She didn't know if he'd ever be back.

* * * * *

Jason stared across the table at his naked slave, posed gracefully in her chair. Did she realize how enticing she looked? He'd made her cook naked and eat naked, and now she sipped her after-dinner tea naked.

Ah, that mouth of hers.

They'd been together a month now, but she was so open, so giving that it seemed like longer. She revealed her heart to him at the most intimate moments, and he…he was falling hard for her. He tried to guard against it because her future was unsettled, but then she'd give him a look or reveal some secret longing, and he'd fall a little more.

Then there was the sex, the hours-long BDSM scenes. The horny, capricious rules, like requiring her to be naked while he stayed fully dressed. They maintained this clothing differential whenever they were alone together because it turned both of them on, and because it emphasized her status as his slave. They pulled the drapes closed and went about their business, doing all the things normal couples did, except that she wasn't allowed clothing. He'd memorized every detail of her luscious body by now, from her curves to her exotic features, to the dusky olive tone of her skin. Her nakedness seduced him more than any fetish wear or negligee ever could.

Now that they'd been tested and she was on birth control, he could take advantage of her nakedness anytime, anywhere, and he did. He took her on the couch, on the floor, in the shower. On the dining room table in the middle of a meal.

But not today. She'd put so much effort into cooking him Mongolian-style lamb and dumplings, and roasting vegetables, and brewing aromatic milk tea.

"I feel like I'm back in Ulaanbaatar. All that's missing is the alcohol," he said, winking at her. "And my drunken haze."

"You were cute in that drunken haze, but I like you better sober."

"I was 'cute,' was I?"

She blushed, ducking her head. "Cute in a very dominant way."

They shared a laugh, both of them lingering in the candlelight. He tried to make time every day to talk and learn more about her. She had a tendency to shyness around him, and he wanted to bring her out of her shell. The urge was always for bed, for slave games and kneeling, but there was a certain titillation in making her sit and converse with him too.

"What do you miss most about Mongolia?" he asked.

She looked around the items on the table. He hoped she wouldn't name a food. He wasn't talking about those kinds of things. She hugged herself and glanced over his shoulder. "I suppose I miss the cool air. It's hot in Paris."

"In the summer, yes. Cooler days will come in a few months."

She looked at him and they both remembered—she might be on some other continent come winter. They hadn't talked about their future together. It seemed too soon to make plans, but time was flowing so fast.

"Baat hates the weather here," she said, a neat avoidance of the topic. "He can't get used to it."

"I don't think he wants to get used to it."

She frowned, picking at a corner of her napkin. "I invited him to come to dinner."

"Let me guess. He scowled and said no." *Thank God*, he added silently. Jason couldn't stand Baat, and Baat couldn't stand him. He knew Sara and Jason were in a relationship and he didn't approve. It got to the point where Baat refused to practice when Jason was around, asking, rightfully, what business Jason had in the aerial facility. Then there was Baat's insistence that they be placed in Las Vegas, in *Cirque Brillante*, probably to separate Sara from Jason. But nothing would be decided until after the Exhibition, and the big boss had the final word.

Lemaitre had suggested *Brillante* from the start, but that was before he'd developed his little *tendre* for her. Jason wondered if he'd change his mind to keep Sara close at hand. Lemaitre hadn't made any overt passes toward her, perhaps out of respect for her and Jason's relationship, but he showed up to her practices far more than was normal. It was because of Lemaitre that Jason hadn't given in to Sara's pleas to visit the Citadel—yet. The Cirque boss held court there, in a bacchanalian, BDSM-equipped back room, and one didn't turn down an invitation to participate.

"What's wrong?"

Sara's quiet question drew him from his thoughts. "Nothing's wrong. Just thinking about work stuff. And how many dumplings I ate. Too many." He shook a finger at her. "They were too delicious. Your fault."

She smiled her sweet, flirty smile. "I'm glad you liked them. And thanks for trying the *suutei tsai*, even though you didn't like it."

He shuddered. Mongolian milk tea didn't taste anything like the name suggested. It mostly tasted like salt. "Sit and drink the rest of yours while I clean up."

She only sat because he ordered her to. Otherwise she'd be fluttering around him trying to do everything like a good slave girl. Honestly, there wasn't much to do. She cooked as neatly as she did trapeze combinations.

"So, what kind of work stuff are you thinking about?" she asked. "Is everything okay?"

"Are you worrying about me again? Why don't we both agree that your Master can take care of his own career? Just as you take care of yours," he added, collecting the plates.

"I know you can take care of yourself. You were a coach, weren't you? Before you were a director?"

"Yes."

"Were you ever a performer? Did you grow up in a circus family?"

Jason turned on the water and leaned on the counter, waiting for it to get hot. "No, I grew up in Sacramento. Slight difference."

"You did acrobatics in Sacramento?"

"I took gymnastics." He shrugged. "Only because my sisters took it and I was bored hanging out at the gym with my mom. I got better than either of them, but I never used it for performance. I did get a scholarship to a university. To UCLA."

"For gymnastics team?"

"No, I got too tall to compete." Jason could feel himself flushing. "The scholarship was for cheerleading."

"Cheerleading? What's that?"

He thought a moment, considering how to explain cheerleading to a trapezist from the Mongolian wild. "It's a quasi-sport, an American thing. I did back flips and tumbling and tossed girls up in the air and caught them. Like banquine, I suppose, but less classy. There was lots of yelling. Megaphones."

Her forehead wrinkled at *megaphones*. "Do you have any pictures?"

"No. There's no photo evidence. And if you ever tell anyone I cheered, I'll spank your ass until it catches on fire."

She took a sip of tea. "You shouldn't be embarrassed. It was a form of performance, yes? I'm sure you were very good at it. Very handsome and strong."

He tucked the last of the plates in the dishwasher. "I'll put it this way. Cheerleading doesn't scream masculinity. Or intellectualism. But it earned me a free degree, which my parents appreciated."

"You have a university degree?" This seemed to shock and delight her. He returned to sit with her at the table, puffing out his chest.

"I have an *advanced* degree, little slave girl. A Masters in Sports Science and Administration. Are you impressed?"

She grinned at him. "I am very impressed."

"When you don't grow up in the circus, like certain lucky people, you have to get fancy degrees and claw your way into the life."

She snuggled against his side as he scooted his chair closer to hers. "I never went to college," she said. "I only went six years to compulsory school, and then two years of tutors in the circus. I'm not that smart. I could never figure out math."

Jason laughed. "There's this stereotype that all Asian people are good at math. But then, you're different. You can see that just by looking at your eyes."

She covered her face. "My stupid eyes."

He pulled her hands away. "What do you mean by that?"

She was always so relaxed, so mild, but for a moment he saw fierce anger in her features. "You think they're pretty, but I've always hated my eyes. They make people stare. I want to get those contacts. The ones you talked about, that can change your eye color."

"You'll get contacts like that over my dead body. Your eyes are beautiful, Sara."

"To you they are," she retorted.

It wasn't a tone he liked, or any tone he'd ever heard from her, but he realized she was upset. "Are you going to get all snippity with Master?" he asked lightly. "I wish you wouldn't. I gave you a compliment. You should accept it gracefully."

"I'm sorry." She blinked and looked down into her cup. "Thank you for saying my eyes are beautiful. I'm glad if you find them...pleasing."

"Come here."

She gazed up at him in consternation, but he wasn't going to punish her. She looked like she needed a hug. Something was on her mind, something she wasn't sharing. Work stress? The Cirque could seem overwhelming to new recruits. He stroked her hair as she nestled her face under his chin. He whispered to her that he loved her, that she was beautiful and strong. He caressed her all over, massaging, soothing, squeezing her ass that always carried bruises and marks from their various sessions.

"Is everything okay in your world?" he asked when he felt her relaxing. "Is there anything you want to talk about?"

She paused—hesitated?—but then she shook her head. "Everything's wonderful. Thank you for asking." Her fingers curled on his arm, tracing his bicep. He wanted to take her upstairs and fuck her to oblivion. *In a little while. Talk to her first.* Part of his job as her Master was to look after her, and develop her into the best person she could be.

He hugged her close and rested his chin on her hair. "If you want to get a degree, little one, you can. I'm sure you're smart enough, and the Cirque has programs for that."

"The Cirque helps people go to university?"

"If they want to. People can't do circus forever. Some performers get tired, or injured. The program helps them develop alternative careers."

"I'll need to get a show first, I guess. Before Mr. Lemaitre will pay for something like that."

"You'll get a show. There's no reason why you wouldn't."

"Unless something happened."

"Like what?"

She was quiet a moment. "What would happen if Baat got sick? If something happened and he couldn't perform?"

He eased her back, searching her face. "Why? Is something wrong with Baat?"

She looked away, shaking her head. "No, but what would happen? Or what if I got sick? What happens when one person in the act can't continue?"

"Circus people don't get sick very often. What's going on with Baat? Is he giving you a hard time?"

"Not really," she said. "I'm just asking what would happen if...if something happened."

Vaguest question ever. He tried to quiet her concerns. "If there are problems between partners, we try to work things out. It's best to stay with the partner you have, unless things are really bad. In that case, the act is scrapped completely. Which is probably for the best."

"They get rid of the people?"

"They might offer them some other type of act. It depends on the performer, their level of skill, their variety of experience. How long they've been with the company." He forced her gaze back to his. "But you shouldn't worry about any of this. Lemaitre will keep Baat here. Everything will be fine."

"But what if he gets sick? What if he gets...cancer or something? Something where he really can't perform?"

"Cancer? Oh, Sara. I think you should worry less about crazy stuff and start enjoying your new career. You and Baat will blow everyone away at the Exhibition, and you'll get placed in a show, and then Baat won't be so grumpy. Once you're performing every night, with the crowds and the applause, he'll come around. He'll see how much better it is than Circus Mongolia, or anywhere else, for that matter. For now, hang in there, okay?"

"Okay, Master. I'll try."

"I'm here for you, baby, always, if things ever get too much. But I don't think you should worry about Baat getting cancer. It's not going to happen. And I'm not going to worry about you telling Theo I used to be a cheerleader, because that's not going to happen either, right?"

She giggled and pressed her face into his neck. "Don't you think Theo would want to know?"

"Literally, I would spank you until you died."

She laughed harder and pretended to shudder. "I wouldn't be a very good slave if I displeased my Master."

When she talked like that, it set him on fire. "You please me, little one." She looked up at him with her sweet, adoring gaze and he thought, *Jesus Christ, I'm so in love with you. Way too far in love with you, for being four weeks into this.* He fondled her breasts, then down between her legs, swallowing a groan as she ground against his erection through his increasingly snug jeans. He set her a little away from him before he lost his train of thought. "You please me so much that I have a surprise for you. We're going to the Citadel with Theo and Kelsey this weekend. They've invited us for dinner, and drinks afterward at the club."

Her face lit up with excitement. "The Citadel? Really?"

"Yes, really."

She sobered, thinking over his words. "We'll just have drinks?"

"Maybe more, you naughty girl." He laughed and slipped a finger inside her, then two. "We'll see when we get there. It's best to take things easy your first time."

But Sara was never one for taking things easy. She was his reckless, fearless slave, and she belonged in the world of the Citadel. Theo had already pledged to help keep her away from Lemaitre. With the two of them—and Kelsey—looking out for her, Jason trusted that everything would be okay.

Chapter Eight: Citadel

Jason leaned across Theo and Kelsey's kitchen table and brushed his lips against her cheek. "Stop fidgeting, little one," he said. "And eat something. You'll need the energy once we get to the club."

Sara flushed, embarrassed to be chided by her Master in front of their hosts. Not that Theo and Kelsey didn't understand their dynamic—Theo was the Master and Kelsey was the slave in their relationship. They were also married, which fascinated Sara. Theo and Kelsey were an established couple with a long history. Though she and Jason were close, he was only her Master of a few weeks. She stole a look at him as he chatted with Theo about company business. She couldn't help imagining what it would be like to be Jason's wife, to share a life and a home with him, and entertain friends in a tiny Parisian kitchen. She thought it would be heaven, even if he sometimes scolded her to stop fidgeting.

Next time he glanced up, she was obediently eating salmon and bites of a spicy, grainy tomato mixture, even though she didn't like tomatoes. Jason liked to make her try new things, foods or activities or sex acts she said she didn't like. It upset her at first, but most of the time she ended up liking them afterward, even the sex acts.

Especially the sex acts.

Oh God, she was fidgeting again. Jason was finally taking her to *le Citadel*, Mr. Lemaitre's private nightclub for members of the Cirque. Jason made a big deal of it, buying her a sleek, tight black dress for the occasion, and an ivory satin corset with stockings to wear underneath. He said Lemaitre preferred black, but he preferred white, and so did she. Sara liked to play the innocent. She loved when Jason called her *little one.*

The corset was beautifully elegant, with ribbons and lace, and wide garter straps that caressed her legs when she walked. Jason told her not to wear panties, so she felt naked under her fitted dress. The corset kept her sitting straight and held together, almost as if she were in bondage. She felt exotic and frazzled, on display, like a doll dressed for Master's pleasure.

Kelsey and the men were similarly dressed in black, per Mr. Lemaitre's dress code. Leather and latex was also allowed, even encouraged. She'd heard gossip about what went on at the Citadel...dancing, drinking, partying, and lots of fetish and sex. When she pressed Jason to expand on that last part, he only told her *le Citadel* defied definition, and that she'd have to wait and see.

But this meal was going on forever. Jason, Kelsey, and Theo were old friends and they liked to talk. Kelsey was from California, like Jason, with a bright, fun personality. She had beautiful, long, white-blonde hair that Sara wanted to touch, only to see if it was as soft as it looked. So far she hadn't been brave enough to touch it, although Theo stroked it often as he talked to his wife. They shared so many fond kisses and caresses, and a lot of jokes and laughter too.

Now Kelsey was telling Jason about her shoulder surgery, which she'd only had done to be proactive, because her left shoulder was tricky sometimes ever since she dislocated it. They talked about other injuries, and how diligent Lemaitre was in taking care of his performers. Then Theo made some crack about him taking care of them too well sometimes.

The conversation ground to a halt and all three of them glanced at her. She lowered her head and shoved a forkful of fish into her mouth. "This is really delicious. All the seasonings and the vegetables and...what is this stuff?" She pointed to the grainy substance.

"Polenta," Kelsey said. "It's supposed to be good for you, but if you don't care for it, let me get you something else. I asked Jason what you liked to eat, but he said to make whatever I wanted."

"Because I eat whatever he tells me," Sara said with a half-smile.

"Ah, it's easy to be the one on the bottom, yes?" said Theo. "Just do as you're told."

Kelsey batted her husband. "It's not as easy as you think. Maybe we should try switching sometime."

"I'm always happy to do switching," he replied with a dangerous smile. "But it might not be the type of switching you hope for."

Jason burst out laughing at Kelsey's flustered look. "Really, Kels? You would want to top Theo? He'd curse and complain the whole time, and top like crazy from the bottom."

"I'm a masochist, not a miracle worker." She made a face at her husband. "Don't worry, you're secure in your mastery."

"Has *anyone* ever topped you, Theo?" asked Jason. "Lemaitre?"

Theo shook his head. "We have a history, *oui*, but not that type of history. I don't make a good bottom. I leave that to the experts." He reached to take his wife's hand, an easy gesture that spoke volumes about their comfort with each other. *Someday. Someday you might have that with Jason.* She hoped so…but she'd have to leave after the Exhibition, go to another city and another show, unless she could get into *Tsilaosa.* Jason said they'd find a way to continue their relationship, but it would be difficult, so far away from each other.

When conversation came back around to the Cirque, Sara asked Kelsey and Theo about their experience with *Cirque de Minuit* in Marseille, and if they knew anything about *Cirque Brillante.*

"I know it's in Las Vegas," Kelsey answered in a sympathetic tone. "That's really it."

"Vegas can be fun," added Theo. Jason didn't say anything, just stared into his drink.

"I wish I could stay here and be in *Tsilaosa*," she blurted. "You were in that show a long time, weren't you, Theo? Did you enjoy it?"

Now all of them were staring very intently at the table. "I wouldn't say I enjoyed it," Theo said. "I prefer doing *Minuit* with my wife."

"I wish there was a way for me to be in the Paris show so I could stay here." She knew she sounded whiny. Jason was giving her a cease-and-desist look. "There's no trapeze act in *Tsilaosa*," she persisted, "when almost every other circus has one. I don't get it, and no one will tell me why."

Theo pushed his chair back and stood. "I'm going to get some air." He strode through the kitchen, pausing by the back door. "You can tell her, but I don't want to hear the story again."

Sara watched in distress as he closed the door behind him with a click. "I'm sorry," she whispered. Jason looked perturbed. Kelsey seemed on the verge of tears. "I'm so sorry for whatever I said."

"It's a little late now," Jason said.

Kelsey touched his hand. "Don't get angry with her. She's right, no one has explained. Why wouldn't she question?"

Jason sighed and rubbed his forehead. "Are you going to tell the story, or me?"

"You should tell it. I'll cry if I tell it."

Sara stared at her plate, mortified that she'd ruined their dinner party. She could see Theo on the back porch, staring out at the black night.

"So," said Jason in a heavy voice. "*Tsilaosa* had a trapeze act once. Duo swinging trapeze, with Theo and a girl named Minya. She was from China, and she was in a relationship with Theo. Not a serious one. Well, to Theo, it wasn't serious. It was more serious to her than he realized. I mean, wouldn't you say that's what happened?"

He looked at Kelsey and she nodded, too emotional to speak.

"Anyway," Jason continued, "Theo and Minya went up one night and they...they missed a connection. Minya went into a somersault but she turned the wrong way. Theo managed to catch her but he didn't manage to hold her. Or rather..." He looked under his lashes at Sara. "She let go. Later, they found out she let go. She'd cut the safety line before she ever went up, to be sure nothing saved her. She chose to fall."

Sara stared. "On purpose?"

"On purpose. I guess we'll never know why. Because she was mentally ill. Because she wanted to hurt Theo. I don't know. Because she wanted to die for some misguided reason."

"She died?"

"She fell almost eighty feet, little one. Yes, she died."

"I was there," said Kelsey. "I was watching from backstage. I'd only just joined Cirque, and I saw her fall and hit the ground." She covered her mouth, her eyes filling with tears. "And I remember looking up and seeing Theo waiting there, hanging down from the trapeze with his arms out, like he might still catch her."

Sara's eyes filled too. She could barely process the vision in her mind. Theo's partner had killed herself in the middle of a performance and left him to deal with the grief. She looked out the back window, at Theo, happy, joking Theo who stood so stiff and still.

"I don't think there'll ever be another trapeze act in *Tsilaosa*," said Jason. "It's bad circus voodoo. After Minya fell, Lemaitre burned the safety lines she cut, replaced the rigging, everything. It's been expunged from Cirque history, and that's why no one ever talks about it. Why no one would answer your questions."

That didn't seem right to Sara. "Wouldn't it be healthier to talk about it? It's not fair to Theo, to treat it like some dark, shameful secret. He didn't do anything wrong."

Kelsey dried her eyes on the edge of her napkin. "I think he understands that, but it still hurts. It's still bad voodoo, like Jason said." She and Jason exchanged a look, then she went to the living room and returned with a light blanket.

"These cool summer nights," she said, holding it out to Sara. "Why don't you take him a blanket while Jason and I clean up?"

It wasn't a cool night at all, but Sara took the blanket and headed toward the porch. Her and her big mouth. Now Theo was sad, and a million questions swarmed in Sara's head, questions about relationships and depression, and circus superstitions. When she opened the door, Theo turned to her and all the questions fled. All she could think was, *this poor man.*

She held out the blanket. "Kelsey sent this for you. In case you were cold."

He turned his head a little toward her, then away. She didn't know what to do. She didn't know if he was irritated, or sad, or whether he wanted company right now. She stepped outside anyway and stood beside him, and waited for the appropriate words to come. But the only words that came were, "I'm sorry."

Theo grunted, his noise that meant *I don't know what to say right now*. He opened the blanket and wrapped it around Sara's shoulders. "You don't have to be sorry."

She tried to hand it back to him. "It's supposed to be for you."

After some repositioning, they stood within the blanket shoulder to shoulder, each clutching one end. "I don't know what to say, Theo," she began. "Except it wasn't your fault."

He gave a short, bitter laugh. "Everyone says that, but it was partly my fault. I wasn't attentive. I didn't care for her feelings. I was too much her Master and not enough her friend." He drew in a great, halting breath. "That is the thing, you know, with power exchange. You can't wander too far from the heart. People try, but..." He squeezed her hand under the blanket and let it go. "I doubt you'll get to stay in Paris, *ma brillante*. It's not meant to be."

"Why do you call me that? *Ma brillante*?"

"Because of your eyes. They are brilliant blue, *non*? So unexpected." He blinked at her, then looked away. "You remind me so much of Minya sometimes. You look so much like her, but she didn't have your eyes. You are happy, Sara?"

"Yes."

"Jason makes you happy? If he doesn't, you have to tell him. Don't be so submissive that you lose yourself."

She made a sound of agreement past the tightness in her throat. "I won't lose myself."

"You know, you must follow your own path. Make your own way. Jason will come to you. He'll come to Vegas, or wherever you end up. He won't mind leaving his job."

"He shouldn't have to," she said with an edge of impatience. "Maybe it's time to let go of this tragedy. Time to let Minya's ghost rest. I'm here, and you, and many trapezists who could delight Paris for years to come. Because of her, we can't go up there?"

Theo gazed at her, his eyes liquid dark in the night. "Really, you are not very much like Minya. You are stronger than she was. Stronger here." He touched a finger to her heart. "You came out of Mongolia all alone, with nothing, to join the biggest circus in the world. You put up with your unpleasant trapeze partner, day in, day out, and choose the most rigid Master to serve. And you are not afraid of Lemaitre, are you?"

"No, I'm not afraid of him. But I don't think he likes me."

"Why do you say that?"

"Whenever I see him, he frowns at me. He frowns when he watches our act. He never talks to me. I wonder sometimes if he's disappointed he asked me to come."

"He's not disappointed, I promise. He just knows you belong to Jason." He chuckled. "He has an affinity for exotic young beauties, so be careful. Stay close to Jason when we're at *le Citadel*."

She turned to Theo in surprise. "We're still going?"

"Of course we are. Do you think I haven't noticed you fidgeting out of your skin with anticipation? Just because you ask rude questions about my past and depress everyone, it doesn't mean we can't still go out and have fun."

She'd been prepared to go home with Jason and endure a punishment for ruining the dinner. Going to the club would be so much better. "Thanks, Theo," she said. "I'm glad you're my coach. I'll miss you when you go back to Marseille. Kelsey too."

"Oh, we'll be around," he said, waving a hand. "Sometimes we come to Paris only to visit the original Citadel. It's the biggest, best one. There's dancing and lights, music, free drinks, and an entire back hallway of special, private rooms." He waggled his eyebrows. "And they are for exactly what you think."

* * * * *

Jason tried not to be exasperated with Sara. He understood that a lot of her missteps were due to cultural reasons. In Mongolia, people got in each other's business. Whole families lived in one-room structures, so they watched out for each other, and demanded explanations when things were off.

Still, if she didn't let the trapeze thing drop, he was going to beat her naughty little ass until she couldn't sit for a goddamn week. Hashing over the Minya thing made everyone unhappy, and each time she talked about staying in Paris to do trapeze, the scab was torn off anew.

At least Theo didn't hold a grudge. By the time he and Sara returned to the kitchen, he was smiling and Sara was out-of-her-mind excited to leave for the Citadel. It was hard to stay mad at her when she was so enthused. Jason, Theo, and Kelsey were hardened attendees by now, but it was fun to see it through a newbie's eyes. As Kelsey said, they all remembered their first times. Kelsey's first time, she'd gotten so drunk she went up to Le Maître—while he was in full character and fetish gear—and flirted with his "pets." She'd cooed over them and scratched behind their ears like they were really pets, while Theo looked on in horror.

They told the story to Sara on the way over, painting a picture until she doubled over with laughter, tottering on her heels.

"I'll try to remember not to do that," she said, taking Kelsey's hand. "Just stay by me, and tell me if I'm about to mess up."

The two girls walked hand in hand the rest of the way. It was sweet. Kind of hot, although he knew Sara did it in complete innocence, because Kelsey was easy to talk to and because they were close in age. Sweet, happy women, and behind them, their perverse other halves dreaming of sexual bedlam.

"They'd be pretty in bed together, eh?" said Theo under his breath.

"Or tied to a bed together."

"Or put in a cage together. Have to give each other orgasms before they could come out."

Jason laughed. "You always have to one-up me. Anyway, I thought Kelsey was straight?"

"She's as straight as I want her to be. She's been with women." His perverse grin deepened. "She does what I like, which is why I love her so much. Is Sara bisexual?"

"We've never talked about it, but she's generally open to new things."

"Nice to have those types of slaves."

"Yep."

"But also dangerous, at a place like *le Citadel.* Don't give her too much to drink this first time."

Jason had no intention of letting Sara get shit faced, and he wouldn't be drinking much either. Drinks were free because no one went overboard with them. Most people didn't go to the Citadel to get shit-faced. When you stepped through the doors, it was all about the rush of sensual, hedonistic physicality. So many bodies, all of them healthy and athletic. So many creative, unfettered minds. It was a heady combination...and it was Saturday night.

The doorman waved them in, and Sara accepted earplugs from Theo and Kelsey as they navigated through the crowds outside the coat room to the pounding, smoky heart of the club. The bar was on one side, and a raised platform dominated the other. The evening's festivities were already in full swing. Revelers writhed and jumped on the dance floor amidst the fake smog and lights, many of them barely dressed. Clothing grew more optional as the night wore on. When Le Maître arrived, people would move to the back rooms to play, although you only entered the Back Room—the main dungeon—at his invitation.

Later on, Jason would take Sara back and show her the tamer play rooms, maybe even scene with her a little. He was eager to show off his beautiful slave, in her ivory corset that complemented her skin tone to perfection. He preferred her naked in his bedroom, but here, he wanted to let her shine.

As Jason expected, Sara took two sips of her drink and lost interest, distracted by all the activity going on around her. "May I go dance? Please?" she asked.

The four of them headed to the dance floor in a group. Jason saw women he knew, women who'd submitted to him before, but the company rumor mill had done its work connecting him with Sara, and none of them approached him. Theo and Kelsey were an established couple and they stayed in each other's arms, tuning out everything else. Sara was less focused, but that was okay.

She leaned close so he could hear her over the music. "Thanks for bringing me here."

He ran his fingers up her waist, tracing the bones of the corset beneath her dress. "It's my pleasure. Are you having fun? You look happy."

She glanced beside them, at a towering, powerfully built leather-sub and his pink-haired mistress. Beside that couple, a threesome was alternately dancing and locking lips. Jason pulled Sara closer, running his fingers up and down her back, over her hidden lacings. Even in the darkness, her blue eyes stood out like glittering jewels. Eternal eyes. "I'm so happy," she yelled over the music. "I love this. I loved dinner with Kelsey and Theo too. I feel so...included."

"Of course you're included." Kelsey's voice rang out while Theo bumped them, interrupting their kiss. Soon all four of them were dancing together and laughing. Sara reached out to stroke Kelsey's hair.

"It's so pretty," she cried. "So light and beautiful. I've wanted to touch it all night."

Kelsey seemed delighted to let Sara stroke her hair, and Jason and Theo were both delighted to watch. "When are you going to start kissing?" Theo asked in his usual blunt style. "That's what everyone wants to see."

"When we go to the back rooms, maybe," said Kelsey with a gleam in her eye. "We are going to the back rooms together, aren't we?"

"We'll see," Jason answered, bemused by Kelsey's hornified enthusiasm. He and Kelsey were friends, nothing more. He'd be able to tease her about this later, whether they only played BDSM games, or went all the way, having sex between the four of them. Since she was currently, actively kissing Sara, Jason guessed there was a good chance of sex.

"I should never give her alcohol," Theo said to Jason.

"Or maybe give her a little more." Jason watched Sara for signs of distress, but she'd abandoned herself to Kelsey's embrace.

"Back rooms?" asked Theo.

"Back rooms," agreed Jason. He took hold of Sara's hair and drew her attention from Kelsey. "Do you want to go play?" he asked. "Exchange power with Theo and Kelsey? There may be other people there."

"Other people we'll play with?" she asked.

"Probably not. You never know, when things get rolling. But listen." He took her face to be sure she heard him. "We don't have to do anything. We can just hang out and dance."

He liked to push her to try new things, but public, group play was one of those things a submissive had to choose for herself. There were rules at the Citadel to protect everyone who played there, and everything was consensual. All the sex was safe. The emotional part of it was harder, accepting that you could be part of a very happy couple and still play with outside partners. "Did you like kissing Kelsey?" he asked, staring at her lips. "It looked so pretty. What if Theo kissed you? Would that turn you on?"

She looked shocked at the suggestion, but also curious. "I don't know. I'll try anything you like, Master. I want to see what happens in the back rooms. You said I had to see it for myself."

"So I did."

He beckoned Theo and Kelsey, and the four of them headed down the hall to peek into the various private spaces. The walls were stone and the doors heavy, age-scarred wood. Even over the music, you could hear impact and screams, and thrilled shouts. Halfway down they encountered a cluster of people watching a scene. Jason heard Lemaitre's voice, Lemaitre's laugh.

They tried to move to the side, but the revelers saw them and parted. Le Maître was tormenting a slave at his feet, a cowering, willing beauty, probably testing her limits before he invited her to his private play space. He was shirtless, his low-riding leather pants revealing his enviable physique. Sara gaped at him, never having seen Michel Lemaitre outside his crisp, bespoke CEO suits. Jason barely heard her gasp, but Le Maître heard it. His eyes locked on Jason first, then Sara.

He hauled his slave up and shooed her down the hall, then grabbed Theo and barked in his ear in French. Theo jerked away, gone white and grim. He turned to Jason and spoke to him, also in French.

"He says Sara has to go."

"What? Why?"

"He won't say why, but he means it. He said not to bring her back again." Theo looked furious, but at *le Citadel*, Le Maître's word was law. "Come, let's go," he said to Sara and Kelsey in English. "There's no room for us back here tonight."

"What's wrong?" asked Sara. "We have to go? Now?"

"We have to leave," said Jason, taking refuge in activity. If he didn't stay busy, if he didn't concern himself with bundling Sara up and getting her out of there, he'd go after Lemaitre and punch him in the face. Theo seemed to understand that. He stood between Jason and Lemaitre until the scowling Master of the Citadel turned on his heel and stalked back down the hall. The door to his inner sanctum slammed.

"Nice," muttered Kelsey under her breath. In the end, she was the one who calmed Sara, who hugged her and said, "Come on, we'll find something else to do."

The four of them left the club and clustered together outside the door. Jason seethed as he watched a lackey deliver a note to the doormen, probably an edict that Sara wasn't to be re-admitted. Fucking Lemaitre. Sara wasn't underage, she wasn't in disgrace, and she was in an active Master/slave relationship. She was beautiful and daring and she belonged in *le Citadel* with her colleagues and fellow pervs.

"I don't understand," she said, burying her face in Jason's shoulder. "What did I do? Why does he hate me?"

"He doesn't hate you, baby." He tilted her face to his and gave her a kiss. "I'm sure this is a misunderstanding. I'll make him explain tomorrow. But yes, this sucks donkey balls."

"It's outrageous," said Theo. "Completely outrageous."

Kelsey beckoned to her husband and whispered something in his ear. He listened a while, nodded, then turned to Jason. "Come back to our place? Kels says we can do as well as Le Maître. Even better."

Jason thought she was probably right. He looked down at Sara, smoothing the miserable lines from her forehead.

"Don't worry. You're going to have your Citadel experience tonight, little one," he promised. "Or as close to it as we can get."

Chapter Nine:
Even Better

For some reason, the Zamoras had a disco ball mounted over their bed.

"I'm not going to ask," said Jason, holding up his hands. "I don't want to know about your freaky sex life. It'll be a nice touch with the Christmas lights, though. Almost like the real thing."

Sara was warmed to the bottom of her soul by the effort they were putting into this, all to make her feel better. It took fifteen minutes for Theo and Jason to crawl into the attic and find some holiday lights, and fifteen more minutes for them to hang them in the Zamora's bedroom. In the meantime, Kelsey browsed her mp3 files and put together a sultry, sexy play list, playing snippets of songs for Sara's opinion. Setting up "Club Zamora" almost, *almost* helped her forget the look on Mr. Lemaitre's face when he'd kicked her out of the Citadel.

She couldn't understand it. Why?

Jason said they could figure it out tomorrow. He was certain it was all a mistake, but Lemaitre's anger hadn't seemed like a mistake to Sara. Didn't she have a right to be there, just like everyone else?

"Are you still thinking about the Citadel?" asked Kelsey as she arranged candles around the bed. "Because we're going to have fun, tons more fun than we would have had there. I'm sure the guys will make us orgasm a zillion times."

Sara smiled at her friend, curious how everything would play out. Did the Zamoras play harder or softer than her and Jason? Would they all have sex together, or would they trade partners? Would she and Kelsey kiss some more? Sara wouldn't mind that. Or would there be no sex at all?

"Is that for the smoke?" Jason coughed as Kelsey lit the candles, one after the other. "This doesn't have to be exactly like the Citadel."

"*Ma chère*," Theo said to his wife. "Go get some wine. It's time to set the mood."

Sara moved to go too, but Jason stopped her. "Not you." He eased her dress up and off, so she only wore her corset and stockings. Then he pointed to the floor. "Right there."

She swallowed hard, sinking to her knees. Jason stared at her until she assumed the correct position: legs spread, back arched, eyes on him. Theo glanced over, still rearranging the lights, and she flushed with a delicious kind of embarrassment. She knew she was dressed in a way that pleased Jason, and that she had a strong, attractive body. She knew they were all about to do a scene together but she still felt pangs of shyness. Theo wasn't her partner. He was her coach.

"*Très jolie*," he said, nodding at her. She didn't know if he meant her appearance or the enticing way she was posed, but his approving smile made her feel warm inside. At last Theo arranged the strands to his satisfaction, and strode to the wall to turn off the overhead light. The blinking, twinkling colors gave the room an otherworldly air. As if on cue, Kelsey returned with goblets and a bottle of wine. She set them on a side table and then Theo and Kelsey started to undress each other.

Sara wasn't sure where to look. Was it okay to stare? They were beautiful—both their physiques and the tender way they interacted. Theo was so dark and Kelsey so pale and light, and both of them had amazing bodies. Theo stripped Kelsey of everything, even her pretty black bra and panties. She had tight pink nipples and a little patch of blonde fuzz over her pussy. Sara wanted to check out Theo's cock but wasn't certain about matters of etiquette. Jason knelt behind her and nudged her face in their direction when she tilted it away. "Go ahead and look at him," he said with a hint of laughter. "See what you're in for."

Like Jason, Theo was strong and powerfully built, and his cock looked every bit as long and thick as her lover's. It rested on a thatch of dark hair that matched the tapered hair on his chest. Theo pulled Kelsey close and tilted her head back for a deep kiss as the lights flickered and reflected off their bodies.

While she watched, Jason knelt again and pulled her arms behind her, and cuffed her wrists at the small of her back. "Chest out," he reminded her. "Good girl. Let's get you in the right frame of mind."

She was afraid he meant the nipple clamps, and she was right. He folded down the cups of her corset and flicked her nipples until they went pert and hard. She gasped, fighting through the pain as he attached the first biting clamp, then the other. She gazed a little jealously at Kelsey, who got to pour wine and enjoy her husband's embraces while Sara had to sit, bound in her slave pose, wearing clamps with a heavy, dangling chain.

"It's not fair, is it?" he said, following her gaze. "But Kelsey's shoulder is still recuperating. That means you'll be doing most of the fucking, sucking, and hurting tonight."

Oh, really? Sara didn't want her friend's injury to worsen, but to be the main event for these two huge, dominant, sadistic guys? But they were doing this for her, because she'd been booted out of the Citadel. If anything, she should be grateful. She *was* grateful, just a little bit scared out of her mind.

Jason held his glass to her lips, and she took a deep drink for courage. The wine tasted rich and spicy, and the flavor lingered on her tongue as the men discussed things like limits and protection. Since both couples were clean and fluid-bonded, they decided not to bother with condoms for oral, only vaginal and anal penetration. *Anal penetration?* That little discussion did nothing to relax her. Kelsey touched Sara's nipples in sympathy and kissed her, and Jason gave her another sip of wine.

"She looks nervous, your little slave," said Theo. He came and knelt in front of her, and gave her some wine too. "You're afraid?"

He stroked her cheek, then squeezed her waist, admiring the corset, but she couldn't stop shaking. She knew Theo well, but she didn't know *this* Theo, whose voice sounded seductive, whose eyes promised wicked things. "What are you afraid of?" he pressed.

You. Jason. All of this.

"I want to please you," she said. "And…and please my Master."

He studied her. She could always read everything in Theo's eyes…if he was annoyed, if he was pleased, if he was amused, but she couldn't read them now. "Just be a good girl, no? That's how you please your Master." He kissed her, a warm, searching kiss that was over before she could pinpoint how it made her feel. Desired? No. Protected? Maybe. It had been a kiss to calm her. She felt a little calmer, but not much. He gave her more wine, and she took a great big sip. Then she heard Jason chuckle beside her.

"Are you trying to get my slave drunk?"

Theo glanced up at him. "No, she has to choose this with all her wits." He looked back at Sara, holding her gaze. "You want? You're sure? All of us together, having sex, having a scene?"

"Yes…" She paused. He was looking at her so intently. She wanted to call him *Sir* or *Master* or something to signify that she agreed to submit to him. Jason squeezed her shoulder.

"You can call him Master if you like. For now. *Only* for now."

His teasing warning brought some lightness to the heavy moment. Sara smiled into her coach's dark eyes. "Yes, Master, I want this."

He made a soft sound of approval. "What a brave girl you are."

Argh. As soon as she relaxed, he said something like that to send her into a panic again. She met Kelsey's gaze. Her friend smiled from behind Theo's shoulder, telling her without words that everything would be okay. What had she promised? A zillion orgasms? Sara would settle for zero, only to experience this moment of being a sexual plaything, a bound victim for two men's pleasure. Master's toy to share.

Play with me, please. Before I lose my mind.

At last, Theo and Jason put down their glasses and turned up the music, not as loud as it was at the Citadel, but loud enough to drown out some of her inner dialogue. *Now. They're going to touch me now, and do...what?* Sara's trembling turned to outright shaking. Both their cocks were hard and getting harder. Jason knelt behind her a third time and this time he smoothed a blindfold over her eyes. She made a sound of protest as the pretty lights went black.

"I know, baby," Jason murmured. "But I don't want you to be distracted by anything. I want you experiencing every touch, every sensation without knowing where it's coming from. It's a popular game at the Citadel."

She turned her head, disoriented by darkness. "How can I serve you if I can't see you?"

"You'll know what to do. We won't leave any question as to what's required."

A moment later, she felt cool fingers on her face, and a warm cock prodding at her lips. She didn't know whose it was, but she opened her mouth and accepted its thrusting length. She experienced a moment of panic—*I can't do this*—but then someone's hands twisted in her hair and arousal followed, an automatic reaction to the pain. That hand was telling her to surrender. Surrender to their power and her helplessness.

I want to surrender. She lifted her face to whoever was using her, opening her mouth wide even as she feared the penetration. The cock drove deeper, thrusting fast, then it was gone, leaving her breathless. Fingers wrapped around her neck and another cock slid into her mouth. The same cock? A different one? She had no way to tell.

She heard French, a hushed conversation, then Kelsey's soft voice. Quick footsteps crossed the room while Sara tried to please whoever was in her mouth. She licked and sucked, gagged a little and made a moan of a sound, an apology or maybe a plea for more. She got more almost immediately, a deeper thrust, a steady face-fucking for several moments. Then that cock was gone, and another in its place before she could even close her mouth.

"Do you like this, little one?" Jason asked. That must have been his fingers twisting in her hair, because they tightened.

"Yes, Master," she gasped as soon as the cock in her mouth allowed her to breathe.

"You love to serve us, don't you? You love to submit to your Masters' needs."

She nodded, since her mouth was too full to speak. She wanted so badly to please, but she couldn't see and she couldn't breathe very well, and the cocks kept coming. Then she heard a new sound, a quiet buzz.

"Your friend Kelsey is going to make you come with a cock between your lips," said Jason. "I don't care whose cock. You have...what do you think, Theo? Five minutes?"

She felt fingers under her chin, pulling her straighter. "Three minutes," came Theo's deep voice. "She can manage in three. She's already so turned on."

Three minutes?

"Three minutes then," Jason agreed. "Spread your legs wider for Kelsey. That's a good girl."

Sara felt probing fingers between her thighs, sliding through her sopping pussy lips. She wasn't sure she could come at all. She felt so overwhelmed, so controlled by the men's grasping hands and their cocks impeding her breath. The vibrator only provided a low buzz, but Kelsey found just the spot to put it. Sara groaned deep in her throat, rising, arching her hips to maintain the contact on her clit.

Another hand on her shoulder, forcing her down. The face-fucking transformed from dominance to struggle. She had three minutes to come, three minutes to make her body obey her Master's will, but he also expected her to continue servicing him and Theo.

"Watch your teeth," Jason barked when she lost her concentration. She jumped as he jerked the chain between her nipples. *Owww.* She curled her toes, opening her mouth wider at the same time she sought the gentle hum of the vibrator.

"This is what they do at the Citadel," said Theo. "They make naughty, horny slaves do naughty, horny things until they forget who they are. This is only the beginning, eh?"

He sounded so much like her coach, but he wasn't her coach. He was her tormentor now, like Jason, and Kelsey was her only saving grace. Sara wailed and nodded when her friend found her clit with the tip of the vibrator. Kelsey kept it there, right *there*, and Sara tensed, spreading her legs, still sucking, still gagging and drooling all over herself. Growing pleasure warred with her aching jaw, as she sobbed through the men's repeated forays into her mouth.

"You look so beautiful," Kelsey whispered in her ear. "You make such a beautiful slave."

"You have a minute to come," said Jason.

Their thrusts intensified, but so did Sara's arousal. She choked as one of them grabbed her head and jammed himself deep in her throat. Her clit throbbed, needing more, more... The cuffs hurt her hands, but then her peak was there, right there. She cried, she moaned, she bucked against the vibrator, and then she orgasmed, coming all over Kelsey's hand as she sucked the cock in her mouth. She didn't care. The hand in her hair relaxed, smoothing it back from her face. Whoever was in her mouth drew away, leaving her gasping. The blindfold felt damp where her tears had soaked it. The vibrator clicked off and, after terse French directions from Theo, Sara felt Kelsey move away.

"What a good girl," said Jason, and beneath her shivering and lack of breath, Sara felt joyful. Someone took off the clamps, slapping her breasts as blood rushed in to make them tingle with an almost unbearable fullness. "Oh, please, Master," she sighed. *Please hurt me some more.*

"What next?" asked Theo.

"I liked your cage idea," said Jason. "But we don't have a cage big enough for both girls, and Sara's already come once."

"This is true. Perhaps it's time for Kelsey to catch up."

Sara was lifted and guided across the room with a hand at the back of her corset. She heard instructions, apparently meant for Kelsey. *Lie back. Lace your hands behind your head. Spread your legs. Wider.* Someone, probably Jason, bent Sara over the bed. He guided her head between her friend's thighs.

"Time for you to lick Kelsey's pussy, little one. Make her come for you. Kiss her nice and sweet, just like you did while you danced."

Sara had never gone down on a woman before, but if she had to fumble through this, she was happy it was with Kelsey. Sara wasn't exactly turned on, but it made her hot that she was being forced to do this. The slavey side of her wanted to please, wanted to give Kelsey the best orgasm ever. She gave her friend a few tentative licks, discovering the taste of her. She was very, very wet.

"Oh, God," Kelsey breathed, and Sara wished she wasn't blindfolded so she could see her face. She decided not to go right for her clit. Instead, she toyed with her and teased her, drawing the moment out. The men were silent, doing God knew what. Watching, she supposed. She decided she would make it as pretty as she could for them. She arched her back and licked Kelsey all over, reveling in her soft, high-pitched moans.

Theo said something in French that Sara couldn't decipher and Jason spoke French back to him. Then, *whack!* She heard the sound of impact, but didn't feel any pain. Kelsey jumped, her leg jerking. Another whack and Kelsey tried to pull her legs closed.

"Open," Theo barked. "Legs still."

Sara raised her head, trying to figure out what was going on, why Kelsey was whimpering rather than moaning, then she felt the excruciating snap of a leather strap across her ass cheeks. "Don't stop," said Jason. "If you can come while you're getting double-faced-fucked, Kelsey can come while she's getting whipped on the inside of her thighs."

Sara cringed on her friend's behalf. Whips hurt so bad, and the soft skin of the inner thigh was so sensitive.

"The sooner you make her come," said Jason with another stroke of the strap, "the sooner Theo puts the whip away. Do you understand?"

"Yes, Master." *Pressure. Oh God.*

So much for taking her time, for making it last. She buried her face in Kelsey's pussy and decided she'd better find her clit immediately. She had a general idea what she was doing but—

Whack!

Kelsey bounced against her face and groaned.

"I'm sorry. I'm sorry," Sara said.

"It's okay," Kelsey replied. "It feels really good, it's just—"

"Less talking, more licking," Jason warned, and both girls yelped as they received their Master's punishment. Sara explored her friend's sex, licking, sucking, searching for that spot that would make her moan again. If only she could see! If only she could use her hands to part Kelsey's pussy, but they were still cuffed behind her so all she could use were her lips and tongue. She finally found a place that made Kelsey babble in between tortured cries. It was *cry, beg, cry, beg* on Kelsey's end, while Jason strapped Sara from behind every twenty seconds or so.

Please come, she thought. *Please come, Kelsey, because I don't know what else to do.*

"I don't think you're trying hard enough," Jason said. "Kelsey's thighs are sore and red and so is your ass." He gave her the hardest stroke yet, and she wailed against Kelsey's pussy.

"I'm sorry, Master. I'm doing my best."

"Maybe you need a good, hard assfucking to motivate you."

"I'm sure she needs that," Theo chimed in. "The lube is in the drawer."

"Hm. I might use a little lube. If she gets that tongue moving."

Theo's only response was another series of whacks to Kelsey's thighs. Sara lapped at her friend's pussy, trying not to flinch as Jason dripped lube on her asshole and pressed his cock against it. With the blindfold obscuring her vision, everything felt more intense—Kelsey's flinching and crying, the heat of her friend's pussy, and the pain as Jason pushed in the head of his cock. She tensed around it, then whined through the aching burn as he slid all the way in, then out again.

It might have been too much, if Kelsey's cries hadn't started rising in intensity. "Yes, yes," her friend begged. "Don't stop."

Sara didn't stop, and Theo didn't either. *Whack, whack, whack.* Jason drove into her from behind, reaming her asshole, while Kelsey's cries rose to a scream and then broke in a gasp of relief. "Don't stop, don't stop," she said as her legs tensed against Sara's shoulders. Sara tongued her clit until her friend's orgasm peaked and her jerking pelvis came to rest.

Was that it? Apparently not, since Jason's cock was still buried in her ass. He pushed her up onto the bed. Her face and corset slid against the sheets until someone took her shoulders and lifted her. Since Jason was fucking her ass, it had to be Theo. He slid beneath her so she felt his warmth through the satin of her corset, and his sheathed cock against the inside of her thigh.

"Oh God," she cried. Next thing she knew, she was rearranged between them and Theo's cock was pressing against her pussy. This was definitely something she hadn't done before. Gentle hands stroked her hair and guided her face to the side, and soft lips pressed to hers.

"You'll like this," said Kelsey. "Just let it happen. This is how things go at the Citadel. You do things you never dreamed you'd do."

"I don't know if I can do this." She winced as Theo's cock eased a little deeper. She felt so full, too full, but the two pairs of hands on her waist wouldn't let her shift away. "I'm scared," she said, burying her face against Kelsey's cheek.

"I'm always scared when I play in the back rooms," she said, "but I'm always glad afterward that I was brave."

Theo's hand squeezed her hip and then he pushed all the way inside, so she felt impossibly full. He groaned and held still. She could feel him tensing beneath her. Jason moved slowly, just a little. "Take off her blindfold, Kelsey," he said, driving in again. "She should see this."

Sara felt Kelsey's hands at the back of her head, and then she lifted the blindfold away. Lights and motion assailed her vision. The music pounded in the background as Sara stared at Kelsey's light hair and smiling eyes, then at Theo's dark torso beneath her. His muscles rippled each time he moved, and she saw such strain and control in his face. Jason unlatched her cuffs so her hands were free and she braced them on Theo's chest.

"Do you like it?" Kelsey asked. "It's so hot."

Sara couldn't reply. Her voice was gone, her mind was gone. There was only her body, grasping and riding the dual intrusions of her Masters' cocks. Kelsey played with her breasts, pinching and teasing the nipples. Sara twisted to look back at her Master, needing his reassurance.

"Good girl," Jason said. "Both of you are such good girls." He slid a hand up Sara's chest and circled her neck with his fingers. "Come for us, baby. Like we're at the Citadel, only better."

"Ohhh," she sighed. "I...I can't believe it."

"Believe what?"

"That the Citadel could ever be better than this."

Theo grinned beneath her and then Jason grabbed her hips and they were both fucking her, invading her, while Kelsey played with her breasts. It was too much, but at the same time it wasn't enough. She gripped the cocks inside her and lost herself, forgot who she was or where she was. Her orgasm came, painfully hard, like a constriction of every muscle in her body. The pleasure racked her, wave after wave of bliss. Theo groaned and Jason's grip tightened on her hips as she clamped on their cocks with involuntary spasms.

The men came in their own time, each of them pressing inside her to the hilt. It felt okay now. It felt right, like her body was made to contain these two men and their violent hungers. Even after they came, none of them moved or drew away from each other. Lights reflected in Kelsey's eyes, a rainbow of blinking, pretty colors, and Sara thought this night couldn't have been more perfect. A month ago, she never could have imagined such closeness, such friendship with the other couple. Such heights of pleasure, Citadel or not.

"Thank you," she said to no one in particular, as she collapsed on Theo's chest. "I don't know what else to say. Thank you." The last word was the barest breath.

"No, thank you," Theo said in his deep voice, slapping her thigh. "That was very well done."

Behind her, Jason squeezed her sore ass cheeks. "You sound like you're coaching her in trapeze. *Very well done*," he mimicked.

"Good girl, then," Theo said. "Is that better? And you, *ma chère*." He tweaked his wife's breast. "When your shoulder is one hundred percent again, we'll invite Sara and Jason over once more. What do you think?"

Kelsey eyed Sara in admiration. "I'll need a little more rehab before I can handle an onslaught like that."

Jason laughed as he withdrew from Sara's ass and gave her a spank for good measure. "You took Theo and Lemaitre at the same time once. I remember. I was there. People still talk about it."

"Don't remind me." Kelsey shivered. "I'll take you and Theo any day. Lemaitre, not so much." She helped Sara ease off Theo and then both of the women collapsed on the bed. The guys got up to take off their condoms, their cocks still partially hard, and Sara burst into a fit of giggling. She couldn't say why, except that she felt so worn out, and giddy, and happy. Then Kelsey joined in until both of them couldn't stop laughing.

Theo and Jason exchanged looks. "Slave girls," Jason said, shaking his head. "I think the disco ball might be messing with their brains."

Theo stood back to admire the view as Sara snuggled against Kelsey in the glow of twinkling lights. "Better than Christmas, wouldn't you say? Better than the Citadel, *sûrement.* All in all, I'd say this was a very enjoyable night."

Chapter Ten: *Mon Dieu*

Jason spooned the two women off to dreamland while Theo circled the room, putting away toys and extinguishing candles. When he got to the last one, he picked it up, beckoned Jason, and headed out of the room.

Jason left the girls in their sleeping embrace and followed him to the kitchen. "I always want to smoke after really good sex," Theo said. "I want a cigarette so badly, but I promised Kelsey, never again. So I eat instead, or drink wine." He gestured to the chair across from him and Jason accepted a glass along with a buttery, flaky croissant. He was either really hungry, or it was the best croissant he'd tasted in his life.

"Where do you get these?" he asked. "You make them?"

"No. Buy them at the shop. Only in Paris. In Marseille, we haven't found any as good. Kelsey says if we stay in Paris much longer, she'll gain too much weight."

"Ha. That girl can eat anything. She has the magic metabolism. Does she still eat those straws full of sugar?"

"Licky Stix? When she's a good girl, she gets them," he said with a smirk. "Speaking of good girls, what a delightful little slave you have. I'm her coach, so I know she's a good trapezist, but the rest..." His eyes widened. "Such a pervert. I never knew."

"I was Kelsey's coach once upon a time, and I never knew either. Although I think with Kelsey, you had quite a hand in perverting her."

"I trained her to my liking, yes. It was a process. It's always a process, but with some, it's easier than others."

"With Sara, it's been completely natural. We've been perfect for each other from the start, like someone knew exactly what we wanted and created it in the other person. I've never experienced anything like it."

He was gushing like an idiot. And to Theo Zamora, no less. If someone had told him three years ago that he and Theo would be friends one day, sharing partners and talking about relationships, he would have politely advised that person to fuck off.

"Are you going to collar her?" Theo asked.

Jason shifted, frowning down into his glass. "I don't think so, only because she had to wear a collar when she worked at the club. So much baggage there. I was thinking about something a bit more permanent."

"Nipple piercings?"

"No," Jason snorted. "An engagement ring. I mean, when the time is right."

Theo's eyes widened. "Really? Already?"

"Yes, already."

Theo raised his glass in a toast. "*Félicitations.* I understand, you know. Sara is a jewel, something special. When I found Kelsey, it was like finding treasure. I wanted to keep her. It didn't take long for me to know." He took a deep drink, then asked, "What is this club you speak of, with the collar? A Paris club?"

Shit. If Jason wasn't so buzzed and sexed out, he wouldn't have mentioned it. Now Theo stared at him with one eyebrow raised.

"Don't tell anyone," Jason sighed. "But Sara used to work at a sex club in Mongolia. A BDSM club."

"What?" Theo gawked.

"She wasn't *working* there, like in the private rooms," Jason clarified. "Just waitressing to supplement her income. I met her there before I ever scouted her."

"And by 'met her,' I suppose you mean you hooked up?"

"Unfortunately. Or fortunately. If we hadn't, she wouldn't have known where to find me after Baat shot down the initial offer." He paused, remembering the sexual intensity of their first encounter. "It made the scouting side of things awkward, but I have no regrets."

"Wow."

"I shouldn't have said anything. This wine..." He pushed it away. "Don't tell her you know. She wasn't happy about working there."

"Poor Sara." Theo traced a jagged scar in the tabletop. "But we all have skeletons in our past."

"Skeletons in our closet."

"What?"

"The expression is—"

Theo waved a hand. "Skeletons, shadows, *spectres*, whatever. Do you know, she told me outside it was time to let Minya's ghost go?" He turned away, shaking his head. "She has a mouth on her sometimes, that one."

"She does," said Jason. "In this case, I think she hit pretty close to the truth."

Theo was silent a moment, then he leaned back, crossing one leg over the other. "I have peace with Minya, most of the time. As for Sara, all she wants is to stay here by you. She'll throw a thousand ghosts under the bus to do it, to get her Paris trapeze act." He pursed his lips, thinking. "Maybe she can do something else. You can help her make an acrobatic routine. She's very strong. She would learn quick."

"No. Sara belongs in the air. Anyway, I can't sleep with her and be her coach."

"*Merde*," Theo drawled at Jason's look. "Yes, I'm her coach, but I did it for her. Poor Sara, turned out from the Citadel by Le Maître himself, when she was so excited to go." He stared at the guttering candle. "I don't understand why Michel wouldn't allow her there. He allows everyone, especially those he's fond of. It makes no sense." He passed his fingers through the flickering flame, once, twice.

"Self-preservation," said Jason. "He doesn't want to be tempted by her."

"I don't think so. He loves to torment himself with what he can't have. Remember the Venezuelan dancer with the exceedingly faithful wife? He invited them to everything. I think he would have moved into their house if they let him."

"Maybe he was having an off night. Maybe he was on something. Maybe he looked over and thought she was the devil."

Theo sucked his teeth. "First of all, no one could ever mistake Sara for the devil. And second, Michel never plays under the influence. He was sober as the grave."

"What did Sara say on the way out of the club? About him not liking her?"

"She says he doesn't like her, but I think it's the opposite." Theo paused. "I think he likes her too much. The way he studies her… They're two of a kind, in a way. Both reckless, strong and persistent. And they both have those same pale blue eyes."

The candle flame lengthened as it reached the end of the wick. Jason stared at it, turning Theo's words over in his head.

Those same pale blue eyes...

Jason and Theo blinked at each other as the candle fizzled and went out.

"*Mon Dieu*," Theo breathed. "*C'est possible?*"

Jason gripped his head, reeling with a thousand emotions. Confusion, shock, disbelief. Fury like a burning ache. He shot to his feet and stumbled over to the living room, pacing in circles.

Blue eyes.

The same pale blue eyes.

"She's his daughter," Jason said. "Jesus fucking Christ. She's Lemaitre's daughter."

"Be quiet," said Theo. "You'll wake her."

"Oh my God." Jason collapsed on the couch, burying his face in his hands. Sara was Michel Lemaitre's daughter. It all made sense now, the way he knew how to pronounce her name the very first day, his anger when he found her at Jason's, his close attention to her training, his refusal to allow her in the club. And those pale blue eyes any idiot could have matched together.

"Why didn't I see it until now?" he groaned. "It's so obvious. Why didn't I suspect something?"

"None of us suspected," said Theo, walking over with Jason's glass of wine. "They don't look alike, and Lemaitre doesn't seem old enough to have a grown daughter. He's always treated her with such...professional distance."

"God damn him." Jason threaded his hands through his hair. He had to calm down. If he stomped around and ranted, he'd scare Sara and ruin her pleasurable memories of the night. He drained his glass but the alcohol didn't have any soothing effect. Theo sat across from him, deep in thought.

"Why wouldn't he tell her?" he asked Jason. "Why not let her know?"

"Shame. Selfishness. Sociopathic tendencies. Pick a trait." He put down his glass and leaned forward. "You weren't there, Theo. You didn't see how she was living in Ulaanbaatar. She had nothing, no family, no money, no choices. And fucking Lemaitre got a twinge and sent me to bring her here for his goddamn pleasure, so he could gaze on what he'd fucking wrought."

"Do you think it was that way? Do you think he feels nothing for her?"

"Curiosity and pride. I think that's what he feels." He grabbed his head again. "Fucking hell. She's his *daughter*. She's so sweet and lovely, and beautiful, and he doesn't fucking care."

"We don't know for sure she's his daughter. We don't know—"

Sara's voice carried down the hall from the bedroom. "Jason?"

He rose to go to her, but Theo took his arm. "You can't say anything to her. Not until you talk to Lemaitre."

"She deserves to know who he is."

"And if he denies her again?" asked Theo. "Then what? The Citadel rejection was bad enough. If he rejects her in this—"

"I would kill him."

Theo tightened his grip on his arm. "Talk to Michel first. Say nothing to Sara until you know for sure."

Jason pulled away from Theo and strode down the hall to the bedroom. Sara stirred, pulling out of Kelsey's arms. "Is everything okay? I heard fighting."

"No fighting, baby." He leaned over the bed and stroked her hair. "Just talking. Everything's fine, but we should give Kelsey and Theo their bed back. They have a guest room where we can sleep."

"Goodbye, little one," Kelsey murmured as Jason gathered Sara in his arms. He carried her down the hall, where Theo waited, holding open the door.

"*Bonne nuit*," he said. "Stay for breakfast tomorrow?"

"*Oui*," said Jason. "Thanks."

Sara was already half asleep by the time he laid her on the bed. "Stay with me," she sighed, clinging to him. "Please hold me."

He pulled her close, as close as he could along his body, and wrapped her tightly in his arms. "Sleep now, good girl. It's been a long night."

"Did you have fun? Did I please you, Master?"

He stroked the smooth skin of her cheek. Did he see, now, the slightest hint of Lemaitre's angularity in her facial lines? "You always please me," he said, nuzzling her. "You're my special little one, no matter who I allow to fuck you. I love you the best."

"You love me?" she asked, pressing her face against his neck.

He was more certain than ever that he did. "I love you the best," he repeated. "You're my eternal girl."

"Jason," she said drowsily, "Theo is my coach. We'll get in trouble, won't we? If Mr. Lemaitre finds out about this?"

"Mr. Lemaitre won't say shit," Jason replied, trying to keep the fury from his voice. "Don't worry about anything, okay? Master's orders. Now go to sleep."

* * * * *

After breakfast, Jason took Sara back to the dorms and left her with a kiss and standing orders to rest for the remainder of the afternoon. Then he headed to Lemaitre's home in Avenue Montaigne, spoiling for a fight.

He banged on the door just before one. "Michel. It's Jason. Let me in." He banged again, harder. "Michel!"

The door whipped open. Lemaitre glared at him. "Must you shout like a hooligan? You're going to alarm the neighbors."

"I don't care if I alarm the fucking neighbors." He grabbed his boss by his starched white shirt and pushed him into his home. "You fucking bastard. Are you Sara's father?"

Lemaitre shoved his hands away. "Do you dare?" he asked through his teeth. "We're not animals. Stop acting like one." He threw him off and smoothed his shirt with an affronted scowl. "We can talk or we can fight. But we won't fight in my home."

Jason stared at him, too angry to come up with civil words, but he must have looked civilized enough, because Lemaitre turned and shut the door.

Jason glanced around his boss's pristine living space, glad there weren't any naked slaves chained in the corners. He'd been here a handful of times, for dinner parties or emergency meetings. Lemaitre didn't have a sprawling mansion, although he could have afforded it. His sunlit *pavillon* was tucked among others of utilitarian-modern design. The interior was strangely neutral. Everything in Lemaitre's home was white, taupe, ivory, mahogany, or steel. Not what one would expect from one of the most creative personalities in the world.

"Are you going to answer my question?" Jason asked, his hands in fists at his side.

"Perhaps. If you'll sit down and compose yourself." He gestured toward a low sofa upholstered in some smooth, easy-to-clean fabric.

So much sex has probably happened here, he thought as Lemaitre took the seat across from him. He perched on the edge.

"Can I get you something? A drink?"

"You can answer my fucking question. You can tell me what the fuck is going on, why you brought a performer here who's your daughter, and treated her exactly like everyone else."

His words snapped out like cracks of a whip. Lemaitre's only reaction was a slight negative tilt of his head. "Not exactly like everyone else. Everyone else is permitted in the Citadel. She is not."

"So it's true?"

Lemaitre leaned back, scratching the side of his knee. "I expected your visit today, but not this confrontation. You want to know if I fathered Sara? Yes, I did. Am I her father? I think we both know the answer to that."

"You're either her father or you're not, you glib piece of shit."

"I'm your boss," he said, his gaze hardening. "I provide your livelihood. You might conduct this conversation with a little more respect." He stood and crossed to the kitchen, and returned with a crystal tumbler of water. "Drink this. Drink all of it before you say anything else."

"I'm not six years old," said Jason. "I didn't just wake up from a bad dream."

"Still, you're agitated. Water has a way of calming the soul. Drink."

Jason wondered if it was spiked with some kind of designer, Lemaitre-style drug, but he drank it anyway, and he did gradually feel calmer.

"Where is Sara now?" Lemaitre asked when Jason leaned to place the glass on the side table.

"Do you care?"

"I suppose what I mean to ask is, does she know why you're here? What prompted this confrontation?"

"You want to know if Sara knows? No, she doesn't, not yet. Theo and I figured this out last night while she was asleep."

His brows rose. "She slept with you and Theo last night?"

"You don't get to ask that," Jason snarled. "You're not her father, right? You just fathered her." Okay, so maybe the water hadn't calmed him after all. "Sara's still oblivious, and I didn't want to tell her until I talked to you."

"I'm grateful for that."

"But she ought to know you're her father."

Lemaitre held up a finger. "She has a father. A good man who didn't question the eye color, who raised her as his own."

"He passed away a couple years ago, along with her mom. In an accident in Ulaanbaatar, which is a hell of a place to drive."

Jason could tell by the shock on Lemaitre's face that he hadn't known. A moment later, he'd neutralized his expression. "What a tragic loss. But Sara loved that man as her father. She's twenty-two years old. Why would she want a new father now?"

Jason didn't have an answer to that. He knew Sara loved her Mongolian father, despite the circumstances of her parents' deaths. But a father was a father, and if Lemaitre was her father…

"Don't think I haven't thought about this," Lemaitre said. "I've agonized over it. I decided it was kinder not to tell her."

"It's kind until she shows up at the Citadel and sees you in action, and fantasizes about becoming your slave."

"I trust you'll see that doesn't happen." Lemaitre's gaze skewered him. "What were you thinking, bringing her to the back rooms?"

"Why wouldn't I? You realize she's..." His voice choked on the words. "She's just like you, Michel. Exactly like you. She likes to play hard."

"So play hard with her at your home. Keep her out of my way."

Jason made a disgusted sound. "All this time, I thought you wanted her. Like, sexually."

"That's on you and your filthy, jealous mind."

"You sent me to Mongolia, never even telling me she was your daughter. I met her in a fucking sex club."

"Again, this is on you."

"Waitressing, Michel, because she needed money. I think it's on you. I think it's shitty that you didn't look after Sara, considering you brought her into this world."

His lips tightened. "I looked after her as well as I could from half a world away. I fell out of contact with her mother a couple years ago. I didn't know about the accident. When I saw Sara's name with the outfit in Ulaanbaatar, I contacted you about going to Mongolia the same day. I thought it would be wonderful to have her close." His eyes were twin pools of pain. "It has been wonderful. But now...I suppose..."

"What?"

"I'm begging you...please…don't tell her I'm her father. If you tell her, it will ruin everything."

"Everything? By everything, you mean this cold and vaguely censorious relationship you have with her?"

"I have to be cold and vaguely censorious. I'm her boss."

"You're her father, you raging asshole."

"I'm not her father. I don't deserve to be, and she doesn't deserve the infamy of being my daughter. What about my reputation, my history? All those clubs set up in my name?"

"That's your excuse? That you own sex clubs? What's more important to you?"

Lemaitre let out a long breath and dropped his face into his hands. He rubbed his forehead and looked back at Jason. "If you love her, if you care for my daughter, don't tell her. I don't want you to tell her."

Jason burst up off the couch. "Fuck that. You should be the one to tell her. If you won't do it, I will."

Lemaitre stood too, meeting him nose to nose. He grabbed a handful of Jason's shirt and lowered his voice to a ragged growl. "Think about it, won't you? Think! I can be an excellent mentor for her. A protector, a friend. But I would be a miserable father. What would she prefer?" The man's grip loosened. He spread his fingers on Jason's chest, his lips turning down in a shadowed frown. "If you tell her, the only job you'll be able to find is with Circus Mongolia. I promise. Don't cross me in this."

Jason stared at his boss. Dark-haired, intense and powerful, exuding sexuality even in the most conservative situations. Perhaps he was right. He was, at his essence, the terrifying Le Maître, and an unsuitable father for anyone. Particularly the woman Jason hoped would eventually become his wife.

"Jesus fucking Christ," he muttered. "Get your hands off me."

Lemaitre complied with an icy mien, as if none of this was his fault. He drew himself up to his full height, brushing at an imaginary piece of fuzz on his shirt.

"This has been a rousing conversation, but I have other appointments. Do we have anything else to discuss?"

"How long will you keep it from her?" Jason asked. "Forever?"

"If I wish to." He made a careless gesture. "Things may change."

"It's all about what you wish, isn't it? In everything."

"I've never made a secret of that, have I?" He gave Jason a ghost of a smile that reminded him, heartbreakingly, of Sara's smile. It took Jason a moment to recover.

"Just tell me you're feeling something right now," he said, studying the smooth lines of Michel Lemaitre's face. "Tell me you're struggling with some measure of guilt, or shame, or self-reproach over this."

Lemaitre gave a soft laugh. "Some measure? You may believe I'm feeling many measures of all those things. Mostly a depth of regret I hope you'll never experience."

Lemaitre allowed Jason to see a flash of his pain, just an iota, then he hid it, masked it with a true performer's skill. *We all have skeletons in our past.* Hadn't he and Theo discussed that less than twelve hours ago?

"I won't tell Sara," Jason conceded grudgingly, stalking toward the door. "For her sake, not yours."

Chapter Eleven: Bound

Sara worried things would be awkward with Theo when they got back to work on Monday, but nothing changed. He was as hard on her as ever, and she was thankful for it. If not for Theo, her and Baat's act would have fallen apart by now.

As the weeks flew by, as the Exhibition loomed, they practiced with greater and greater intensity, and it was Theo who forced Baat to do the work and get things right when he slacked off and spouted attitude. Theo also stayed after practice a few days a week to teach Sara solo moves for fun, tricks and flips he knew from his past career in trapeze. She got really good at them, and tried without success to convince Baat to incorporate them into their routine. He wasn't interested. She could tell he was still drinking every night, although he claimed he wasn't.

As long as he was sober in practices, she didn't care, but his muscle tone wasn't what it had been in Mongolia. At the end of their second month, Mr. Lemaitre assigned him an extra physical therapist, which irritated Baat even more. She carried the guilt of his alcoholic spiral around with her, a dirty little secret she couldn't share with anyone, not Theo, not Jason, not Kelsey. Not Mr. Lemaitre. She didn't want Baat to get fired because then she'd lose her job too. What then?

Mr. Lemaitre held no love for either of them, that was clear. He never explained why she wasn't welcome at his club. Jason said it was because she was too young, but she knew plenty of Cirque employees her age who hung out there. Well, whatever. She felt safe and welcomed in Jason's home, and in his bedroom. Through their private scenes and heartfelt conversations, she came to know him not just as her Master, but as an honorable man she loved.

All too soon, hot July turned into an even hotter August, and their act neared completion. Theo raised her and Baat's practice trapeze, two stories, three stories, four stories off the ground in preparation for the real thing. Then it was five stories up, and the Exhibition was only a week away. They received their costumes, a dazzling emerald leotard and feathered headpiece for her, and matching knee pants for Baat. Jason was with her at the fitting, his expression filled with the same gravity she felt.

Costumes, the Exhibition, an ever-rising trapeze. It all meant one thing, that she'd be leaving Paris—and Jason—very soon. Theo said Jason would follow her, but what if he didn't? He took his duties at Cirque very seriously. Even if he did come, what if he missed Paris and wanted to come back?

The more unsettled she felt, the more manic and gleeful Baat became. He couldn't wait to leave Paris. He'd already invited his friends from Mongolia to visit him in Vegas when their act was added to *Brillante*. Never mind that it wasn't a sure thing, never mind that they still had to impress the bigwigs with their performance in the Exhibition. Baat was as cocky and self-assured as ever. He believed he had a free ticket to Las Vegas and nothing would stop him from making plans.

The Thursday before the Exhibition he met her outside the locker rooms, happy, smiling despite the fact she'd lost her temper with him several times during practice.

"Hey, guess what?"

Sara looked at him sideways. "What?"

"Chuluun sent me two bottles of *har* to congratulate us on *Cirque Brillante*. You can have some if you like."

Har made her think of Jason and the BDSM Fun Club, and all the things that were wrong with Ulaanbaatar. "No thanks," she answered curtly. "First of all, we don't have the job yet, and second, I prefer to keep all my brain cells."

"Fine, more for me. I'm tired of this stuff the French call alcohol. I have to drink so much more here to get drunk."

Oh Baat, how can I fix you? She hid her grief in irritation, turning away with a frown. "Why do you need to get drunk? Why can't you just drink enough to enjoy the buzz, like a normal person?"

"Because I'm in Paris and I don't want to be. And because my partner nags me and annoys me."

"Your partner cares about you. Your partner wants you to be able to perform for ten, fifteen more years. Your partner thinks you have serious problems."

He snorted, waving her concerns away. "Hey, you want to come over for dinner after the Exhibition? No drinking, I promise. Not until later, anyway."

"You think Chuluun would want you to share the *har* with me?"

"Why not?"

"I thought everyone hated me for ruining the circus. I thought all the children starved."

He made a face at her. "What are you talking about?"

"You told me the circus was going out of business. You made me feel horrible." At his blank look, she blew out a breath. "Look, I'll probably go out with Jason afterward, and Theo and Kelsey. They have to go back to Marseille in a few days."

Baat's erratic temper surged. "You've turned into such a bitch. Such a haughty, nasty bitch. You're too good to hang out with your old friend Baat, yes? I get it. Fine, celebrate *our* act with your *Amerik* and his asshole friends."

She looked around, glad no one else understood Mongolian. "They're not assholes," Sara said, signaling for him to lower his voice. "And Theo's your coach."

"Do I fucking care? He won't be my coach much longer. When we get to Vegas, you and I will be able to breathe again. We can train without Theo and Lemaitre hovering over us, and we can finally correct all the shit they did to ruin our act."

"Everything they did improved our act."

"You would think so. Are you in love with them too? Why don't you take all three of them to your bed? You seem to have developed a taste for Western cock."

She tried not to react, tried to not give him the satisfaction as they left the Cirque lobby and stepped into the blinding sunlight outside. He couldn't know that she and Jason occasionally played around with the Zamoras. Could he? It was their secret. She didn't think Baat even knew about the Citadel. He was too isolated from everyone else, due to language and cultural barriers. *Yes, because of you. Because you ran away and dragged him here.*

"Maybe we can share one drink," she said, softening. "Right after the Exhibition, before I head out with Jason. They'll probably have things to discuss with Mr. Lemaitre anyway."

"Eh. If you don't want to hang out with me, then don't."

Baat turned away in a huff, heading for his dorm, shoulders hunched against the draining summer heat. He looked so lonely. He probably was lonely, which was why he drank. She knew all of this, but she didn't know how to fix it without losing all the things she'd worked for.

You're selfish, a voice inside her whispered. It was a terrible thing in her culture, to be selfish and self-serving. *All you care about is yourself. What you want. What you need.* No wonder Baat acted so hateful toward her.

But things would get better. They had to. If it took *Cirque Brillante* in Las Vegas to get Baat back on his feet again, Sara would gladly go. Once they were there, she'd make him seek help, get him healthy again. She hoped against hope that all of this would be worth it in the end.

* * * * *

The night before the Exhibition, Jason took her out for a celebratory dinner at a posh restaurant near the Eiffel Tower. Sara dressed up in a black brocade dress, with a garter belt and back-seamed stockings, and black stiletto shoes Jason loved. "No power exchange tonight," he said when he picked her up. "I just want to take you out and be proud of you. Have a special dinner with the girl I love."

No power exchange? It was impossible for them to be together without power exchange. Even his request for no power exchange was a power exchange, because she had to submit to it against her will. But she did, because he wanted it. She made polite, appropriate conversation, laughed and made jokes, and stared at him from under her lashes. He looked so beautiful in his stylish suit and tie. She didn't want to lose him, but she didn't know if she could hold onto him when their lives started to change. His fingers… Oh, his fingers as he traced the stem of his glass. The restaurant was all crystal and white, so elegant. She couldn't shake the feeling that she didn't belong here, that she wasn't good enough for this sparkling elegance.

That she wasn't good enough for him.

Near the end of the meal, he leaned close and caught her gaze. "What's the matter, Sara? Are you worried about tomorrow? You shouldn't be. Theo tells me your act is super tight. I've seen you do the whole thing in practice. It's amazing."

She tugged at the napkin in her lap. "I'm not worried about tomorrow. It's more the uncertainty that comes after, going to a new place and a new show. I wish we could stay here together in Paris." At his frown, she added quickly, "I know why I can't."

He put down his fork in a very controlled movement and took a sip of wine. "I hoped we could speak about that. About what's next for us."

He had that look, that exacting look he got when he'd made a decision and was about to tell her what was what. She clasped her hands in her lap and swallowed past the paralysis in her throat. He looked so serious and resolute that Sara wondered if his next words might be "*we're through*." Maybe that was why he'd asked her here, why he'd told her no power exchange.

Calm down, Sara. He's not breaking up with you. They belonged together, even if it was long distance, even if things were difficult for a while. Jason reached for her hand and rubbed his thumb across the back.

"As you know, I've been reluctant to make any plans for our future," he began. "Or more specifically, to tie you down with any hard and fast plans. We've only had three months, Sara. It's not enough time to ask you to make big decisions, or for me to make big decisions."

"But it's been a good three months," she pointed out. "I feel closer to you than I've ever felt to anyone in my life."

"I do too, baby. And this is circus life. It's about dealing with change, evolving, adapting. You're just beginning your journey and a lot's going to happen in the years to come. It's all good, it's all normal. And in my heart, I've made a decision."

"What decision?" she asked, her heart thudding double speed.

"That I want to be with you, wherever you go. I want to come with you and support you however I can."

She let out a breath, clutching her chest. "Oh, Jason. I thought...I thought you might break up with me."

He smiled at her, reaching in his pocket. "If I was going to break up with you, I wouldn't have brought this."

He took out a little box and slid it open. The first thing Sara saw was the stone, a striking pale blue jewel nestled in black velvet. It was set into a ring, elegant in its simplicity, just an aquamarine oval supported by four gold tines. Sara was so taken by its beauty she forgot to breathe, and ended up sucking in a big gust of air.

"Ohhh." That was all she could say for a moment.

"The blue's for your eyes. I hope that's okay. I know you don't like your eye color, but I think they're ungodly beautiful, and I can't look at this color anymore without thinking of you." He paused, turning the ring over in his hand. "I adore you, Sara, and I don't want to let you go. If that's okay with you."

"If it's...if it's okay with me?"

"I don't want to put pressure on you, because you have a lot of other pressures right now. This isn't an engagement ring. This is a promise, something to bind us together. A symbol to remind us we're working toward something. Marriage, hopefully, but you're young and your life is changing. I think it's too soon for you to decide."

"But I know—"

He held up a finger, silencing her. "I know you think you know. But look, I'm a stickler. You know that about me. When you commit to me, that's going to be it. So let's take a few more weeks. Even a few more months, because we have all the time in the world. I want you to be sure."

She gazed down at the glittering ring between his fingers. Her tears made the blue jewel sparkle, transformed the hues into something complex and even more brilliant. She blinked the tears away and looked back at him. "I didn't have a life before you. So even if it twists and turns, I want you to be part of it."

His expression was so gentle, so kind. He took her left hand and slid the ring onto her finger. "There. Every time you look at your hand now, you'll see that I'm part of it. Well, except when you're doing trapeze. I hear rings are a no-no when you're grabbing someone's fingers fifty feet up."

Sara laughed and moaned a little, and gawked at Jason's ring. She'd been so worried about their future, but this was actual, material proof that Jason wasn't planning to drift away.

"What about your job?" she asked, touching the stone.

"Don't you get in trouble every time you worry about my job?" He squeezed her hand. "Lemaitre and I will work something out. There's bound to be some opening wherever you go. Or I could travel, do more scouting. As long as it's not Mongolia," he teased.

"Oh, Jason." She whispered his name, imprinting this moment in her memory. "You're so wonderful. Thank you." She had a million more things to say but words wouldn't come, only a swirl of emotions. Impulsively she stood and threw herself on her knees beside his chair, staring up into the beloved lines of her Master's face.

"Sara, honey." He looked around, drawing her up again. "This is a classy restaurant. I love you, but you can't do that here." He settled her on his lap for a quick, tender kiss and then nudged her back over to her seat. "Later," he promised. "When I get you home."

After that, though, neither one of them could concentrate on the atmosphere or the food. Jason paid the bill and Sara floated out of the restaurant on his arm. She wanted to flash the ring at everyone they passed on the way to the door. *Look, look! Look what my Master gave me.*

When they got to his house, they didn't go upstairs right away. He kissed her inside the door, then in the living room, then in the kitchen, and in the hallway against the wall. Each time he kissed her, he took off another item of her clothing—her shoes, her dress, her slip, her tights, her bra and panties. Everything but her ring. Every kiss seemed to bind them closer together. Every kiss said, *this is for life.*

When she pressed against him, aching for his possession, he lifted her in his arms and carried her upstairs to his bedroom. There was no slave pose this time, no slowly building scene. They were on some other plane tonight, where he tossed her on the bed and ripped off his clothes and came at her. She melted as he pinned her hands over her head. He spread her legs with his knees and paused with his cock at the entrance to her pussy.

"Sometimes I don't want to hurt you," he sighed. "I just want to be as deep inside you as I can be."

"Oh, Master, yes." She tried not to cry out as he pushed inside, but it felt *so good*, the way he stretched her pussy. *The air ducts, remember? Don't be noisy. Don't scream for more, more, more…*

"More," she cried. "I want this forever. I want you inside me forever."

He let go of her hands and muffled her babbling with another kiss. *Yes, please, yes.* She wrapped her legs around him and clung to him, tangling her fingers in the softness of his hair. Body to body, he took her with a violent, demanding passion that left her breathless. She squeaked when he bit her on the lip and then begged him to do it again. His cock filled her, harder, deeper, lifting her with each thrust.

He's turning me inside out. They were back to exchanging power, back in their comfort zone, and now there was even more joining them together. A commitment, a promise. Was this really happening to her? It seemed her life was a constant swing of the trapeze, from depressing problems to the joy of Jason's love. He'd given her a *ring*. They were bound together as he said, perhaps even bound for marriage one day. In all the big world, from Mongolia to California to Paris, they'd found each other, found a perfect match of personality and desire. And love, always love.

She stared into her Master's eyes and for long delicious moments, the Exhibition, Vegas, Baat, none of it mattered. All that mattered was Jason and his mastery of her, and his life force pressing inside her, and their soul-deep bond.

Chapter Twelve: Exhibition

Sara and Baat had a short practice the next day with Theo, a final run-through. It went pretty well, as well as could be hoped with nerves and anxiety. "Just relax," Theo told them. "Be proud of your strength. Be proud of what you can do. Most of all, let the directors see the possibilities in your art."

Sara loved the sound of that. Possibilities. It seemed all of life was possibilities, especially now that she wore Jason's ring. She showed it to Theo and Baat after practice. Baat, as usual, couldn't care less, but Theo smiled and congratulated her. "He loves you very much," he said, then he leaned closer. "You know what this is, yes? A collar for your finger. Lucky girl."

Lucky didn't even cover it. Sara felt euphoric. Here she was at the world's top circus, in love, inspired, and about to perform in an Exhibition for the top brass. Around them, hallways and rehearsal spaces buzzed with activity. Several new acts were making their debut today at the Cirque's multi-purpose auditorium, including acrobatic acts that Jason had worked on. He was busy prepping those athletes, so she didn't have a chance to be with him before her performance. He was still with her though. She put on her emerald green finery and glittering makeup with last night's "performance" playing vividly in her mind. All the passionate kisses, and the way he'd held her close… She loved when he was rough and masterful, but she loved his romantic side too.

Even with her daydreaming, Sara was ready early, almost an hour before stage call. Baat had disappeared after he rolled his eyes at her ring. She hoped he was somewhere getting charged up. If only this performance would go well... If only they could get to Vegas, where both of them could be happy. Baat liked partying, he liked showgirls, even the casinos.

Hmm. Baat and casinos. Sara wasn't sure about that.

She wandered the halls, buoyed by her fellow performers' encouragement and smiles, and ducked into one of her favorite conference rooms, a quiet, uncluttered space. She sat down in the dark, being careful not to snag the rhinestones on her costume.

"*Mademoiselle*. What a pleasure."

The deep, rumbling voice was Lemaitre's. She leaped to her feet and searched the shadows, finding him not ten feet away. "Why are you sitting here in the dark?" she gasped.

"Why are *you* sitting here in the dark?" he countered. Even in the dim light, she could see his smile and his casual shrug. "Like you, I came to escape the hullabaloo outside. To gather my thoughts before the Exhibition."

His voice sounded tired. This was nerve-wracking for her, but how much more nerve-wracking for him? She only had one act to concentrate on. Mr. Lemaitre had to coordinate all of the coaches, staff, and performers, as well as his team of directors, and somehow keep everyone content.

"How have you been, Sara?" he asked in the silence. "All is well?"

She looked down at her costume, which was really his costume. Everything she had came from him, even Jason, in a way, because Lemaitre was the one who had sent him to Mongolia. She tried to think of what to say to such an exalted person, something clever and engaging that might make her stand out from the other performers, but she couldn't summon a word. All she could think about was the way he'd scowled outside his back room at the Citadel, and the way he'd ordered her out.

"Everything's fine," she said, trying to keep her voice light.

"Are you looking forward to performing today?"

"Yes, we've been working hard. I hope you like the act."

He smiled again, a tight smile that made her wonder if he was thinking about the Citadel too. *I don't need your sex club. Jason loves me.* She didn't have her ring on. She couldn't wear it while she was performing but she wished she had it to flash in Lemaitre's face.

"Hard work is good," he said in his smooth, French-inflected lilt. "Will you walk with me to the theater?"

He posed it as a question, but she couldn't realistically say no. He opened the door for her and light streamed into the room, illuminating the sparkles on her costume.

"How beautiful you are," he said, gesturing her into the hall beside him. "But green isn't your color. You should be wearing blue."

"They didn't give me a choice."

"Ah, yes. Sometimes at Cirque you have no choice. Not the choices you want, anyway." He guided her around a milling group of performers, ignoring their curious looks. "There is always the conflict of what the ego wants, and what is required by the greater group."

At once, she thought of Baat. *Selfish. You're so selfish.* Did Lemaitre think so? Maybe that's why he didn't allow her at the Citadel. She made some ambivalent noise as they turned into a quieter hallway.

"And how are things with Mr. Beck?" he asked. "Still pleasant in your world?"

What business is it of yours? If he was fishing due to his own interest, he could forget it. She'd never give up Jason for a cold, haughty Master like him. "Things are great with me and Jason," she said, lifting her chin. "He gave me a ring last night."

Lemaitre's eyes went wide. "A ring? An engagement ring?"

"Well, no." Sara felt a flush spread out from her ears. "He said I'm too young, that we need to wait a little longer. But it's a promise ring. A bond between us."

"A bond." Lemaitre pursed his lips. She could tell he was unhappy, even when he forced a smile. "What a nice way to put things."

"We're in love," she said. "We'll probably get married, just not...yet."

"It's good of him to give you some time to grow. In the scheme of life, you're little more than a girl."

"I'm twenty-two."

"An infant then."

"No, a grown woman."

"Hm." That was all he said. *Hm,* with that lofty tilt of his aristocratic nose. Why was she arguing with him? And why must he stare at her so intently every time she met his eyes?

"I should go find Baat," she said as they approached the theater lobby. Lemaitre nodded and bid her goodbye, and then she felt guilty for being so snippy with him. It wasn't that she didn't like Lemaitre. He just made her uncomfortable with his probing questions and assessing stare. He might be Master over everyone at his circus, but he'd never be Master over her.

She touched her ring finger, remembering last night's heated whispers and caresses, and headed backstage to prepare for the show.

* * * * *

Jason and Kelsey sat eight rows back, near the middle. The previous seven rows were filled with a chatting, laughing, babbling assembly of Cirque bigwigs and directors who'd flown in from all over the world. The Exhibition always had a celebratory feel. New acts, new artists to admire and nurture, fresh material for aging venues. So why did Jason feel nervous rather than celebratory?

"Stop bouncing," said Kelsey, pressing down on his knee. "Everything will go fine."

Jason's acts were ready, Sara was ready. He didn't know why he felt this agitation. Maybe because Theo was in an especially long conference with Michel Lemaitre down on the end of the first row. He couldn't see Lemaitre's face, only Theo's carefully controlled reactions to whatever he said. A moment later, the conversation came to an end and Theo climbed the stairs, sliding into the chair on the other side of Kelsey.

"What's the news?" Jason asked.

Theo grimaced. "Lemaitre is waffling about *Cirque Brillante* again. He wants Baat and Sara to go, he wants to wait, he's not sure if it's the right place for them." He bent closer, lowering his voice to a whisper. "I think he doesn't want his little daughter too far away from him."

Kelsey shook her head. "Someone should tell her. Just tell the poor girl. I would want someone to tell me."

"It's not my secret to tell, or yours," Theo warned his wife. "It will come out eventually, when the time is right. Let them work out their own affairs."

Jason stayed silent. Would it come out? When he looked at Sara now, he saw so much of Lemaitre in her features, he couldn't believe everyone didn't know. More and more, he agreed with Kelsey. The deception bothered all of them, especially Jason. He ought to tell her, but what would happen then? What would be the emotional damage for Lemaitre, Sara, even Jason when she realized he'd kept quiet about it? It could be devastating. When he thought about it that way, he thought Theo was right. Lemaitre was the one who should have to tell her and deal with the fall out. It was his affair, no one else's. As loyal as Jason was to Sara, he wasn't sure it gave him the right to "out" his boss.

Kelsey held his bouncing knee again. "Stop it, seriously. Or go sit somewhere else."

Shortly after that, the lights dimmed and the Exhibition got under way. The first act was a strength act, anchored by two women rather than two men. Every fifteen seconds or so, Kelsey breathed "wow" until Theo held up a finger to silence her. The next act was a completely crazy hoop thing, then a banquine routine that Jason had consulted on.

Between each act there were pauses for performers to introduce themselves, to take questions, to display their equipment, then the next act would need time to set up. Jason waited impatiently as the show dragged on, enduring Theo and Kelsey's bemused looks. Finally the stage crew pulled out Sara and Baat's safety mat, cleverly disguised as a dragon boat. Their red trapeze drifted down from the rigging on automated pulleys, Baat sitting on one side, Sara posed on the other. Their preview act was loosely based on an Asian-nature theme, complete with plinking Chinese music and a river and moon projected onto the stage.

Jason relaxed as the act got underway. The presentation was beautiful, with the red and green colors and their striking dark hair. Sara looked strong and confident, and even Baat looked good in his laced-up emerald leggings. Jason had never seen it all together with the costumes and music, and thematic staging. Her costume made sense now. She looked like an ancient jeweled goddess under a mysterious moon. Jason could see Theo's expertise all over the act, in Sara and Baat's movements and transitions, in the small, meaningful things they did. He became so lost in the flow he didn't see the first mistake happen. He only saw Sara twist and grab for Baat's arm in a jerky movement.

"Was that supposed to happen?" Kelsey whispered.

"No," Theo said, leaning forward in his chair.

Sara regained her momentum, found her groove again, and the act resumed. But moments later, it seemed to unravel completely. Their moves became stilted, tentative. Jason could see the panic on Sara's face even from the eighth row.

"Stop. Stop," Theo whispered. "Something's wrong."

Sara did a somersault and Baat almost missed her ankles, grabbing for them in an uncontrolled way. Theo shot to his feet in the darkened theater, jumping over chairs and spectators and rushing toward the stage. "Stop! Stop the act. Something's wrong with him."

Jason bolted after Theo, pushing past anyone in his way. Theo called to Baat from downstage. "Stop! Lift Sara up to the bar." Jason could hear Sara hissing at Baat over the rising hubbub from the audience.

"Shut off the music," Lemaitre boomed across the theater. "Stop the act."

Sara stopped then, hanging limp from Baat's hands. *He's going to drop her. Fucking Christ, what if he drops her?* A moment later Sara had swung herself up to the bar, and climbed to perch on the narrow length of wood. Baat settled beside her, slouched over, glaring down at the audience. Slowly, the trapeze began its ascent into the rafters.

"No, not up. Lower it," barked Lemaitre. "Bring them down."

The theater was in an uproar. Twenty people were on stage now, ranged around the apparatus, and forty more milled in front of the seats. Jason stood right under Sara. He'd catch her if he had to. Out of the corner of his eye, he saw Theo slip away through a side door, his shoulders up around his ears.

"Sara," he whispered. When the trapeze arrived at stage level he caught her in his arms, hugging the solid, intact shape of her. "Are you okay? Is everything okay?" He went into coach mode, checking her joints, her shoulders and elbows, wrists and hands. "I thought you were going to fall. What the hell happened up there? What was Baat's problem?"

She shook her head, bursting into tears. "I don't know. I don't know what happened."

While Jason tried to console Sara, Lemaitre spoke to Baat, demanding explanations. His gaze burned dark as the depths of hell. Since Sara was bawling too hard to translate, the men fell into pantomime. One of the directors made a drinking sign, the universal gesture of tossing one back, and Baat nodded ruefully.

Jesus Christ. *He'd been drinking.* Baat had taken Sara fifty feet in the air and performed with her while he was *inebriated.*

Jason didn't think. He let go of Sara and lunged at Baat, tackling him to the painted safety mat. The man's breath blew in his face, saturated with alcohol. This cushy surface was bullshit. Jason wanted Baat to hurt.

"You could have killed her," he yelled, throwing him off the mat and onto the floor. "What the fuck is wrong with you?" He ducked as Baat threw a fist, then they were rolling across the stage, grappling, punching each other. Jason didn't feel anything, didn't think anything, just pummeled Baat with the metal taste of adrenaline in his mouth. Baat snarled in Mongolian, his diatribe rising over panicked shouts and screams. Jason didn't care what Baat had to say. All he cared was that Baat had gone up on the trapeze with Sara while he was full-on drunk, and almost dropped her on her head.

It was bedlam, with artists and staff shouting, and Sara bawling, and someone blowing a whistle, loud and shrill. Finally Lemaitre wrenched him and Baat apart and stood between them. "Enough. That's enough." His voice rang out sharp as a gunshot. The entire auditorium went silent, except for a few muffled sobs. "No more trapeze in Paris," he shouted. "This is why. It's cursed, and I tell you now, never again." He shoved Jason toward Sara. "Leave and take her with you. You," he barked at Baat. "Go somewhere and clean up."

Baat was bleeding, a steady stream from his nose and a swollen, mangled lip. Sara hid her face, a picture of misery in her resplendent green costume and headpiece. The trapeze rested on the stage, the ropes arrayed around it, tangled and twisted. This one wouldn't rise again.

"Come on," Jason said as calmly as he could. "Exhibition's over." With one final, vicious glance at Baat, he took Sara's arm and guided her through the crowd of sympathetic gawkers to the locker rooms, and then outside into the oppressive August air.

Chapter Thirteen: How You Learn

Sara shed her costume beside Jason's bed while he paced back and forth. Every now and again he stopped and rubbed his eyes, and shook his head.

"Where should I put it?" She held out the green leotard and the headpiece she'd crumpled in her hands on the way over.

"It doesn't matter," he said. "Throw it on the floor. They won't be used again."

No more trapeze in Paris, Mr. Lemaitre had yelled. *Never again.* Sara folded the costume, her tears blurring the sequins and rhinestones together into a green blotch. After all her hard work, and Theo's hard work, and everyone's hard work to put the act together, she and Baat were finished. Over. This was a nightmare and there wasn't any way to wake up.

"They won't allow him back, will they?" she asked, swallowing a sob.

Jason turned to her, his eyes blazing. "Do you want him back? Really?"

She didn't dare answer. Jason wasn't only angry at Baat. He was angry at her too. He'd held her and soothed her all the way home but now...now he wanted answers, and she didn't have them. She realized now that she'd fucked up, that she'd protected Baat one too many times.

"Did you know?" he asked, crossing to stand in front of her. "Did you know he was drunk when you went up there with him?"

She hugged her arms over her chest. "May I have some clothes? Please?"

"No, you may not have any clothes. Stand there and answer my goddamn question. Did you know he was drunk?" Jason's voice resounded through his bedroom and she thought to herself, *they'll hear you through the air ducts.*

She stood quailing in only her thong panties, feeling doubly exposed to his anger. "No, I didn't know he was drunk. He didn't act drunk."

"Did you know he'd been drinking?" Jason asked with a mien of forbearance. "Did you smell it on his breath? Hear it in his voice?"

She covered her face, then looked up into Jason's accusing eyes. "I knew he drank at night, after practice. That's all I knew. I didn't realize..." She babbled out words, trying to exonerate herself. "I never imagined he'd drink before a performance."

"But you knew he drank. You knew he had a problem."

"Everyone drinks here—"

"Wrong!" She flinched at his sharp tone. "Nobody drinks here before a performance. Nobody. Nobody drinks to inebriation, to the point where their judgment is clouded. No one here is a fucking alcoholic."

"Everyone drinks in Mongolia," she cried, hugging herself tighter.

"Does that make it okay? Your parents died in a drunk driving accident, Sara. I don't understand this. I don't get this attitude of looking the other way."

"Why are you so angry with me? It was Baat's fault."

"But you knew. You knew he had a problem and you kept it from me. From everyone. You're the only one here who spoke his language, who knew this was going on. It was your responsibility to let someone know he didn't have his shit together."

Tears squeezed from her eyes. "Yes, I know. I just didn't... I didn't..."

"Yes, you didn't," Jason muttered. He glared at her, his hands braced on his hips. "This will reverberate through the entire circus. Lemaitre's going to pop an artery over this, and Theo—Theo walked out as soon as you were safe on the ground, to go have a mental fucking breakdown. He's curled up in a rubber room somewhere, rocking in a ball. And you! You could have *died*, Sara. Minya the second. That would have been a fucking *thing*."

He stalked away from her. She'd never seen him so angry before. She wanted his tenderness back, his calming arms around her. She hunched over, swiping at the tears on her cheeks. "I'm sorry. I didn't know what to do."

"Tell someone. Get a new partner. Deal with your problems."

"But what if something had happened?" she asked. "What if the new partner didn't come, what if I lost my job?"

"Lost your job?" He came back to her and grabbed her shoulders. "What if you lost your life? Don't you get it? Baat could have killed you. Why was that okay, that risk? Why did you let it go on? You knew he had a problem, why didn't you say something?"

"Because I was trying to protect him. In Mongolia, families support each other. Baat's the closest thing I have to family."

"No. This has nothing to do with family or supporting each other. Don't play some cultural card with me."

"He wasn't that bad, not as bad as you think. His friend sent him Mongolian spirits. He wasn't used to them. You remember how potent they are."

"Don't, Sara. Don't make excuses for him."

"In Mongolia, drinking is normal. All men do it," she persisted. "I know that doesn't matter to you, I know you don't believe me—" Her words cut off in her throat. He'd told her not to make excuses. Her excuses were nothing but lies, anyway. "Yes," she said, defeated. "I knew and I kept quiet. I was afraid of losing the act. I was afraid of being sent home."

"They would have sent him, not you." Jason let go of her. "If you'd talked to me, I could have told you that. If you'd confided in me, in anyone..." He shook his head, his lips set in a grim line. "You betrayed my trust, and Theo's, and all of Cirque du Monde when you kept quiet about Baat's alcoholism. What else aren't you telling me? If you'll stay silent about a big thing like that?"

His gaze was awful, piercing and accusatory. She shook her head. "There's nothing else. I swear. It was only...only Baat. I was so afraid of being fired. I thought when we got settled into a show somewhere, he would get better."

"Now he'll get better, because Lemaitre will get him the help he needs. A process that could have started a long time ago."

Every word pained her. Each syllable of his displeasure felt as painful as a stroke of the cane. She'd deceived and disappointed her Master and she didn't think she could survive how awful it felt.

"I'm sorry," she whispered, sobbing into her hands. "I'm sorry I made you so angry."

"No." He pulled her hands away from her face. "My anger is not the issue here. The issue is that I might have lost you tonight. We all might have lost you because of this choice you made, and you're the only fucking Sara we have. Do you understand that?"

She couldn't answer him. She was crying too hard. He pulled her into his arms, letting his breath out against her cheek. "Jesus, little girl. Why did you do this to me?"

"I'm sorry," she wailed. "I'm sorry, I'm sorry. I'm so sorry for what I did."

"I'm sure you are," he said, hugging her tighter. "Still, you'll have to be punished for this."

She shuddered, shrinking in his arms. He was so angry. It would be a terrible punishment.

He tipped her head back, gazing into her eyes. "You've been through enough for one day, but you'll be punished tomorrow. Severely. Because I never, ever want you to keep a secret like this again."

She hid her face in his chest, clinging to him. "Yes, Master." She wanted him to punish her because she deserved it, but she already knew she'd never keep anything from him again. It felt too awful when he caught her at it.

He drew away and offered her a tissue to wipe her tears. She blew her nose into it too. She was a sniveling mess. While she cleaned up, he undressed and drew back the sheets.

"Lie down on the bed."

She did as he asked and he came over her, spreading her legs apart. His lips brushed against her ear. "You know I'm only angry with you because I love you so much."

His quiet words started her tears flowing again. He kissed them as they fell, moving his lips across her cheek. He positioned his cock between her legs and pushed inside her. Pleasure mingled with shame.

"Open for me," he said when she tensed away from him. "I might have lost you, Sara. I want all of you now."

She spread her legs wide, as wide as she could, and trembled as he took her. His thrusts were steady and rough, a slow torment that roused her to a climax even though she felt she didn't deserve one. She cried all over him as she came, squeezing on the length of him inside her. A moment later he groaned and wrapped her in his arms. Just before he came, he looked in her eyes and mumbled something under his breath. She thought he might have said "eternal," but then his mouth was on hers and she couldn't think about it anymore.

* * * * *

When Sara woke, the passionate lover of the night before had been replaced by a stern and silent Master. She spent breakfast exiled at his feet, in slave position, accepting bits of food when he offered them. They didn't converse and she didn't get much to eat, but she didn't want it anyway. She was too frightened of the punishment to come. And after the punishment, she'd still have to face the other consequences, like Theo's displeasure and Mr. Lemaitre's judgment. She wouldn't be able to work with Baat anymore, and that scared her most of all. What would happen with Cirque, with her career?

She looked down at the pale blue stone on her finger. What if Jason reconsidered his pledge to her, now that he saw how selfish and deceitful she could be? All along he'd been there for her, but she'd tried to deal with everything on her own. Stupid, so stupid. She gazed up at him, wishing she'd been honest. But so many of her fears were tied up in him, or more specifically, losing him. She didn't want to go back to her old life without him.

When Jason finished eating, he shifted in his chair and drew her between his legs to serve him. She licked and caressed his cock, bringing him to full hardness. He pushed his plate away with a scrape and grabbed a handful of her hair, burying himself deep in her mouth. When Jason took over there wasn't much to do but endure his aggression and try not to gag too much. She was glad they'd begun the day with this. Kneeling at his feet, choking on his deep thrusts, all of it put her in the mind for powerlessness, and accepting the punishment she'd earned. As soon as he came in the back of her throat, he ordered her up the stairs.

In his bedroom, he made her submit to the ignominy of a ball gag in her mouth. She hated gags for so many reasons: because they silenced her, because they were ugly, because they made her drool, but mostly because they signaled a hardcore session with a lot of pain.

But punishments had to be about pain, not pleasure. She sank down into her slave pose at the foot of Jason's bed and watched forlornly as he gathered equipment. Strap, paddle, belt, cane. One magnum-sized condom. She shuddered as he lined them all up in a row.

Then he went for the spreader bar and returned. "Stand up and bend over the bed."

She hated that his hard voice and gaze turned her on when she was supposed to be remorseful. She spread her legs for the bar, flexing her toes as he cuffed her ankles at each end. She was too short to reach the floor in this position, so Jason had installed a clasp to hold the bar and prevent her from kicking or falling. Once that was all together she was stuck, bottom raised, all of her on display.

She flushed as he slid a finger through her moist pussy. "Wet, are we?"

She covered her face in shame, even though she knew it wouldn't last, this arousal. He never, ever made punishments feel good.

"Stretch your arms out to each side," he said, then waited for her to comply. "I'm not going to restrain them. Do you know why?"

It was a rhetorical question but she made a small sound behind the gag to let him know she was listening.

"I'm not going to restrain them because you're not going to move them. You're going to lie there and accept everything you get. You deserve it."

She nodded. *Yes, Master. But I'm so scared.*

"The pain is how you learn, little one. So don't dare move those hands or get them in my way. You understand?"

She made a bleak sound of agreement. A couple tears were already pooling beneath her lids.

"I'm going to punish you until I feel you've been adequately corrected for staying quiet about your partner's alcoholism." She felt his hand on her bottom, squeezing, slapping, bringing blood to the surface. All the implements were laid out in front of her on the bed, so she saw when he picked up the strap. Immediately, the first blow fell. It hurt, it stung terribly. He wasn't being gentle. He gave her another, and another.

"Mmm...aww...*oww*." She couldn't stop the begging sounds that erupted from behind the gag, or the helpless squirming of her bottom. She tensed her shoulders to keep her arms as still as possible as the strap fell again and again in an awful rhythm.

"Does that feel good?" he asked.

She shook her head. No, it was too hard and sustained to feel good. When he played with her, he paused between licks, varied the tempo and severity, teased her clit to keep her turned on, but when he punished her, it was just *wham, wham, wham* until her ass was on fire. He used the strap until her cheeks flamed and she was breathless from crying, and then he put it down.

Sara let out a huffing breath. Her ass throbbed along with her racing heart. She tensed her legs and curled her fingers in the sheets. She was lucky. She had one of those Masters who was impervious to pleading and whining, so there was no pressure to do either one. She only laid still and watched him pick up the slim pine paddle. It had holes in it, which Jason alternately called "sad holes" and "scream holes."

The first whack made her shriek behind the gag. She tensed her ass cheeks but that only made it worse as the walloping continued. It was so hard not to flail around and reach back to cover herself. *Take your punishment. You deserve this.*

After ten hard smacks he stopped and caressed her pussy with the paddle's edge. When the wood slid over her clit she bucked involuntarily. A moan tore from her throat. He answered with a tsk.

"The problem with punishing you is that you think pain feels good."

She shook her head, but yes, he was making her feel good. She swallowed a sob as he slid the wooden edge over her entire slit. Then he put the paddle down and picked up the belt, and doubled it over. "Do you think Theo felt proud of you yesterday?" *Whack!*

The belt's sting was much more concentrated than the paddle. Each lick left a burning streak of pain building on the one before it. "How do you think Theo's coping, after everything he went through with Minya? Do you think he enjoyed almost watching you fall?"

Sara shook her head, keening behind the gag.

"Maybe I should have invited him over here so he could have his own go at you. Really, Sara. After everything he did for you."

He brought the leather down on her ass again and again in the same spot until her hips danced on the padded foot board. Oh God, she couldn't bear it, but there was no way to escape. She curled her arms up beside her head, grabbing her hair.

"No. Arms to the sides," he said, belting the backs of her thighs until she complied. "Stick your ass out and be still. You're learning a lesson here. If you don't learn it now, we'll have to do this again another time."

Sara sobbed and shook her head. No, no, not again. But there would be times she would mess up and have to endure these punishments. That was the life she'd chosen, a life of submitting to her Master's will, and his corrections when necessary. At last he put down the belt. Sara fought for breath, brushing her teary cheeks against the bedcovers. Her entire ass and thighs ached with waves of pain, but there was more to come. That was the worst part.

He picked up the last implement, the cane, and tapped it slowly against the bed. It wasn't the one he'd gotten in Mongolia—he only used that for happy scenes. This was his punishment cane. "I don't want you to sit comfortably for a while, so you'll get ten hard strokes."

Ten? She'd never survive ten, not on top of the pain she'd already suffered. She started bawling, squeezing all her fear and panic out through her eyes. He counted each stroke aloud, which made it even more awful. "One." "Two." "Three."

She screamed behind the gag as each whack came burning across her already fiery skin. *I can't. I can't.*

But this is how you learn to never, ever do it again.

"Four." Horrible. "Five." *Nooo...*

Sara's nails bit into her palms as she endured each slice of fire. "Six." She hated Baat for causing her this pain. "Seven." She hated Paris and Cirque du Monde, and even Jason a little because he was hurting her so bad. "Eight." No, not hurting, punishing. Even if his stern voice and cane strokes would give her nightmares later, this is what she'd earned. She screamed at nine, and then he paused and she waited, dreading the final shot. It was the worst of all, a stroke across her parted ass, resonating through her tender center. It brought her no pleasure, only agony.

But that was it. If he told her ten, he gave her ten. As much as it hurt, it had been a controlled and bearable punishment. Her body relaxed as he put down the cane. He stroked her ass, squeezing the painful welts he'd given her. He delivered a few final smacks with his hand, dull, hot spanks that wrested a moan from behind her gag. He ran his fingers up her spine and tugged her head back by the hair. A few jerks of his fingers and the dreaded gag was off.

She felt his legs warm and hard against the backs of her thighs. His grip tightened in her hair. "What do I always do at the end of punishments?"

It took her a moment to find her voice. "You fuck my ass, Master."

"Are you allowed to come?"

"No, Master."

"And we don't use lube, do we? Beyond what's on the condom."

"No, Master." Her voice caught a little on the words. "Only good girls get lube."

"What are you waiting for?"

With a small sob, she reached behind her and parted her ass cheeks.

"Wider," he murmured. "Like I taught you. Don't make me get the cane again."

It was so difficult to do, and yet he required it, so the choice really wasn't hers. She pulled her cheeks wide and offered her asshole to her Master, to punish her as he pleased.

"That's better," he said, spreading one hand at the small of her back. She clenched her teeth and tried to relax as he used his other hand to press his thick girth against her hole. The slippery stuff on the condom always got the head in, but the rest... She muffled her whine in the covers as he forced himself deeper. "Does that feel good?" he asked.

"No, Master," she said on a sob.

"Because punishments don't feel good, do they?"

"No, Master, they don't." Punishments hurt like being pried open from the inside. Once he was fully seated, he told her to put her hands at the back of her head, and then he took her sore ass cheeks, one in each hand, and drilled her in a steady rhythm meant for his pleasure, not hers.

It didn't *hurt* hurt. He wasn't injuring her, but each time he moved into her body it was uncomfortable. It stretched her asshole and taught her a very stark lesson. *I'm in charge of you, and I hurt you when you're bad.* He could have sodomized her for an hour and she would have taken it. In reality, he fucked her only a few minutes before his strokes quickened to a more focused pounding. She heard a grunt and a sigh, felt him drive all the way inside her and fall over her back. He stayed that way, his balls hanging down against her clit. She wanted to grind her hips back to intensify that tickle of pleasure, but she didn't dare. He'd fuck her again and really make it hurt, because this wasn't about her.

A few moments later, he leaned back and withdrew, and went into the bathroom to throw away the condom. She knew better than to move a muscle without his permission. She stayed sprawled where she was, feeling sore and punished, just as he wanted her to feel.

Finally he returned and released her from the spreader bar, and stood her up. He held her arm a moment, until she got her legs back, and then he made her look in his eyes. "I only punish you because you need it," he said.

"Yes, Master."

"Now walk over to the drawer and get the black clover clamps."

Her whole body went hot and cold but she obeyed him, because revolt wasn't an option. She found the dreaded set of clamps and carried them back by their chain. Her rising panic finally spilled out as she placed them in his hand.

"I'm sorry. I'm so sorry. Please, no, Master."

There might have been a small inkling of sympathy in his gaze. She couldn't tell for sure through the tears obscuring her vision. He flicked her nipples, leaning down to lick the treasonous things to attention in preparation for the clamps. Her whole body hurt, her asshole hurt, her pride hurt, and when he closed the biting teeth on her nipples, her breasts hurt too. He tugged down on the chain, ignoring her groan. "Tell me what you learned today."

"Not to keep secrets. Harmful secrets," she said, gasping through the pain.

He jerked the chain again. "Not to keep any secrets. Slaves don't keep secrets from their Masters. Not good slaves, anyway." He wiped away her tears and tilted her chin higher. "Are you going to be my good slave from now on?"

"Yes, Master. Please..." She pulled in her shoulders, giving him her most piteous look.

He kissed her on both her eyes, then gave her a little squeeze on the neck that made her nipples throb harder. "Does *please* ever work for you, little one?"

"No, Master. It never does."

"Hush then. You've got ten minutes in the corner with the clamps, hands at the small of your back. Then we're through and you're forgiven." He let go of her neck and gave her a crisp smack on the bottom. "Now go."

Chapter Fourteen: Struggles

Sara went to headquarters the next day at her usual practice time, even though her body still hurt. Even though she didn't want to. It was Theo's last day and he told her to come in for one last session. Jason had work of his own, a meeting with Lemaitre and the other directors. They had to deal with the aftermath of the ruined Exhibition. Everyone was freaking out. The artists whispered to each other, retelling the story of Sara and Baat's botched act and the fight afterward, embellishing it, making it even more awful. Several artists hadn't gotten their chance to perform because of Baat.

Because of her.

Baat wasn't there, so Sara bore the brunt of everyone's disapproval. Even Theo was cool to her, putting her through an especially grueling warm up. *You deserve this. You fucked up.* He'd ordered the trapeze lowered to its former height, another humiliation. When she finished the exercises he ordered, she swung herself up onto the bar and winced.

Theo crossed to stand under her. "You are injured? What hurts?"

"My ass," she said through her teeth.

She thought he might offer sympathy, even anger on her behalf, but he only nodded. "I would have done the same. I'm tempted to give you a few whacks right now. I lost two years of my life, watching you dangle from his fingers."

Even her coach had no pity for her. She hugged the rope and leaned her head against it. "The mat was underneath."

"The mat saves your life," he snapped. "Not your career. You still might have broken an arm or leg. You might have been paralyzed. A small chance, but a chance."

Sara swung her legs, peering down at the blue surface of the practice floor. "My career might be over anyway. I'm supposed to talk to Mr. Lemaitre today at three-thirty. About Baat and my future here." She wished she could crawl into a hole somewhere. Lemaitre would be angry, and Theo, her wonderful coach, was leaving just when she needed him most.

He took in her bleak expression, reached up and patted the side of her leg. "Come down. We need to talk. Your butt is too sore for trapeze anyway."

She swung down by her knees and winced again at the ache in her muscles. Theo took her by the waist and plucked her from the bar, setting her on the ground. Even the soft mat hurt her ass. She stretched out on her side and rested her head on her arm.

"Poor punished girl. It could have been much worse, you know," said Theo. "You could have been in the hospital with some terrible injury. Broken neck." He kept his voice light, but a muscle worked in his jaw.

"I'm sorry for what happened, Theo. I know it was hard...hard for you to see."

"Yes, well, you shouldn't have gone up with him. You should have told someone about his drinking."

"Jason already lectured me and wrecked my ass." She rolled onto her stomach, burying her head in her hands. "Please, I'm sorry. I'm so sorry for everything." She started crying and hated herself for it. It wasn't professional to cry in front of your coach. She thought he might stalk off in disgust, but he sat and waited. She peered over at his fingers tapping the mat. Those fingers had dropped someone once, someone who'd died.

"I'll make it up to you." She rolled back over, wiping her tears. "What can I do?"

"You can stop crying like a baby, and start talking to me about your new act."

"What new act?"

"Your new solo act you're going to have to learn now that your partner's gone."

She blinked, sitting up. "I'm going to do a solo act?"

"You already know some tricks. When you go to Lemaitre, you can ask him for this opportunity. You can ask him for anything you want, and if he thinks you can do it, he'll say yes."

"But..." A solo act? Just her doing tricks on the trapeze? "I don't know if I can do that, carry a whole act by myself."

He scowled at her. "I will spank you again, right now, on your painful ass. I don't care who sees."

She scooted back from him, just in case he was serious. "But you're leaving. Who's going to help me?"

"How about helping yourself? You're the only one in your partnership who ever had a heart for trapeze, for performance," he scolded. "And you've been practicing tricks for weeks, solo tricks you could use to anchor your own routine. This *I-don't-know-if-I-can* nonsense makes me angry. Of course you can do it. You only need determination, and ideas."

She stared into Theo's avid gaze, an idea forming in her mind. "I could make up my own story. Couldn't I? Would that be okay?"

"Of course. Make it what you want."

She could make it a story of her struggles, a story of a lonely, blue-eyed girl from Mongolia torn between two worlds. A story of a girl who couldn't please everyone, no matter how hard she tried. The story of a girl trying to balance selfishness and ambition on the way to achieving her dreams. She threw out ideas as they came to her, egged on by Theo. He helped her refine her vision and put the depth of her feelings into words.

Before long, the two of them had sketched out a loose story for an act. They began to talk about transitions and tricks, even costuming and colors to support the theme. Blue. They both agreed the colors had to be blue.

Sara got so excited, she took to the trapeze and started practicing, ignoring the pain in her ass cheeks. This was more important. This was progress and inspiration. This was expiation, a way of making things right. She'd create a solo act and perfect it, and Jason would be proud, and Lemaitre would forgive her—

Lemaitre! She looked at the clock, shocked to discover they'd spent two hours practicing. It was already three.

"I have to go," she said. "I have to shower and change before I meet with Mr. Lemaitre." She started for the locker rooms, then turned back and gave Theo an impulsive hug. "Thank you. I feel so much better. But...if he's mad at me... If he tries to fire me..."

"He's not going to fire you."

"But he might be mad."

"He's probably stressed out, yes. You and Baat stressed out a lot of people." He squeezed her extra hard, then tilted her head up. "Listen, *ma chère*. If Lemaitre starts scolding, tell him about your big plans for the act. Tell him everything. The theme, the story, the colors." Some shadow crossed his face, and he hesitated. "Most of all, share the things you shared with me, about your struggles and fears, and your loneliness. These are things he should hear too."

Sara didn't know if she could be that open with Mr. Lemaitre. She looked at the clock and ran for the showers. She wished she had time to find Jason and tell him about her new ambitions for solo trapeze, but that would have to wait.

* * * * *

Sara ended up running the last half of the way to Mr. Lemaitre's office, so she arrived winded and disheveled after all the care she'd taken with her appearance. The receptionist asked her to sit a moment while she notified him she was here. Sara waited in a row of chairs outside his office, her heart beating with nervousness. Would he be angry? Kind? Encouraging about her future? If she had to beg to stay on, could she do it?

Yes.

She smoothed back her hair, blowing away an errant strand when it fell in her face. She loved the color and beauty of the Cirque

CEO's office, but it was always so quiet. She drew in a deep breath and before she let it out, the receptionist looked over and signaled her to go in.

As soon as he greeted her by the door, she sensed she wasn't in for a scolding. He used her full Mongolian name and gestured her toward a chair, and then sat down behind his massive desk.

"Thank you for your promptness," he said. "We have many things to talk about. Yesterday..." He stopped and leaned forward. "First of all, how are you feeling?"

"Feeling? You mean, physically?"

"Let's start with that. You didn't sustain any injuries?"

Only to my ass, she thought. "I'm doing fine," she said aloud. "I practiced with Theo today and everything went well."

"I'm glad to hear it. And emotionally? How are you holding up?"

He asked so gently, so kindly, when she'd expected anger. "I've been feeling guilty," she admitted. "And a little scared."

"Scared of what?"

"Losing my job. Finding my way forward. I was with Baat a long time."

Her emotions were so close to the surface. Her throat tightened and she dug her nails into her palm so she wouldn't cry. It was bad enough to cry in front of Theo, but Lemaitre?

"You mustn't worry about your friend," he said. "Baat is bound for an alcohol rehabilitation center in Ulaanbaatar. They have excellent programs there, and Baat agreed it was a necessary course of action."

"Oh. Thank you. I...I tried to get him to stop drinking so much. I didn't know how to help him."

"I knew how to help him." There was the censure, the intimation that she ought to have said something.

"I'm sorry, Mr. Lemaitre. I'm sorry for causing all this trouble."

He sighed and leaned back in his chair. "Let's be clear—Baat caused the trouble. You exacerbated it by staying quiet. But Jason tells me you've been corrected on that point."

She flushed twenty shades of red and shifted on her sore ass. Lemaitre seemed to take pity on her and produced a note from his desk. "Baat wrote this for you. I understand it's an apology. He did realize by the time he left how badly he'd wronged you. Please, read it. I'll wait."

Sara looked down at the note written in Baat's broad hand. It held an apology, but so much more. *When you took the Amerik's ring, something in me broke. I always loved you.*

I never meant to hurt you, but Sarant, I hurt. I'll get better. Please forgive me one day. She stared down at the words, shocked.

"Does it say he loves you?" Lemaitre asked in the silence.

She couldn't speak, only nod her head.

He made a soft, sad sound. "I don't read Mongolian, but I expected he was writing more than a simple apology."

"I never realized. I've been so blind." She pressed the back of her hand to her lips to still their trembling. "I don't understand, though. Baat was like a brother to me."

"Ah, well. He saw things differently. But he never told you, so how could you know?" Another reprimand, couched in a cool, soft voice. "The two of you, keeping dangerous secrets. Cry if you like, Sara. It's a lot to process."

"I don't want to cry." She shook her head, feeling anger more than anything else. She'd never known Baat, not really. Why had he hidden his feelings from her? And then drowned himself in drink? "He should have told me. He should have been honest," she said.

Lemaitre studied her, his lips drawn down in a frown. "Perhaps he didn't feel capable of being honest. Perhaps he thought it would hurt you to know."

"Hurt me? To know the truth? To know how he really felt about me?" She rubbed her eyes and grasped for calm. "Please, I just want to know what happens now. Can I stay here?"

"With Cirque du Monde?"

"Because I had this idea for an act. A solo trapeze act. Theo and I developed the basics so I can work on it after he leaves for Marseille." She rushed to get the words out before he could cut in. "It's about a girl. About a girl caught between the world she was born in and the world where she wants to belong. And she has all these frustrations, and fears, and horrible anxieties and this loneliness, because she doesn't fit in anywhere. But she also..." She stared down at her ring, twisting it on her finger. "She also has love. And that scares her most of all, because it can't save her. She knows she has to find her own way, her own strength, but it's so hard."

He looked at her a long time, then he asked, "Is this act about you?"

"Not really," she lied. "Well, a little bit. But it could be anyone's story."

"Yes, it could be," he agreed. "Fear. Love. Loneliness. They're universal themes."

After all her efforts, the tears came anyway, a crushing wave of emotion she hid as well as she could. While she swiped at her eyes, Lemaitre came around his desk and sat beside her. "Is that your ring? May I see it?"

Sara held it out, trying to still the shaking of her fingers. He touched the stone. "Beautiful." He gave a sigh and took her hand. "A ring is a serious commitment, especially for one so young. You're sure he's the one for you?"

His nearness shook her. His touch startled her. It felt encroaching. Inappropriate. She got the same feeling she'd gotten in the hall that day, that he had an interest in her beyond boss and artist. Baat's secret love was bad enough. She had to set this man straight. "Mr. Lemaitre, I'm not too young to know what I want. And I want to be with Jason. I'm in love with him, totally and completely. I'm not available. At all."

"Available?" He processed her rejection, narrowed his eyes and made a face. "*Mon Dieu.* I suppose I've brought this on myself."

He looked so upset that Sara tried to console him. "I'm sorry. It's not that you aren't attractive—"

He held up a hand. "I beg you, please."

"It's just that Jason and I are meant to be together. From the moment we met, we've had this bond."

"Sara." Lemaitre let out a ragged breath. "Please understand I have absolutely no interest in you. Not interest of that kind. For God's sake."

Oh. Embarrassing. "I just thought… From the way you…"

"Did you never wonder why you had eyes that color?"

The angst in his question caught her off guard. She fell back on her usual explanation. "I was born outside, under a blue sky. My mother said I opened my eyes and the sky changed them forever. That the sky turned them blue."

He stood and went to the window. "What a beautiful story. I'll have to use that in a show sometime. It's just the sort of story your mother liked to tell."

It took her a moment to unpack his words. "You knew my mother?"

"I knew her well, once upon a time. We worked in the same circus for a while, touring Europe. We made a baby together, a little girl. I didn't know at the time. She only told me later."

Sara gawked at him, at his carved profile outlined by the sun outside. It wasn't possible. Her mother only had two children, herself and a brother who died as a child. "But how? When did you know her?"

"About twenty-three years ago." He turned from the window and crossed to her, reaching in his pocket for his wallet. He flipped it open and pulled out a small, dog-eared photo and handed it to her. Sara stared down into her own face, her own features as a girl of six or seven, with blue eyes, wind-chapped cheeks, and a hint of a smile.

He stared at her, saying nothing. She struggled to understand.

"This is— You mean, I'm— You—"

The pronouns got tangled up in her mouth, just like the revelation got tangled up in her brain. "It can't be," she said. "I can't be your daughter. My eyes…the sky…"

"You didn't get your blue eyes from the sky," he said sharply. "Have some sense."

How dare he admonish her when he was the one making up this crazy story? It had to be a lie, all of it, a lie. "My mother loved my father!"

"She certainly did," said Mr. Lemaitre. "That's why you grew up with him instead of me. A mercy, I'm certain."

Sara's thoughts reeled, along with an avalanche of emotions: confusion, fury, disbelief, and a terrible sadness. "It can't be true. I don't look anything like you."

He sat in the chair beside her, reserving comment. Sara covered her eyes, the eyes that proved she was his, as much as she wanted to deny it. "Why? Why would she have done that to my father?"

"It was an accident, I assure you." At her grimace, he shook his head. "No, you weren't an accident. You were the result of a sublime, impetuous affair, and it was my fault, all of it. Your mother loved your father, and he loved her. I'm not good at love, or fidelity, or any of those things, so I left her. I left you, because I thought it best." He gazed at her, a look of such guilt and pain that she almost forgave him for his crime. Almost.

"You're as bad as Baat," she said, tasting nausea in her mouth. "You're worse. You hid even more. You hid...*this*."

"I'm sorry I didn't tell you when we first met." He stood and paced across the room. "It paralyzed me, the sight of you standing there. I didn't feel worthy to be your father. I still don't. But part of me hoped you'd figure it out yourself."

"How is it my job to figure it out?" she cried. "People should be who they are. You lied to me. You kept this a secret—"

"You kept a secret too," he said, turning on her. "People keep secrets when they're afraid. When they don't know what will happen."

Sara felt numb. She seemed to know nothing about anything going on in her life. She didn't know what to believe anymore, or what to do, or who to trust. "This is why you wouldn't let me come to the Citadel," she said. "This is the reason you threw me out."

"It's rather traumatic to discover one's daughter has arrived in the midst of your BDSM scene. It was one more reason not to tell you."

"Well, I wish you had explained. I had no idea why you sent me away that night. I thought you were angry at something I did. I thought you didn't like me."

"I care for you very much." That confession seemed to leave him breathless. He leaned against the wall, his arms crossed over his chest. "I've been keeping an eye on you. Protecting you as best I can."

"By avoiding me?"

"I didn't know what to do. I'm not a father. I've never been a father."

"You didn't even come get me yourself. You sent Jason to bring me back for you, like some curiosity from afar."

"No."

"Your little Mongolian souvenir."

"No, it wasn't like that."

"What was it like then?" Anger propelled her to her feet, and she stormed toward him. "You never had any intention of telling me. You probably couldn't wait to pack me off to Las Vegas. Good riddance, right?"

"No." He shook his head. "I dreaded losing you, but I wanted to see you settled. I don't feel capable of being your father but I wanted to nurture this gift you have. I owe that, at least, to your mother."

Her lips trembled. "How nice. Settling accounts."

"Sara." His voice rose on an anguished note. "Please understand, I'm not the fatherly type. I don't know how to do this. Here you are, my grown-up daughter, and you're feeling all these things, and imagining this incredible solo act, and falling in love when I've barely had a chance to know you. You're too much for me, dear girl. You're so much more than I expected you to be."

She blinked at him and took a step back. "What does that mean?"

"I don't know what it means." He spread his arms in frustration. "I'm making a mess of this, just as I knew I would. I understand your anger. I deserve it."

Anger? No. She wasn't angry. She was devastated. She was confused and emotionally gutted. "I think I'd better go, Mr. Lemaitre." Her voice faded on the formal address. He was her father, for God's sake.

"Why don't you call me Michel?" he offered. "Until we figure things out?"

"Figure things out?" she said, looking around his office, at all the mementos that defined this man. Her *father*. "I don't even know you. Everything I thought about you is…"

"I'm sorry."

She took another step back, and another. "I think... I think I'm... I'm going to go and...take some time to process this."

"Of course," he said. "If you need me I'll be here, just as I have been. I'll do anything to help you. None of that will change."

You weren't there last year, when I took a job at a sex club. When I didn't have any family left in the world except for Baat. She needed Jason. Jason would hold her and comfort her, and help her make sense of this crazy revelation. She took one last look over her shoulder at the man who was her father, but not really her father.

The man who didn't want to be her father. That's what hurt her most of all.

Chapter Fifteen: Who We Are

Jason was in the middle of a multi-artist tumbling team when he noticed Sara at the door of the gymnastics facility. He saw all the hands coming up to hide whispers. Everyone knew by now that Baat had a problem with alcohol and that Sara had stayed quiet about it. He wanted to protect her, to explain her side of things, but the only real explanation was that she'd messed up.

He'd punished her because he had to, because he couldn't move past the choice she'd made without venting his fear and frustration, his anger that she hadn't confided in him. Since then, he'd tried to buoy up her spirits, but she had a long way to go to regain everyone's trust. As she walked toward him, she received more than a few judgmental looks.

He asked the gymnast team to break for a moment and jogged over to meet her by the wall. "Sara, I'm busy. Things are crazy here." She looked pale, wrung out. Her eyes were rimmed in red. "What happened?" he asked. "What did Lemaitre say?"

"He didn't say anything bad." She paused and rubbed her forehead. "He just said..."

"What?" he prompted when she hesitated.

She stared up at him. "He said he was my father. That I'm his daughter. That's why...my eyes... That's the reason they're blue."

Jason touched her face, wishing he could smooth away the pain etched on her features. So Lemaitre had finally fessed up. Why now, on top of everything else she was going through?

"Oh, baby." He drew her into his arms, cradling her close. "So, how does that make you feel? What did you say when he told you?"

"What did I say?" Sara stiffened and pulled away from him, her sadness transforming to anger. Fuck. He'd remembered too late to add surprise to his expression.

"You knew." It wasn't a question. Her gaze eviscerated him. "You already knew. You knew and you never told me."

"Sara—"

"When were you going to tell me? Didn't you think it was important?"

"Sara—"

She looked around at the gawking performers lounging on the mats. "Who else knew? Everyone? Did everyone know but me?"

He held up a finger, cautioning her. "If you don't lower your voice, everyone is going to know."

"Well, I guess it's not much of a big fucking secret, if you already knew."

He let out a soft sigh. "I knew, and Theo. And Theo told Kelsey."

"But not me, right? Because why would I need to know?"

His sweet little slave was livid. The worst part was, she had a right to be. "Honey, I would have told you but Lemaitre begged me not to. He thought it was best. He asked all of us not to tell you."

"When did you know?"

Heads turned at her sharp, shrill question. He angled himself so he stood between Sara and the performers. "This might not be the ideal time to discuss this."

"No, I want to discuss it. When did you know? Did you know from the start, when you came to Mongolia?"

"I didn't, I swear. I didn't figure it out until he kicked you out of the Citadel."

"And you didn't see the need to tell me?"

"Listen, you haven't heard the whole story." He grabbed her arm, meaning to find a more private place for the discussion, but she pushed him away.

"Don't 'listen' me. Don't touch me."

He backed away from her, at a loss. This wasn't how their dynamic worked. *You don't have a "dynamic" anymore. You've lost her respect.*

He knew he'd lost it before she gave voice to it. Her pretty English syllables stabbed him in the heart. "You're a hypocrite, Jason. You lectured me. You punished me for keeping secrets."

"For keeping secrets about something that endangered your life," he shot back. "It's not the same. I punished you because you could have died."

"I don't trust you now. What else aren't you telling me? If you'll stay silent about a big thing like that?"

He recognized the words as his own. She had him, she was right. He was a liar and a hypocrite. He'd expected truth from her while he kept deep, dark secrets she deserved to know.

"Lemaitre asked me not to tell you. He threatened me," he said, pleading his useless case. "He's my boss, Sara."

"But I'm your lover. Your slave. You gave me a ring, you bound us together."

"Sara."

"I trusted you."

"I promised to keep it a secret," he said. "He thought it would be better if you didn't know and I agreed with him. He won't be a good father to you."

"I guess that means it was okay for you to hide this from me. See, I never realized this before. It doesn't matter. Being truthful and honest, and trusting people. It doesn't matter. Nobody is who they say they are. Everybody's just..." She gave a wild wave. "It's all an act, right? Circus!"

"Please, baby, take some deep breaths. It's been a crazy couple of days. We're all exactly who we are, and I love you, and everything's going to be okay."

"No. We're not all exactly who we are," she said, her voice shaking with emotion. "Because Baat isn't who I thought he was, and my father isn't who I thought he was, and Lemaitre isn't who I thought he was, and my Master...he isn't who I thought he was either."

He wanted to take her in his arms, make her believe he'd never meant to hurt her, but some wall had appeared between them, too jagged and high to climb. "I'm not perfect, okay? I'm human. I was trying to protect you. I didn't think Lemaitre..." This was the worst thing. "I don't think Lemaitre intends to be your father. I didn't want you to be hurt."

But it was too late for that. She was hurt, hurt so badly she couldn't look at him.

"What did he say to you?" he asked. "That fucking asshole. I didn't want him to hurt you."

"He didn't, not intentionally. But I think you're right. He doesn't want to be my father." Her delicate throat worked with emotion. "He was more interested in...how did he put it? 'Nurturing my gift.'"

"Can I hold you?" he asked. It sounded like begging. "Can I try to help you feel better? I love you, Sara. I want you to be happy."

"The thing is..." She brought her hands to her drawn cheeks. "The thing is, I don't know if I'll be happy for a while. I think I need some time. I'm going to go home and be alone for a few days, because right now, I don't know what's going on with my life. I don't know how I feel." She slid a sideways look at him. "And I don't want you telling me how to feel."

Because I don't trust you anymore. She didn't say the last words, but Jason heard them clear as a blue Mongolian sky. "If you need time, take time," he told her, but she was already walking away from him.

She didn't need his permission anymore.

* * * * *

Jason tried to give her time. He lasted forty-eight hours without calling or texting her, without trying to find her at the practice facility. He had plenty of work to do, plenty to keep him busy, but her words haunted him. *I trusted you.* Trusted. Past tense.

In the end he had to seek her out. Theo and Kelsey were gone to Marseille, Lemaitre wasn't answering calls. There wasn't anyone else to look after her, and looking after her was his job. In his heart he was still her Master, with all the duty and caring that entailed. They belonged together. They'd both agreed to that from the beginning. He'd just explain again that he never meant to hurt her. Maybe she'd listen now that she'd had some time to calm down.

With that in mind, he headed to her dorm, feeling chilled even though it was a warm night. As he walked, he made plans in his head: what he'd do if she didn't let him in, what he'd do if she did let him in. What he'd do if she pushed him away and slammed the door in his face. But when he knocked, it wasn't Sara who swung the door wide.

Jason stared at Michel Lemaitre. His tie was askew, his shirt collar crooked. He didn't look like himself.

"Where's Sara?" Jason asked, pushing past him. "I need to see her."

"Sara isn't here."

Jason stalked around, checking the bedroom, the bathroom, the closets. "If she's not here, what are you doing here?"

The older man sat back down on her couch. "They are my dormitories, and she was my daughter. I suppose I can brood here if I like."

Was his daughter? Panic exploded in his brain. "Where is she? What happened?"

Lemaitre held up a hand. "Nothing's happened. She asked to go with Kelsey and Theo to Marseille, and I said yes."

"She went to Marseille? She left? Already?"

"Very much the same way she left Mongolia. Once she makes up her mind, she doesn't stick around."

Jason paced to the kitchen and back, reeling with disbelief. She hadn't consulted him, hadn't told him anything. She'd taken off without so much as a goodbye.

"You sent her away." He advanced on Lemaitre again. "You did this. You sent her to Marseille."

"No. I wanted her to stay here. I wanted us to have some time to..." His voice trailed off. "But it's good. This is what she needs at the moment. Theo will continue to work with her there until her solo act's ready."

"What solo act?"

"You haven't been paying attention, have you? Perhaps that's why she left without this." He stood and walked to her desk, and picked up a narrow blue ribbon. When Jason walked closer, he realized it was tied around her ring, the promise ring he'd given her.

She'd left him. They'd come unbound.

Jason took the ring and turned it over in his palm. He didn't want to believe she'd left him, but there it was. "There wasn't anything else?" he asked, looking up at Lemaitre. "A message? A note?"

"Just the ring." He clapped Jason on the shoulder. "Don't take it too hard. I don't think she would be so upset with you if she didn't love you so much."

Jason stared at the delicate circle with its pale blue stone. He couldn't even fit it on his pinky. "Leave it here for her," said Lemaitre. "She'll want it back."

"No, I'm taking it." His voice sounded petty, like a child's, but he wasn't giving up the ring. Right now, it was all he had of her. "I can't believe she just...just left."

"I believe it, because I was here. She was confused, and very angry. Wouldn't you be?" Lemaitre drifted around her living room, looking at her bookshelves, at the few things she'd accumulated since she arrived. "This is a necessary break for her, a time to fly solo for a while. It's good. She's growing." He turned to look down his nose at Jason. "You told her, didn't you, that she was too young?"

"Yeah, but I didn't mean it! I didn't want her to actually outgrow me."

Lemaitre shook his head, tracing a felt flower on her bulletin board. "Then why did you wait? I don't understand you, Jason. You had her. You had her right here, and you didn't claim her."

"Pot, kettle. Kettle, pot. You did the same thing."

Lemaitre made a peeved sound and leaned against the wall. "We're a miserable couple of idiots, aren't we?"

"You never told me about her act."

"From what I understand, it's about a girl stuck between two worlds, with fears and anxieties, and loneliness. Lots of anguish." He gave a rueful chuckle. "She's my daughter. I'd believe it even without the blue eyes."

You don't deserve her for a daughter. He bit his tongue against the words. Perhaps he didn't deserve her as a slave either. "Do you think..." He took a sharp, pained breath. "Fears and anxieties, and loneliness. Is this act about her?"

"Of course it is," he said. "Because there's love in it also. Not that I'd know anything about that."

Jason leaned on the wall opposite him and pinned the great Le Maître with his gaze. "You love her, Michel. Deep down, you want to be her father. You're dying to be her father."

"I can't do it, so it doesn't matter. I don't do love the 'right' way. I don't love like other people."

"Bullshit." Jason laughed and turned away from him. "We all get so caught up in your bullshit. Your drama. You get caught up worse than anyone. The truth is, you loved her the first day, just like I did. Now both of us are sitting here, dumped, like a couple of jackasses." He walked across her dorm room toward the door. "I'm going to Marseille."

Lemaitre sprang away from the wall and grabbed his arm. "You're not. I forbid it."

"You can forbid my left nut, Michel," he said, shaking him off. "It doesn't matter. I'm going."

"I'm telling you as your boss, you're not to interfere in her business. She wants to develop her own act, find her way through this without depending on anyone else. I promised she could."

"And what happens then?"

He shrugged. "It's up to her. Cirque du Monde runs sixteen shows, fifteen of which she's eligible for."

"Not *Tsilaosa*?"

Lemaitre sighed and shook his head. "The trapeze. It's cursed."

"It's not cursed. You don't want her here because you don't want to deal with her. You don't want her in your face."

"No."

"You don't want to fight your feelings. You don't want to have to change from Le Maître, all powerful God and pervert, to Lemaitre, middle-aged father. I know it's scary, Michel—"

"Enough!" Jason could see he'd hit a little too close to the truth. Lemaitre scowled at him, his eyes dark with pain. "Yes, it's the truth. I don't want her here. Yes, I admit it." He bowed his head until he collected himself. "I'm sorry. I know you wanted her near."

"Oh, I'm going to have her near. I'm going to Marseille to win her back, and then I'll stay with her, go wherever her talent takes us. I love her."

"I know you love her, because I've seen you together. I see how you're both hurting now. But if she's truly your slave, she'll come back to you when she's ready. And if you're a good Master, you'll give her the space she needs right now."

Jason wondered how Lemaitre could be so wise about power exchange, about Master/slave relationships, and so stupid about other things, like accepting Sara into his life. Either way, he was right. Sara had requested space and Jason was obliged to give it to her.

"Have patience," Lemaitre said. "She'll be okay. Let Theo and Kelsey look after her for a while."

Chapter Sixteen: Now

Jason's phone pinged while he was at lunch. He flicked onto his messages, hoping it might be Sara. He hadn't heard from her in almost two weeks, since she'd gone to Marseille. But no, it was Theo.

Sara says please stop txting her.
It's sad, dude.

Jason grimaced and tapped out a reply.

Why won't she talk to me?

Because she's busy.

Too busy for one text? "I'm okay, Jason"

You sound like a woman.
Stop.

Jason pushed away his half-eaten plate and hunched over his phone, and tapped out the one question he had to ask.

Have you been sleeping with her?

No reply. Jason applied the capslock.

WELL, HAVE YOU?

Theo's reply came a few seconds later.

I asked but she refused.
She's slept with Kels several times.

What???!!!

Joking.
Idiote.

Then, a moment later, words that soothed some of his ire.

She misses you. She doesn't say, but...

Oh, no. Theo wasn't leaving him hanging with an ellipsis.

But what?

No reply.

Call me when you get a min, Jason typed.

No.

I need you to call me.

No.

Just tell me how she's doing. She's okay?

If she wasn't, I'd tell you.

Is she sad?

There was a long pause, then Theo typed, *Two more weeks.*

Two more weeks, what?

Two more weeks, act is ready.

I can see it?

Yes. In Marseille.
Now stop txting.
I'm busy. She's busy.

Tell her I love her and I miss her, he typed quickly.

No reply.

*****

Sara lay back on the grass in a meadow a few miles outside the city. A small brook outlined the clearing, as well as a ring of great, old trees. Marseille was beautiful in late summer, warm and breezy. A few hundred feet away, two tails of aerial silk wafted in the breeze. Theo had hung them from a thick branch of the largest tree, and he and Kelsey played on them, practicing tricks and showing Sara some of the rudiments of their art.

It took skill and strength, Sara thought. But mostly it took trust. It was just like duo trapeze. She'd heard from Baat, learned he was feeling better now that he'd completed the first phase of his rehab. *Sobriety is a whole new world*, he'd written. *I feel like a new man.*

Sara was trying to feel like a new woman. She wasn't finding success at it, not so far. Oh, her act was coming along, thanks to

Theo and Kelsey's encouragement. The show in Marseille had its own rehearsal space, and *Minuit*'s artists gave her plenty of time to practice. All that was going great, but...

She watched Kelsey and Theo fool around on the silks, speaking a cobbled-together mixture of French and English. Since she was staying at their house, she'd learned a lot about their relationship. They kissed a lot. They touched a lot. They fought a lot too, but they always made up. She wished now she hadn't blown up at Jason, disappeared and left his ring behind as if it meant nothing to her. She wished she'd given her and Michel Lemaitre's newborn relationship a chance, rather than spewing anger and accusations at him.

She wished she didn't have so many regrets.

"You two sure know how to have fun," she called as they swung across the clearing. They were together, a happy couple. Sara was alone, by choice, because she thought it would make everything easier to deal with. Maybe she'd been wrong.

In two days, Lemaitre—her father—was coming to check out her new act. Theo said Jason would probably come too, but what if he didn't? What if he'd found some other slave by now, a slave who was perfect and normal, and truthful and obedient?

She could text Jason and ask him. She could call him right now on the phone but she was afraid. With them, it had always been about what happened when they were face to face. The chemical reaction that occurred when they were in a room together, or gazing into each other's eyes. Would it still be there? Lemaitre said she had to spend this time growing into her new self...but two big parts of her new self weren't there.

Kelsey came over to sit by Sara while Theo showed off, doing a series of pull-ups on the silks.

"Feats of strength," Kelsey yelled. "We want to see them."

He grinned over his shoulder and levered his body into a right angle with the ground. His sculpted muscles contracted into statue-like perfection.

"Whoa," Sara breathed. "How does he do that?"

She laughed. "Jason can do it too. I've seen him." She looked over at Sara, covering her mouth. "I'm sorry. I didn't mean to bring him up."

Sara tried to sound casual. Unaffected. "It's okay."

Theo was doing an actual handstand on the silks now. They applauded and cheered, then lay back on the blanket again. "He's going to break his neck, isn't he?" asked Sara.

Her friend shrugged. "Maybe. Hopefully not. I learned a long time ago that Theo is gonna do what Theo is gonna do, and that's why he's so good at what he does. You're the same way when you're on the trapeze. Fearless. It's good to be that way. It frees you up to create."

"I guess." Sara rolled onto her side, picking at twigs and blades of grass. "But is it hard to be married to someone like that? Someone so fearless?"

"Sometimes it's hard. But love is worth the risk."

"Was there ever a time you didn't trust him?"

Kelsey burst into laughter. "Oh, lady. I could tell you some stories."

"I'm waiting. Tell."

Was Kelsey blushing? She covered her eyes, then looked back at Sara. "Let's just say Theo and I didn't have the most conventional start. The first time we slept together, I wasn't sure if he was going to kiss me or choke the life out of me. I was a fearless little innocent myself, and I got involved with him just after...after Minya died." She looked over at Theo, swinging in the silks. "There were so many whispers, so many terrible things people said. Some people said he dropped her on purpose, that he murdered her—" Her voice cracked and cut off. "Well."

"That seems crazy," said Sara.

"Yes, it does, but for a little while, I doubted." She drew in a sharp breath. "I hate that I doubted, but people are so complicated. In my heart though, I knew the truth. He never meant to harm Minya. He'd never harm anyone. For all his hardass, dominant ways, the man's as gentle as a fly."

It was Sara's turn to laugh, because Theo seemed anything but gentle. He spent most of his free time berating her in practice sessions.

"He's a tough coach," said Kelsey, reading her thoughts. "But he only means the best for you."

"I know."

They fell silent, watching Theo practice tricks and drops that looked terrifying, although Sara knew they were safe. After a while, Kelsey turned toward her, brushing her hair off her face. "We can talk about him if you want. About Jason. About trust. That's why you were asking, wasn't it?"

Sara stared at the ground, at the little pile of twigs she'd broken and rearranged. "I miss him so much. I wanted to be with him forever."

"You can still be with him forever."

"But I fucked up, Kelsey. I left him. I've ignored his calls, his texts." She covered her face. "I never even said goodbye."

"You were angry. He kept a big secret from you."

"But I kept a secret from him too." Kelsey was sweet, taking her side like a loyal friend, but over the past couple weeks Sara had come to realize how unfair she'd been to her Master. "When I kept a secret, Jason punished me and we moved on. He *forgave* me. When Jason kept a secret, I closed myself off and ran away. If I love him, why did I do that?"

Kelsey sighed and touched her hand. "You didn't run away. You took the time and space you needed to process some serious upheaval in your life."

"Maybe," Sara said, burying her head in the blanket. "But I don't know where things go from here. I'm scared to face him. I don't know what he'll say."

Theo descended the silks and started toward them, only to be waved away by Kelsey. "We're talking about girl things. Periods and stuff. Can you wait a sec?"

He turned and walked in the other direction, and settled to lounge beside the tree. He laid his head back and closed his eyes, so calm, so at peace with the world. Why couldn't Sara find that peace? "Men have it easy," she muttered. "Especially dominant men. They ask for whatever they need and they always get their way."

"That's not true," said Kelsey. "You can ask for what you need, too. You can get your way. What do you need from Jason?"

"I need him to always do the right thing. I need him to be perfect."

Kelsey glanced at her husband, who spied on them from under his eyelids. "They're never perfect. So no, you can't have that."

Sara covered her face with a groan. "I made a mistake, leaving him. I wasn't thinking. I was confused about who I was."

"Are you still confused?"

"Yes."

Kelsey reached out to squeeze her shoulder. "Again, this is pretty normal. Do you love him? Do you think he loves you?"

"I don't know. He kept secrets from me. He should have told me Lemaitre was my dad, don't you think?"

"I didn't tell you either. Theo didn't tell you. We're all guilty, but you're only angry with Jason. It doesn't seem fair."

Kelsey was right, as much as she hated to admit it. "I'm not even angry anymore," she said. "But I don't know what to do now. All these things happened—"

"And you didn't know how to handle them. Okay, that's called life. It happens with me and Theo all the time. We survive, we regroup, we talk things out. We get over them and grow past them and it becomes part of the fabric of our love. You know?"

The fabric of our love. That was a pretty way to put it, especially for two silks artists. Now that Theo was on the ground, the silks were flying free, almost close enough for Sara to touch. But her and Jason's love wasn't like fabric. It was more like a trapeze at the moment, off-balance, swinging back and forth.

"Maybe I just need to hang on the bar for a while," Sara sighed.

"What? I don't think alcohol's the answer," said her friend with a frown.

"No, not that kind of bar. I was thinking about trapeze. You do tricks, but then you take breathers where you 'hang on the bar.' And you relax and exist and just...hang." She shook her head and rubbed her forehead. "I've been so stressed, so worried about everything. About Baat and Jason, and the act, and the Citadel and Lemaitre, and Las Vegas, and my future. Maybe I need to stop stressing about everything so much and just..."

Kelsey smiled. "Hang on the bar for a while?"

"Yes. And apologize to Jason, and forgive him, and ask if we can try things again."

"You realize Jason texts Theo every day. *How's Sara? Is she happy? Is she okay? Does she miss me?*" Kelsey chuckled. "You two can have a nice, long discussion about how much you love each other when he comes to Marseille to see your act."

Oh yeah, her act. The main reason she was here. "I think Jason will like it," Sara said, "but I'm nervous about performing for Mr. Lemaitre."

"You mean your dad?"

"I can't think of him like that. He made it clear in Paris that he wasn't interested in a father-daughter thing."

"Aw, Sara. He's interested. He cares about you."

"Does he text Theo every day?" she joked bitterly. "He hasn't tried to contact me once."

"Well..." Kelsey thought a moment. "If I had to guess, I'd say he's taking a little breather on the bar."

"Maybe the bar at the Citadel," Sara said. "Or some other sex club. He has his priorities."

Kelsey shuddered. "Oh God. I just realized something. I slept with your *dad*. I was his plaything for a whole week."

"Theo allowed that?"

"Theo loved it, watching Lemaitre torture me. I won't tell you the particulars since he's your father and everything. Believe me..." She shuddered again. "You'd be traumatized for life."

"He's not very nice, is he?"

"Lemaitre? Sometimes he's not, but he has a huge heart under all that Lord-and-Master posturing. I know, I've seen it. Even if he won't be your father, I'd accept him as a friend."

Theo glared over at them, spreading his hands. "You're still talking about your periods? There is so much to say?"

"I love you, honey," Kelsey called out, laughing.

He rolled his eyes at her and then gestured to Sara. "Come, *ma brillante*. Your turn on the silks."

Sara watched the fabric twist in the wind. "I better not. I've only ever done trapeze."

"Go try it," said Kelsey, nudging her. "It's fun. If you want, I'll go with you."

"Can it hold both of us?"

"It could hold an elephant, silly. Come on."

Kelsey gave her some rosin and showed her how to make hand and foot "traps" so she could hold on once she climbed up. The fabric looked so soft billowing in the wind, but in her hands it felt hard and strong, like it could literally hold an elephant. Theo climbed up too, on the opposite silk, and he and Kelsey demonstrated how to do some of the moves in their act. In *Minuit*, their act was dark and tragic, but here on the silks, they laughed and teased each other, and the day was warm and bright.

"It's fun, no?" asked Theo, swinging away from her. He was back a moment later. "More fun than girl talk."

"Nothing's more fun than girl talk," Kelsey said. "Except flying. Hey Theo, make us fly, please?"

"Um," Sara said as Theo nodded and started down the opposite silk. "What is this flying thing?"

"You'll love it," Kelsey assured her. "Everyone should try it once."

Theo let the other tail blow free and took the girls' silk. "Kels, Sara has her hand lock?"

Kelsey made sure Sara was secure, then looked down at her husband. "We're good."

Sara wasn't totally good, but Kelsey winked at her and told her to relax. Theo grabbed a big handful of the tail and pulled it to one side, then the other, creating a wide, swinging, circular momentum that really did feel like flying.

"Oh my God," Sara yelled. "This is crazy."

"I know, right?" Kelsey laughed like a maniac. Below them, Theo smiled and guided their flight. Each time he pulled the tail out a little farther, so they went in greater and greater circles, until the sky above them spun in a dizzying whirl. *Life is about hanging on*, Sara thought, clinging to the silk. *Sometimes it's just about hanging on for the ride.*

She half-laughed, half-cried thinking about Jason coming to Marseille, and hung on for dear life until Theo took pity on them and let them down.

* * * * *

Jason flew to Marseille Sunday afternoon with Lemaitre. The trip to the picturesque coastal city only took an hour and a half in his private jet. They didn't chat. Lemaitre worked on his laptop, occasionally pausing to stare out the window. Jason drifted, lost in memories of his times with Sara, both the good and the bad.

What now? he wanted to ask Lemaitre. *You started all this. How will it end?* They all moved through Cirque's world by his hand, like human chess pieces on an extremely colorful board. If Lemaitre approved Sara's act, then he'd send her to perform somewhere and Jason would go with her. That was going to happen. The rest of it—the hows, whens, and whys—were still up in the air, like Sara's red trapeze.

Or would it be some other color now?

He didn't know. Even Lemaitre didn't know, and Theo wasn't talking. All he would say to Jason's pleas for information was, "You'll see."

"Oh God," he muttered under his breath. He was so nervous for her, so stressed. Lemaitre turned to him but didn't comment. Jason assumed the Cirque CEO would be staying in his Marseille residence while they were here, probably with a select group of his local slaves, but Jason had booked a hotel room closer to the theater and Theo and Kelsey's place. Closer to Sara.

Jason wasn't offended when Lemaitre declined his invitation to dinner, but he was frustrated. It left him alone with his anxious thoughts. He ended up dining alone at a sidewalk café and walking around afterward. He wandered in and out of a couple jazz clubs, but his heart wasn't in it so he headed back to the hotel. It wasn't even eight.

He took a long, steamy shower and distracted himself with some emails before bed. The sooner he went to sleep, the sooner tomorrow would come, and that was the day he got to see Sara again. Surely she'd talk to him. He could tell her all the things he should have said before, that he was her Master and she belonged to him, and that he had a cage with her name on it back in Paris, and that she'd been a very bad girl to run away.

No, he couldn't say that. He wanted to, but no.

He had to tell her the other stuff, like how he couldn't concentrate on work, and how often he checked Marseille's weather. He had to tell her how sorry he was for squandering her trust, how empty his life was now that she'd gone. He'd tell her he'd do anything to win her back, even if it meant just being Jason and Sara for a while, without the Master/slave stuff.

His phone pinged and he glanced down to find a text from Theo.

You're here? Marseille?

Yes, he typed.

Where?

Hotel Arbruste
Rm 17
Come by?

If Theo would meet him for a drink, he could pump him for details about Sara. Maybe he'd even take a message back to her. He waited a long time for Theo to reply, and when he did, it wasn't the answer he expected.

Sara wants to come.
It's okay?

He read the text twice to be sure he wasn't seeing things.

She wants to come here?

Yes, okay?
I'll bring her.

Theo was going to bring her. *Sara.* Sara was coming back to him, just as Lemaitre had said. Whether she was coming as a slave or lover or friend, Jason didn't care. He typed back the only word he could think of.

Now. Now.
Now now now now now.

Chapter Seventeen: Re-Bound

Jason wanted to run downstairs so he could meet her as soon as she arrived, but there were several entrances to the hotel. God forbid he missed her. In the end he waited in the room, pacing, going out of his mind. He looked down at his phone, reading and re-reading Theo's texts.

Sara wants to come.

It's okay?

He didn't say why Sara wanted to come, especially the evening before her big performance. What if she wasn't returning to him? What if she didn't want to be his slave anymore? What if she was quitting Cirque du Monde altogether, and coming to tell him goodbye?

Theo would have warned him if that was the case. No, she was coming back to him. When he heard the knock he flew to the door, fumbling with the lock just as he had so many months ago in Mongolia. *Hold on a second. Don't go.* When he opened it she was standing there beside Theo, blinking her beautiful eyes.

"*D'accord*," said Theo as they stared at each other. "Be good, you two."

Jason would have thanked him but he was already down the hall, and Sara was in his arms, hugging him, burying her face in his neck. "I'm sorry, I'm sorry," she repeated over and over. His eyes fluttered closed. While she was away, it had been like missing some vital organ, his heart or his lungs, but now she was back and he could breathe again. He inhaled against her hair, remembering the smell of her, the shape of her, the weight of her against his body.

"I missed you," he said, clutching her close. "God, I missed you so much."

"I missed you too." Her fingers dug into his skin. "I'm sorry I left without saying goodbye. I needed time."

"I know."

"I'm sure you were angry. But I'm back now, if you want me."

"Of course I want you," he said. "But how are you?" He touched her hair, her face, her eyes, learning each part of her again. "Are you okay? Did you have the time you needed? I'm so sorry, Sara. I'm sorry I hurt you and lost your trust."

"You were trying to protect me. I realize that now."

He was supposed to explain all that, but she understood already. She possessed some new peace, some serenity he hadn't seen in her before. She had changed during her time in Marseille. Grown, matured, whatever. She was different now.

He squeezed her, trapping her in his arms. "I want you back, little one. Right now. We belong together. Even when we fight, even when we make mistakes, I want you beside me. I can't be happy without you."

None of these words were enough to explain the depth of his feelings so he kissed her instead, a long, deep, searching kiss as he held her close. *My lips. My beautiful body. My Sara. Mine.* She kissed him back, pressing against him like she wanted to blend into his body. His cock filled and rose between them, and he shook with the effort not to throw her down and take her. Instead he broke the kiss and tilted her head back, and looked into her eyes.

Such longing. She might have changed but she was still all there, his precious slave girl, adoring and eager to please. "I missed you," he said, and this time it was a growl of frustration.

She ducked her head. "Are you going to punish me for leaving? I deserve it. I should have forgiven you, the way you forgave me."

He wove his fingers into her hair and squeezed until her lips parted in a whine. "I understood that you were upset," he said against her cheek. "Maybe someday I'll punish you on principle. But right now, I'm more of a mind to reward you for coming back." He undressed her, yanking off her shirt and jeans, tossing them over the hotel chair. She scrabbled at his button and zipper. They probably should have talked more, become re-acquainted with each other before they got naked and started playing, but this had been their mode of operation from the beginning. She wanted to be on her knees and he wanted her on her knees, staring up at him, waiting for instructions.

"Master?" She clung to him as he stripped off her bra and panties. "You won't...you won't be too nice to me, will you? Because you missed me?"

He chuckled and took her elbow, holding it behind her back. "Are you trying to top me from the bottom? Who decides how 'nice' I am?"

"You do, Master."

"Yes, I do."

"I'm sorry," she said as he pinched and then slapped one of her nipples.

"Maybe I'll be so nice to you that you can't stand it. So nice that it makes you sick."

"You could never make me sick, Master," she cried, a smile playing at the corner of her lips.

"All right, sillypants. Enough." He twisted her arm a little further, pinched her nipple a little harder and pressed his lips to her neck. "Who are you?"

She didn't hesitate. "I'm your slave. I love you, Master."

His cock ached at every word. He ordered her to the floor and waited for her to assume her slave pose. She sat back on her ankles and parted her legs wide, arched her back and stuck her breasts out. So pretty. His cock rose hard and insistent in front of her face. She stared at it with such worship, such hunger. How on earth had he found this girl…and how had he ever let her go?

He grabbed the back of her neck to bring her up on her knees and used his other hand to guide his cock into her warm, wet mouth. Her tongue slid along the underside, teasing, caressing. The pleasure almost took his legs from under him. He eased deep in her throat. She gagged, but then stared up at him as if to beg for more. The sensation would have been enough, but her enthusiasm made it ten times hotter. A hundred times hotter. Way too hot, actually. If they didn't stop, this encounter would be over before it started.

"Hold on." He drew away, fighting the urge to plunge back into her mouth. "I want your shoulders on the floor. Ass in the air. I want to see everything," he added. "So spread those legs."

She complied, assuming the position he'd first put her in at the hotel in Ulaanbaatar, before he knew who she was, before he realized she'd be his for life. Her shoulders rested on the floor, her hands above her head. She spread her knees and arched her ass up just as instructed. It was a position of offering, of utter vulnerability.

Mine. All mine.

He made her wait like that, exposed to his gaze, for a full minute before he spoke. "Who are you?" he asked for the second time.

"I'm your slave, Master," she answered in a trembling voice.

He knelt beside her to trace the neat line of her spine, the curve of her hips, and then he slid a finger into her pussy. Ah, so wet. He drew the moisture over her clit and caressed it. She moaned, but she didn't move. She was his, truly his.

"You don't take pleasure unless I give it to you, yes?"

"Yes, Master," she sighed.

"Do you want me to stroke your clit? Do you want me to make you come?"

She twitched then, the slightest bit. "If it pleases you. I want what you want."

Jason let out a soft laugh. "I wish I had a cane. That's what I want, to mark you. You don't have any marks at all. You were away from me too long."

"Yes, Master."

He stood and went to his jeans, and pulled his belt from the loops.

*****

Sara pressed her cheek to the floor. How she'd missed this...the fear and intensity, the pleasure and pain rolled into one. Jason was the only man who'd ever excited her like this, to the point where she would do anything, endure anything at his hand. As he pulled his belt from his jeans, she got wetter and arched her ass higher. *Hurt me. Please.*

She sensed more than heard him draw his arm back, and then there was pain. *Oww...* He'd started with a medium-strength stroke just under her ass cheeks. She made a sound that was half agony, half jubilation. More pain followed, *whap, whap, whap,* fire licking against each cheek and then across her whole ass. Oh God, it *hurt.* The strokes rose in intensity because he meant to mark her. He placed them on top of each other to bring the strongest sting. All she could think was, *more, please more.*

He stopped, rubbing the edge of the belt against her swollen clit. Now, she couldn't help it. She arched back against it. It was greedy and undisciplined but she ached for his cock and her self-control was running low.

"Do you still want whatever I want?" His low voice rumbled with an edge of menace. "Because now I want to hurt your pussy. I want to whip you right on your thrusting little clit."

"I want what you want, Master. Even if it hurts."

He rearranged himself so he was standing over her, facing away from her shoulders. He leaned down and slapped her pussy a few times, and already, that hurt enough, but he wasn't finished. She whimpered as he slid his belt between her legs. Why did he make her wait?

She knew why. So she'd have plenty of time to get scared. By the time the leather snapped down against her slit, she was beside herself, and the pain... The stroke felt sharp and awful, especially against flesh that was buzzing with need. "Oh," she cried. "Please, Master."

"Please, again?"

She made fists beside her head. "Yes, please."

He whipped her clit again, and again, and she couldn't help but jerk. He trapped her hips between his legs to keep her still and then he whipped her continuously, sometimes on her clit, sometimes on her pussy lips, sometimes on her inner thighs. She stopped trying to be brave and let the cries and groans come. In his bedroom, he would have told her to hush, or gagged her to silence, but here he let her make her sounds. Soon, they weren't groans, but pleas for satisfaction. *Please fuck me, please fuck me.*

"Do you want to come, little one?"

"Yes, please," she begged.

"I want you to come while Master's hurting you with his belt."

Oh, God... She could do it, but it was so humiliating, to make herself come jerking off against the edge of his belt. *You're his slave. You do what he likes.* She moved her hips as he slid the belt across her clit, alternately cracking her and tapping her, and then caressing her in a slow glide.

"Yes, baby," he sighed. "You come however I want, whenever I want. You look so beautiful, so hurt and turned on at the same time."

"Oww!" She cried out at the blow, as her clit exploded with pain. But then he stroked her and she could feel her orgasm blooming, a sharp promise of release. "Please, please..."

Every time she said *please*, her pussy paid the price. Even with his legs bracing her, her hips were going wild, seeking a climax just out of reach. *His belt's going to be a mess*, she thought. Good thing he had plenty of them. He could do this to her every day for a month if he wanted to, and never run out.

He could do this to her forever, if he pleased.

That was the thought that tipped her over the edge. Jason, her Master, her tyrant, her wonderful lover, he could control her forever. He could give her hurt, or orgasms, or even both at the same time. She gasped, her fists pounding the floor as her walls contracted. She wished he was inside, and then he *was* inside, driving into her, snapping his hips against her aching ass. Her clit felt hot and achy too, but it was the good kind of ache. His cock felt so huge inside her that her orgasm continued on. It was too much, almost too much.

"I want you to come again," he ordered. "Like you just did, only harder."

"I can't." Her body collapsed. She absolutely couldn't do *anything.* He jerked her hips up and smacked her on the ass.

"You can and you will, because I want it. Answer me. '*Yes, Master.*'"

"Ow...yes, Master," she cried as he spanked her again. She was so sensitive, so tense in the aftermath of her orgasm but he gave her no quarter. He took her pussy like he owned it, driving in, filling her walls so she felt every inch of his advance. *He does own it, Sara. He owns you.*

He gentled, slowed his driving rhythm and pressed his hands to the back of her shoulders. Her clit ached and pulsed and her ass cheeks burned where he held them. "I love you," she whispered into the floor. "I love you, I love you."

"What?" He pulled her head back by the hair.

"I love you," she said through bared teeth. She started to cry, not from pain or his deep, pounding strokes, but because she loved him so much. She'd missed him so much.

He pulled out of her and lifted her from the floor. Next thing she knew, she'd been tossed across the bed. She held up her hands and he grabbed them as he climbed on top of her. He pressed his cock inside her, holding her down so she couldn't move. "You're mine," he said against her ear, which meant so much more than "I love you." She fought against him, testing him, but he didn't let her go. His muscles slid over her skin, his power subduing her along with his cock buried inside her.

"I'm going to come again," she gasped. Because he was inside her, one with her, and it felt like heaven. She believed with all her heart that he cared for her and that she could trust him, even if he made mistakes. She'd made mistakes too. In the end, what mattered was that they loved each other and fit together in some perfect, eternal way.

He let go of her hands and she wrapped them around his shoulders, and snapped her hips against his. He held her so tight she could feel his heart pounding against hers, and then the pounding transformed into the waves of her climax. The waves grew stronger, not weaker, until she felt the pleasure everywhere—her body, her mind, her soul. Jason arched deep inside her, grasping at her as he reached his own release.

Sara went still beneath him, boneless in the aftermath. Jason shuddered through his orgasm, then he unraveled too, relaxing against her. He smelled warm and male, and so familiar. She buried her face in his hair and wiped away the last of her tears. *No more crying,* she thought. *I have nothing to cry for.* She was back with her Master where she was meant to be. She felt happy and protected. Safe.

And a little bit smothered.

"Master," she gasped. "I can't breathe."

He rolled sideways and brought her with him. She looked over into his deep blue eyes and thought, *they're so beautiful. If his blue eyes are beautiful, mine can be too.*

He traced a finger down her cheek. "Okay now? You can breathe again?"

Yes, she could breathe again now that he was here. She put her hand over his and traced his fingers. Her walls clenched, involuntary aftershocks from the power of her orgasm, caressing his cock that was still buried deep inside.

"Mercy," he said, laughing. "I just got you back. Don't kill me."

"I would never," she whispered.

He leaned to kiss her forehead and ended up kissing all over her face, all over the residual tracks of her tears. "Who are you? I want to ask it a million times."

"I'd answer a million times. I'm your slave. I love you so much."

"I love you more than that," he said, shaking his head. "I love you too much to find any peace of mind, but that's okay. You're worth it." He screwed his face into a threatening mask. "But if you ever leave me again...so help me."

She squirmed as he gave her another set of spanks. Then he levered himself up to check out her backside. "That's more like it. Your ass needs color. Always."

"Yes, Master."

He pulled away from her, fixed her with a look and said, "Stay."

She watched from the bed as he went over to his luggage and pulled out a box she recognized. Her promise ring was inside, still tied with her little blue bow. He came back to the bed and dangled it in front of her eyes. "I'll give this back to you on one condition."

She stared at the blue stone as it caught the light. "What condition? Anything, Master."

"No, listen first. You can have this back if you agree to marry me. Not right now. Not even this year if you don't feel ready. But eventually I want you to marry me because I want you forever, Sara. I want this to be our engagement ring." He captured it in his fingers, hid it from her in his fist. "But only if you want. Don't say yes just to please your Master."

She didn't like that the ring had disappeared. She wanted it on her finger right away, immediately. "Yes. Please. I want to be yours forever."

"You're sure?"

She took his hand, trying to peel his fingers open. "Yes, I want it."

"Marriage is forever. I won't let you go."

"No, I don't want you to. Mmph." She pried at his fist. "Please let me wear it."

He finally relented and opened his hand, uncurled his long, strong fingers and allowed her to have it. She shoved it onto her finger, blue ribbon and all. He took her hand and untied the bow, slipping it from beneath the band.

"Why did you tie this around the ring?"

"So it wouldn't get lost. So you would notice it there."

"I didn't find it. Your father did."

She closed her fingers and avoided his searching gaze. He tilted her head up so she had to look at him.

"He was there that night, Sara. The night I went looking for you, the night after you left. He cares about you, baby, he just doesn't know how to show it. Not yet."

She crept into his arms when he opened them, let him cradle her close. She hadn't thought much about her father, because it hurt too much and because it confused her. "I don't care if he cares about me," she said. But that wasn't really true. "I don't know. I don't know how I feel." She buried her head in his shoulder. "I'm afraid to see him again."

"You don't have to be afraid. He wants the best for you." He massaged her shoulders, running his fingers over her back. "Tell me about your act."

"You'll see tomorrow. It's a surprise."

"What does your costume look like?"

"Tomorrow," she said, giggling when he growled and shook her.

"You're not going to tell me anything?"

Her eyes were drifting closed. He was so warm, and his arms felt so protective. After weeks of honing her inner strength, she was relieved to surrender to him again. "I can tell you that I hope you'll like it. And that I love you, and that I'm going to be your wife someday."

He tapped a finger against her cheek. "I knew all that already."

"And your slave. Your slave-wife," she said with a yawn.

"I like the sound of that." He reached down and rearranged the covers, pulling them up so she was even warmer and cozier. "You have a big day tomorrow, little one."

"I hope you like the act. I hope you're proud of me."

"I'm already proud of you."

Those were the last wonderful words she remembered before she drifted into Jason-scented dreams.

Chapter Eighteen: Blue Skies

Jason lingered over Sara in the morning, kissing her, caressing her, stroking all the beautiful parts of her. He'd only just gotten her back, so he wasn't happy about letting her go.

But they had forever to spend together, and his talented trapezist needed to go to the theater and get ready for her act. Sara was excited but nervous. "You'll be great," he assured her, kissing her forehead. "And I'll still love you, even if you totally fuck up. Which you won't."

At the Marseille rehearsal facility, Theo and Kelsey took her into their custody. "We'll see you after the show," Theo said. "Oh, and Lemaitre is looking for you. Not in a good way," he added under his breath.

Shit. Jason wandered around the rehearsal space and then out into the main theater. He scanned the darkened seats and located the glow of a laptop in the far right corner.

"*Viens*," came the voice, and the imperious beckoning gesture.

Jason climbed the stairs to the top and sidled down the row. Long legs and auditorium seats didn't go together. He thunked his knee as he folded his tall frame into the seat a couple down from his boss.

"It's like being on a plane," Jason groused.

"These chairs are designed for an average-sized person. Which you are not." Lemaitre clicked a few more keys and tugged at his lips.

"What's wrong? Chewing someone out via email?"

Jason was joking, but Lemaitre answered him in seriousness. "There are problems in Paris. Attendance is down now that *Tsilaosa* is getting older. They want new acts but I don't know if new acts can save that show." He sighed. "But to let it go? It was my first production. Then other shows want updating, performers want to transfer, or tour, or stop touring, or have babies."

"Yes, they're people. They have lives."

"Aside from the artists, my directors are fighting, stabbing each other in the back and demanding special benefits for their shows and their casts. Then the disaster with the Exhibition." He threw up his hands.

"You're the boss. You'll handle it. Things will work out, they always do." He studied Lemaitre's drawn features. "Don't take this the wrong way, but you look like hell."

"I spent a restless night."

"A 'restless night.' Is that shorthand for brutally and repeatedly sodomizing a writhing bevy of slaves?"

"A writhing bevy of slaves? So poetic. But no. If you must know, I spent last night visiting Kelsey and Theo's place, where I expected to find my daughter." He looked at Jason in consternation. "She was not there."

Jason thought his smile probably said everything. Theo would have filled in the rest. "You should be happy, Michel. Happy for her and happy for me."

"I told you to leave her alone until she was finished creating her act."

"She's finished with it. She's performing it for you in a couple of hours," he said, looking at his watch. "And for the record, I didn't go to her. She came to me, just as you said she would. We got engaged for real last night, which I guess means I'm going to be your son-in-law someday." He shuddered. "That's disturbing."

"To you and to me," Lemaitre snapped. "I hope you plan to keep the promises you made to her. You'll have to leave Paris."

"Or you could keep her there," he pointed out.

Lemaitre didn't reply, just tightened his lips into a hard line.

"I think you'd like to keep her near you," he poked. "And God knows, she'd like to stay."

"She can't. She does trapeze."

"If the trapeze thing's such an issue, how about making a new show? Retire *Tsilaosa* and mount something different. You said yourself it's aging out, and Sara's right, this Minya-curse thing is bullshit. Maybe it's time to scrap everything and start again."

"Hmph." Lemaitre flushed around the ears, a brewing storm about to break. "Last I checked, you don't run this goddamn circus. I do. It's my company. My vision. My facilities. My people."

"Your daughter."

He gave Jason a withering look. "I have an ungodly amount of work to do, and a meeting with staff members in an hour. Perhaps you can find someone else to irritate for a while."

"You never used to be afraid of trying new things," Jason said in a parting shot. "The riskier, the better. I always admired that about you."

A muscle ticked in his boss's jaw, but he made no response.

Well, Jason couldn't make Lemaitre be a father to his daughter. All he could do was shelter Sara from the pain of that loss.

* * * * *

"Jason, I swear to God." Kelsey pressed down on his knee. "You're shaking the entire row of seats."

"I'm nervous, okay?"

"No need to be nervous," Theo said. "Not this time. She's got this."

Of course she had it, but Jason stewed over other things, mainly his conversation with Lemaitre. Jason could try to be everything to her: father, Master, lover, friend. But Lemaitre would always be there in the background, because they both worked for him. He'd be a constant reminder to Sara that he didn't want to claim her. It seemed an untenable situation, but what was the alternative? Going to some other, lesser circus?

"Lemaitre's in a mood," Jason said under his breath as the Cirque owner entered the theater. He was impeccably styled, as usual, in a designer suit and tie, but he didn't look like he had it together. Various staff members trailed behind him, some from Paris and other places, but most from Marseille.

"Who's that?" Jason asked Theo, pointing to an older man he didn't recognize.

"The director of *Brillante*."

While everyone settled into seats, stagehands prepped the act, dragging out Sara's safety mat and lowering her trapeze. It wasn't shiny and red like the last one, but a dull gray color with a thick rope hanging down from one side. A chill chased down his arms. The trapeze was a close replica of the one back in Mongolia.

He started bouncing his knees again, then stopped. He couldn't let nerves get the best of him. He had to be strong and support her efforts, whatever she chose to do, whatever she chose to reveal in her act. Wherever she chose to go afterward, even if it was back to Mongolia.

A few moments later, the house lights dimmed. Sara walked onto the stage in a blue and white leotard, nothing fancy. Her hair was done up in two buns with hair sticking out every which way, for a childlike, innocent effect. Her legs were bare because she needed them to grip the trapeze, but their bareness also added to her character's vulnerability. She stared up at the bar, touching the rope, studying it. Someone in the audience let out a soft laugh, unsure whether to be amused or not.

After testing the rope's strength, Sara began to climb up to the bar, flailing and straining as if it was a great challenge. Acting. She could have scaled it with one arm and two legs tied behind her back. Some of *Minuit*'s musicians provided the score, a spare, atmospheric melody, almost like a child's song. When she reached the top of the rope, she turned toward the audience, clinging to the bar.

Jason squinted, bemused. Her eyes were garishly blue, made up with jewels and what appeared to be bright blue feathers glued to her lids. She fluttered them with an exasperated expression. He laughed, everyone laughed, but some part of him was unsettled by the gravity in her features. From the comedic beginning, things got serious fast.

Sara hopped up on the bar, testing it with her toes. At one point, she pretended to lose her balance and fall, clutching the bar on the way down to save herself. Everyone gasped and many leaned forward in their chairs. It was a good sign her audience was engaged. From there she did another funny split that ended in her hanging upside down. Flutter, flutter, flutter. Those blue feathers fluttered like fake eyelashes gone wild.

She pulled herself up again as the music increased in complexity. Some deeper notes sounded. Sara's tricks grew more daring, more driven. If she was telling a story, it was her own story of experimenting and taking risks. After one release she fumbled the bar and caught the dangling rope instead. The audience gasped, someone even yelped. Theo growled beside him. "It's part of the act. She never misses."

Sara twirled around the rope, out of control but not out of control. She struggled back up to the top, pathetic and heroic. The blue-eyed girl who wouldn't give up.

Jason watched her, lost in the precision of her athleticism, and her body's strength. He'd watched her practice with Theo many times, but she had some heightened beauty when she performed, some artistic mojo that came from within. She did another series of tricks, splits and handstands and contortions of her body as she clung to the bar. She didn't smile. She did no more fluttering. Her features twisted in determination—

Then she fell and grabbed the rope again, sliding all the way down to the edge, so far down her toes almost touched the stage.

It was a performance. Jason knew that, but his heart ached for her. She hung from the rope with her head bowed, facing the audience. The blue feathers rested on her cheeks, the jewels at the corners of her eyes glistening like oversize tears.

She climbed again, pausing with each handhold, looking up in miserable resignation at the trapeze. Aside from the haunting music there wasn't a sound in the theater. No coughing, no shifting or shuffling papers. Jason could see Lemaitre down in the front, his eyes fixed on his daughter.

This time when she climbed up, she only sat on the bar, legs dangling. With the help of the spotlight, the feathers cast a long shadow on her cheeks. A moment later she reached over and unbound the dangling rope from the side of the trapeze, and dropped it to the ground in an exaggerated shove.

Oh, good girl.

Sara's blue-eyed character stood with a new conviction in her manner, and did the tricks again with all the energy of the previous attempts, only this time she didn't fall. She did handstands on the bar, spun around in flips, did a frozen split in mid-air with only her arms to support her. Her skills built to a rousing climax, her full artistry on display. Her strength and courage astounded him.

But then, it always had.

As the music reached a crescendo, a projector turned the scrim behind her a brilliant blue. Sara swung her trapeze, higher and higher. No tricks now. This was a different kind of finale, just Sara's wide blue-feather eyes looking into the expanse of "sky" above her. She'd completed a story arc...the struggle, the comeback, and now, the appreciation of her dreams. The lights faded until you could only see the barest flutter of her jeweled eyelashes, and then went out on the music's last note.

No one moved for long moments. The trapeze sailed up into the rigging with its blue-eyed passenger, and then the half-lights came up, illuminating the theater. Theo stirred beside him, glowing with pride. "My work is done here, no?"

Before Jason could frame some kind of response, Lemaitre was on his feet, heading for the doors.

"Where's he going?" Kelsey asked. "That's not the way backstage."

"Is he leaving?" Theo craned his head as the Cirque director disappeared down the aisle.

"He better not be fucking leaving." Jason jumped up and followed him. Sara had just poured everything inside her heart onto the stage, told her story with the entire audience in the palm of her hand. Michel Lemaitre wasn't leaving, not until he congratulated his daughter for what she'd accomplished.

"Michel," he called, following him down the narrow hallway that led outside. "Michel, stop. What the fuck?" He caught up to him and grabbed his arm. "You can't just leave."

Lemaitre shrugged his hand off. Jason stepped back as the dark-haired man faced him, his features twisted with anguish. Michel Lemaitre was in tears.

For a moment, Jason was struck speechless. In all the years he'd known Lemaitre, he'd never seen the barest hint of softness or sensitivity. Power, insistence, command, even anger, these were the faces he recognized. Not grief.

"You shouldn't be sad," Jason said when he recovered himself. "You should be proud."

"Proud of what?" he said, turning away. "Proud of all Sara had to endure while I cavorted around my theaters and clubs, thinking only of myself? Proud of how I didn't even bother to find out if she was dead or alive?" He walked a few more feet and pushed through a set of double doors to an outside patio. He collapsed on a stone bench and leaned his head against the balustrade. He looked like he'd aged ten years in the last day.

"Why are you still here?" Lemaitre said after a moment. "Go to her. She'll want to see you."

"You think she won't want to see you? You're her father. That means something."

"In our case it means nothing."

He crossed to sit on the bench beside him. "Don't be pathetic, Michel. It doesn't suit you."

Lemaitre turned to him, his piercing eyes clouded with pain. "I made her, Jason. That wondrous, talented artist on the trapeze. She's mine and I adore everything about her…but I have to send her away."

"No, you don't."

"Yes, I do, because I don't know how to *do this*." He twisted fingers in his thick, black hair. "I'll hurt her, even more than I've already hurt her. I'm not nice. I'm not fatherly or nurturing. I've thought about it, and I just can't see—"

Jason cut him off. "You can't see? Jesus, you see everything. You see things none of the rest of us can see. How it is you can't see opportunity in this? Opportunity for growth, opportunity for a relationship that might bring joy to both of you?"

"I can't do it. I don't know how."

"It's not that hard, damn it. Start by telling her how you feel. Tell her what you just told me, that she's wondrous and talented. That you adore her. You should be backstage right now talking to her, telling her how great she is. Telling her you're proud of her. That's what fathers do."

"I'm not her father. I don't have it in me."

The double door scraped open, and they turned to find Sara standing with Theo. She still wore her pale blue costume, her jewels and feathers obscuring her troubled gaze.

"Sara wonders if she could have a minute to talk to you," said Theo to Lemaitre. He nudged her forward at the same time he beckoned Jason to leave with him.

Let them work out their own affairs.

That had been Theo's take on things from the start, and as much as Jason wanted to protect Sara in this moment, he also knew she didn't need his assistance.

"Tell her what you told me," he said to Lemaitre before he stood. "She deserves to hear it. No matter what the two of you decide in the end, she deserves to know how you feel."

*****

Jason came to her and hugged her, and touched her face, and said he was so, so proud of her before he headed back inside with Theo. She was glad, because otherwise she might have fallen apart. Mr. Lemaitre looked unhappy. No, he looked miserable.

"You didn't like the act?" she asked. She wanted her voice to sound strong and professional, but it shook with nerves. "If you want me to change things, I can. The tricks are what's important. With Theo's help, I can adapt them to any theme."

No answer. She wanted to cry. She wanted to scream at him, *why are you like this?* Instead, she started yanking at her blue feathers, trying to peel them from her lids.

"Stop." Lemaitre flew across the patio and stilled her hands. "You'll hurt yourself. You'll hurt your eyes if you pull like that."

Sara looked up at him, this man with her exact same eyes, even the same dark ring around the middle. Was he concerned as her boss, or as her father? Did it matter? She found the edge of the feather adhesive and carefully peeled it away, then the other, more slowly than she would have if he wasn't staring at her with that grimace on his face. She closed the feathers in her hand, feeling the tickle against her palm.

"I'll change whatever you like," she said. "If you didn't like it—"

"I liked it."

"If you want to give me some notes—"

"I don't want to give you notes!"

Sara snapped her mouth shut at his sharp voice. This was so hard, trying to be performer and boss when both of them knew they were something more.

"I can tell you're unhappy," she cried. "Tell me how to change it. I can make it whatever you want."

"Didn't you hear me?" he said through tense lips. "I don't want you to change it. It's perfect as it is. I don't have any notes for you, no criticism or comments. Only one note, really." He lifted his arms at his sides. "I'm sorry. I'm sorry for everything you went through, all your struggles. I'm terribly sorry for not being in your life."

She bristled at his angry, angsty tone. "This act wasn't about you. It wasn't *for you.* It has nothing to do with you, because you weren't there. They were *my* struggles."

"Your struggles because of me. I got the subtext, my dear."

The way he said *my dear* snapped her last nerve. "Don't 'my dear' me," she said, glaring up at him. "You have no right to be upset. It was your choice to leave me there."

"I had to leave you there."

"And it was your choice to bring me here now. *Your* choice."

"I'm sorry. I'm sorry for everything, for all the ways I've hurt you." He blinked at her, a muscle ticking in his jaw. "Why are we yelling at each other?"

"Because I'm angry at you." She spit the words out, then everything came pouring out, all the feelings she'd kept bottled inside. "I'm angry. I'm furious with you and your fucking coldness. I hate you for not wanting me. I hate you for lying to me and being cowardly. And you know what? I'm angry that you don't want me. It's mean, and it's not fair. There's nothing wrong with me. *There's nothing wrong with me.*" She shouted it the second time, like she could convince him. Like she could convince herself. "I want you to want me and you won't. You *don't.* And I don't understand why."

She made fists and pounded them on his chest. *Why? Why? Why?* The word echoed in her brain, or maybe she yelled it out loud. She felt his arms come around her and she waited to be pushed away, but he pulled her close instead.

"Shhh. I want you, Sarantsatsral." He brushed a hand across her cheek and she felt tears, when she hadn't even realized she was sobbing. "Please," he said softly. "You're crying these tears for me?"

She pressed her face against his chest. "Yes. Because of you. I want you to be my father. I've tried not to want it but I do." She burst into another bout of sobs, then she felt his fingers against her hair, brushing through her messy buns.

"Beautiful daughter," he murmured. "I don't understand. How can you want me after all I've done to you?"

"I don't know," she said, drawing back to look at him. "I can't answer that. I just do." She looked down and realized her stage makeup had smeared horrible blotches onto his pristine suit. "Oh no," she said. "Your jacket is ruined. My makeup—"

"It's okay." He pulled a handkerchief from his pocket and dabbed it against her face. When she reached to take it, her feather eyelashes fluttered up between them. He snatched at them and caught them before a breeze could carry them away.

"That was close," he said, letting out a breath.

"I have more."

"But these are special. From the first time you did your act."

More superstition. What a strange, complicated man her father was. "Do you want to keep them?" she asked.

He nodded and slipped them into his pocket, and accepted his handkerchief back. She'd ruined it with foundation and eye shadow but he put it in his pocket too, and then he took her hand. "You know, it was a lot easier for me when you were a concept. My faraway daughter. A secret child I never thought to meet."

"Yes, well, it was a lot easier for me before I knew you were my dad."

"That's what I was afraid of. I thought I could bring you from Mongolia and put you in a show somewhere. I thought it would be enough for me, to know you were happy and safe, and provided for. But now I realize..." He touched her hair again, with an infinitely tender gaze. "I realize I can't bear to send you away."

The whole last month, she'd ached for this kindness, this recognition. She wanted to stay with him and be his daughter…but she wanted to do trapeze too. "What will I do if I stay?" she asked. "There's no act for me."

He released her and leaned against the balustrade. "That's the rub. I'm sorry, *ma petite.* I can't send you into the rafters of *Tsilaosa.* A woman died, a woman who looked so very much like you. It's too much risk. Too much bad luck."

"Her bad luck. Not mine."

"Sara, I can't."

"It's silly, this superstition. I'm great at trapeze."

He turned his head sideways and scowled. "You almost fell at the Exhibition, remember? I still have nightmares about it, and probably always will."

"That was different. It had nothing to do with any weird circus curse."

He said something fierce and blustery in French and stared out at the city for a long while. Then he straightened with a sigh. "Perhaps there is a way. Your fiancé suggested an entirely new show."

"In Paris?"

"Yes. To replace *Tsilaosa.* It's not a bad idea."

"And I could do trapeze in that show?" she asked, clasping her hands together.

Her father took a deep breath. "I might be able to bear it. You're very good at what you do. Very skilled."

His praise thrilled her, but something else thrilled her more. "You called Jason my fiancé."

"He is your fiancé, is he not? He told me he was."

"It's the first time I've heard it out loud," she said with a kind of wonder. "He's full of good ideas, isn't he?"

"Proposing to you was one of them. Even if I think you're too young."

She looked at him from under her lashes. "That sounds like something a father would say."

A glint of humor curved the edges of his lips. "It does, doesn't it?"

They stared at each other, and Sara could see the change in his eyes. Some barricade had lifted. *He's going to be my father. He is.* She felt so relieved, so happy. And a little embarrassed about the things she'd said in the heat of the moment. "I'm sorry I yelled at you and said I hated you. I didn't mean it. And I'm sorry about your clothes."

He brushed at the stains on the front of his suit with a smile. "I hear that babies ruin their parents' clothes with regularity. And that teenage children are full of angry tirades. You're only making up for lost time." He sobered and reached for her hand. "We have a lot of lost time to make up for, but I'll do what I can. Sara…I'll try. I can't promise I'll get everything right."

She moved into his arms when he opened them. "I won't get everything right either. That's how families are, I guess."

And this was how families hugged. This time their embrace wasn't stormy, with pent up emotions. It felt natural. Relaxed.

"So, if I mount a new show in Paris, you'll help me?" he asked against her ear. "You inspire me, you know."

His words settled in her heart, a forever-memory. "Of course I'll help."

He clasped her closer and rested his cheek against her hair. "I'm proud of you, Sara. I love you. I'm glad you're my daughter. I've wanted to say all of those things for some time now."

She didn't say anything. She couldn't. She just breathed in, and breathed out, and thought how wonderful it was to be held again in a father's arms.

Chapter Nineteen: To This

Jason paced the living room and watched out the window, waiting for Sara to get home. As soon as they'd returned from Marseille, he'd asked her to move in with him, so his home was her home now. Both of them were staying in Paris for the foreseeable future, thanks to the new show, and she was wearing his ring. At some point he'd make his eternal girl into his eternal bride, when they had time to sit down and plan a wedding.

That time wasn't now.

A lot had happened in the last few weeks. For one, they'd entered the planning stages for *Cirque Élémental*, a new production based on the elements: fire, air, water, earth. Sara's act fit perfectly in the air category, and several other acts were being developed with complementary themes. She'd worked hard to regain her cast mates' trust after the Baat debacle, and eventually, the whispers and judgments faded away, replaced by different whispers: *She's his daughter. Lemaitre's her dad!*

Lemaitre let the gossip engine spread the news that he was Sara's father. To spare her embarrassment, he led everyone to believe she'd known all along, and chose to keep it a secret since he was the big boss. And after all his doubts and reservations, Lemaitre impressed Jason with his paternal instincts. Lemaitre gave his daughter attention, but didn't smother her. He tried to make up for lost time, but didn't stress over all the history they'd missed.

All of this suited Sara perfectly. She adored her father and called him "daddy," which was sweet if slightly squicky. Both of them were happy, and that made Jason happy too. Lemaitre took Sara out to dinner every Saturday night, and no one, not even Jason, could interfere in this father-daughter time. He tried not to be jealous, and anyway, Sara told him all about their evenings as soon as she got home.

At last he saw her getting out of Lemaitre's car and waving goodbye. After the rat-a-tat of her shoes on the staircase, he met her on the landing and embraced her. He never got tired of touching her. He'd never take her closeness for granted after that long month she was away from him. When he kissed her, she tipped her head back for more.

"Oh, baby," he whispered against her lips. He rubbed her neck and gripped it just to hear her moan. With his other hand he undid the button on her skirt, easing it down along with her black silk panties.

"Where did you go this time?" he asked, starting on the tie at the back of her blouse.

"Vietnamese," she said. "It was delicious."

"You're delicious." She giggled as he nibbled her shoulder. Her blouse came off, and then her lacy bra. Pretty but unnecessary, especially at home where he kept her naked. This undressing was a custom of theirs now, a ritual of his ownership and her slavery. He gave one of her nipples a pinch.

"Any news? How's your dad?"

"He's well. Hard at work on *Élémental*, just as you are."

He smiled. "And you too. All of us are in this."

"He said only one act is driving him crazy. An acrobat. He said you'd know who it was."

Jason did know how it was, but he didn't want to think about that now. Sara whined as he pinched a little harder, then he bent to lick the ouchy away. He had no reason to punish her. Well, except that she liked it. She drew in a breath as he teased the other nipple. "He also said he heard from Baat. He's finished with rehab and doing really well. He's even gone back to work."

"With Circus Mongolia?"

"No, in a touring circus this time. In a larger troupe."

Jason was happy for Baat, but Sara had always been his primary concern. He slid his hands lower and grabbed her ass, squeezing the cane tracks he'd put there last night. Her hips bucked against his front, and she reached—without permission—for the front of his jeans.

"No," he said, pushing her hand down. "Not yet. Talk to me first. So Baat's better and he's working again. Is there any chance he'll come back to the Cirque?"

"I know he won't." She went up on her tiptoes as he fingered her slit. "Daddy—Daddy says he has a new partner with lots of experience. That she's very good."

"God, Sara. It's so weird when you call him daddy."

"Why? He's my dad."

Jason smiled and smoothed the lines from her forehead. "I know he's your dad." He stopped molesting her a moment to gauge her mood, her reaction to this news about her ex-partner. "How do you feel about Baat working with someone else? Does it make you sad?"

"No. I'm glad he's better, and I hope she makes him happier than I did. He deserves someone more like him. Someone who's content to stay in Mongolia, someone not always focused on crazy dreams."

He took her face in his hands and cupped her cheeks. "I'm glad you had crazy dreams. They brought you to me. To this. You're exactly who you should be." He waited for that to sink in. "And you're exactly where you should be, here in my arms."

"I know, Master."

"Do you really know? Or do you need me to prove it?" Her shiver and fearful look started a pulse in his cock, a drumbeat that seemed to pound whenever she was near.

"I love when you prove things to me," she whispered. "When you really prove them hard."

"Upstairs, little one," he said, turning her toward the hall. "Wait at the foot of the bed. I'll be up in a minute." *As soon as I compose myself. As soon as I regain my control.*

If I ever regain my control, now that you're in my life.

*****

Sara skittered upstairs and dimmed the lights to her Master's preferred scene level, and then positioned herself to wait at the foot of his bed. Their bed. It was her bed now too, with her Mongolian leather cuffs bolted to the headboard, and a matching pair he'd ordered for the footboard. The bed was set up to restrain her more than offer relaxation, but that was okay with her.

Since she'd moved in with him, they'd developed all kinds of habits and protocols that kept her in a constant state of longing. The way he touched her, the way he talked to her, the way he kept her naked, the way he sent her upstairs whenever he liked...

He wasn't only a Master, though. He was a caring fiancé too. He took her on dates and bought her gifts, and talked a lot about their future. He could be tough and exacting, and then be so sweet she wanted to cry. She never knew what she'd get with Jason. Sometimes she got both sides of him at once, and those were the most wonderful times.

She heard his footsteps and straightened up her slave pose, arching her back a little more. Her pussy was already wet. It wasn't only the waiting. It was the way he made her do it, in that pose that offered everything, that forced her to be open and displayed for his pleasure. He required that pose because it reminded her she was his, that her body was his to use however he wanted, whenever he wanted.

Oh God, she got so out-of-her-mind horny whenever she thought about it.

Her feelings must have shown on her face, because as soon as he looked at her, he chuckled and started stripping off his clothes. She stared as he revealed each elegant, muscular part of his body.

"Come here, Sara," he said when he was finished. "Look what I've brought you."

She hurried to him on her hands and knees. His gift might have been lingerie, or chocolate, or a hurty new whip. Any of them would have made her happy. But no, it was a coiled length of soft rope, custom-dyed in a pale blue color.

"Oh, Master. It's beautiful." She touched the woven edge. "Where did you find it?"

"I ordered it from a guy I know. I was inspired after watching your act." As he spoke, he knelt and drew her arms behind her, and started tying them together from elbow to wrist. Each tug, each touch, each whisper of his fingertips aroused her more. When he finished, he helped her stand and walked her over to the full-length mirror in the corner, and turned her so she could see what he'd done. He'd crafted beautiful knots, a ladder of them matching her eyes and her ring. As she looked over her shoulder, she caught his gaze in the glass. Her heart was too full to come up with fancy words.

"I love you," she said instead, tugging at the bindings. No, she couldn't get free. Which was good, because she didn't want to get free.

He squeezed and caressed her breasts. "Thank Master for helping you be a pretty, color-coordinated little slave."

"Thank you, Master." Against her better judgment, she added, "Although I think it's more for your benefit than mine."

He snorted. "Aching for a few more marks on your ass?"

She looked back to study those in the mirror too. "Yes, Master. If it pleases you."

Yes, Master. Thank you, Master. If it pleases you. Such a limited vocabulary for the depth of these games they played. He put a finger under her chin and tilted her face up. "Who are you?"

"I'm your slave, Master."

"Are your eyes pretty?"

"Yes, Master."

"Is every part of you lovely and beautiful to your owner?"

"Yes, Master," she said through gathering tears. He always did this to her, made her get all emotional with only a look. A touch.

I love you, I love you, I love you. Touch me.

He moved his hands down her body, over the rope, over bare, sensitive skin. She didn't resist when he pushed her to the floor, arranging her with her cheek against the hardwood and her ass in the air.

"I love you, Sara," he said when she was in position. She made fists as he pushed his cock inside her, inch by lingering inch. In the end it didn't please him to give her any more marks, unless she counted the shadows left behind by the rope when he unraveled it. Even free from her fetters, she knew in her heart she was bound to him forever.

Eternal love, bound in blue.

The End

A Final Note

Thank you for reading this second book in my Cirque Masters series. If you haven't read the first one, you can find Theo and Kelsey's dramatic love story in the pages of *Cirque de Minuit.* The third story, *Master's Flame*, will be available in the spring of 2014 and will feature Michel Lemaitre. Please read the included excerpt for a sneak peak at Michel and Valentina's book.

Many thanks to my beta readers, Linzy Antoinette, Rebecca, and Doris, and to my editors Audrey, and Lina Sacher. Thanks also to Annabel's Army and Annabel's Naughty Brigade, my super-readers, whose tireless support and encouragement inspires me to write another day. I'm grateful for every review and every recommendation, and for the fact that you put up with my silliness on Twitter and Facebook. I love all of you. You know who you are.

An excerpt from *Master's Flame*, the third book in the Cirque Masters series, coming soon

Valentina had to walk fast to keep up with Michel Lemaitre's purposeful strides—and she *had* to keep up, because he hadn't yet loosened his grip on her hand.

Not that she minded. She could barely believe she was walking through the halls of Cirque du Monde's world headquarters on the arm of the powerful, sexy CEO. She'd liked Naples, and liked performing with her family as part of a traveling variety act, but they never left Italy. City festivals and community fairs were small time. She wanted to tour the world and the surest way to do that was to join Mr. Lemaitre's company, with shows in numerous countries and touring productions that traveled the globe.

And the man beside her? He was nothing less than a genius, and that excited her. He exuded some intensity, some electric energy that made her heart pound. No, not her heart. Her sex. The moment she met him, the moment he took her hand so many months ago in Italy, she had recognized him as a sexual creature and responded to him in kind.

Mr. Lemaitre was tall and muscular, his swarthy physicality as attractive to her as his piercing blue eyes. He was in his mid 40's, seasoned, elegant and handsome, the type of man who commanded attention and knew what he was about. His features were prominent, finely carved, their aristocratic haughtiness softened by his head of unruly hair. Glossy black waves tumbled over his forehead and behind his ears, tapered and tamed to a neater arrangement in back.

Tamed. It was an effort for him, she understood, this tame front. His exquisitely tailored suit, his styled hair, even his neatly manicured facial hair spoke of tamed impulses. Control. Nothing fascinated Valentina like an intriguing, complex man. Adei was charming and enthusiastic, but so much on the surface. So *sweet.*

Michel Lemaitre was not sweet. He was something else.

Mr. Lemaitre had stood and watched with no compunction as she enjoyed the pleasures of Adei's agile mouth. She knew it was poor behavior to steal away with Adei, but as always, in the moment, desire won out over reason. Anyway, Mr. Lemaitre had seemed far from scandalized. Another reason she wanted to be here. Performers talked, and Cirque du Monde was known for its culture of sexual abandon. Adei had answered her come-hither stare without a second thought.

"Oh, I'm so happy," she burst out, skipping beside him. "This place is...is wonderful."

He looked over, dropping her hand to allow her to do an exuberant pirouette. "I do not doubt you think so," he said drily, "considering how you spent the last half hour."

"Half hour? It was only twenty minutes."

He raised a brow. "And before, in the showers?"

"Oh. That." Perhaps he was not completely approving. "I told Mr. Beck that man was my father, but he isn't really."

"I rejoice to hear it."

She couldn't pin down his tone. Was he angry, or teasing her? "My father is home in Italy," she said. "I met Lugo at a cafe and he wanted to come."

"He wanted to come, or you compelled him to come?"

"He had nothing better to do. He's very much a...what is the word? Slacker? Anyway, I think he's leaving."

She *hoped* he was leaving. Lugo's avid, clumsy lovemaking had thrilled her at first. She loved big, brutish men who grunted and groped. Then again, she loved cultured, urbane men too. She slid a look at *Signore* Lemaitre, who was large and had dark hair like Lugo, but was nothing at all like him. She wondered what it would be like to share a bed with him. She'd heard that the Cirque founder was omnisexual and intensely dominant.

Fascinating. A fascinating and intriguing man.

He paused, bringing her to a stop. "In here, if you please."

He guided her through a set of double doors into an office complex. There was an outer waiting area with conference rooms and cubicles, and Cirque posters decorating the walls. She loved design and art, and the entire office sang with artistic energy. The area was flanked by a frosted glass wall with a door that read *Michel Lemaitre, Cirque du Monde*. She suppressed a frisson of excitement as he led her inside with a light touch on her back.

"Please have a seat, Miss Sancia." He nudged her toward a worn leather arm chair facing his desk as he removed his suit jacket and hung it near the door. She looked around at the memento-laden shelves, at polished wood furniture that spoke of refinement, wealth, and success. These walls too were decorated with posters and photographs of Cirque performers in rehearsals and shows. She recognized some of them. They were the trailblazers, the outstanding ones. She hoped she would earn a place on his wall one day. He only had to give her a job to do. She would perform the hell out of it, whatever he wanted. She lived for the high of performance, for that soaring feeling of expressing herself. *Please*, she thought, turning her eyes back to him. *Please let me express myself here.*

His eyes locked on hers across his desk and for a moment she felt frightened by the depth of his scrutiny, not that she had anything to hide. She lived in the open, as herself, as much as society allowed. She hoped he would respect that. "Well," she said, as silence spun out between them.

"Well," he repeated with a slight quirk to his lips. "First, I must commend you. Your English is excellent. Much better than my Italian."

She felt pleased at his compliment, although language came easily to her. "I have never had problems learning things."

"I'm glad to hear that."

"I can help your Italian if you like."

He tilted his head at her. Did he hide a smile? "I believe we'll limp along just fine in English," he said. "Miss Sancia—"

"You can call me Valentina if you like," she interrupted. "Or Tina. My friends call me Tina."

"I am your employer, not your friend."

His curt reminder both devastated her and turned her on. "Of course," she said, sitting on her hands to keep them still.

He pushed forward a thick file on one side of his desk. "Miss Sancia, do you know what this is?"

"My dossier?"

"Yes. Do you know what is inside it?"

She bit a lip, thinking over his question. "Complimentary things, I hope. Any police reports…they are not to be believed. I did not vandalize that fountain, merely went swimming in it because the water was so beautiful that day."

"Miss Sancia—"

"And I was only naked because, well, I had on my favorite dress and I didn't want to ruin it. I was not even fully naked. Just mostly naked."

"Miss Sancia—"

"And that other time, no matter what the report says, I did not force the Italian councilman's sons into any inappropriate behavior."

His blue eyes widened. "*Sons*? Plural?"

"Monsieur, I never would have. I merely—"

"There are no police reports," he said, cutting off her rebuttals. "Although we may continue this discussion at another time. This dossier contains my talent scout's notes, photographs, and my own notes from our brief meeting last year. Do you remember?"

She nodded. How on earth could she forget? What was the purpose of this private meeting? Was she not officially hired yet? Had he gone over her dossier and decided she was not, after all, a Cirque du Monde-caliber artist? She was beginning to regret stealing a little "private time" with the handsome gymnast in the unused room. "About before, about the man who was..."

"Going down on you on my conference table?" he provided.

"Yes. It was a matter of impulsive urges."

"Obviously."

"The man—"

"His name is Adei. Please do not disappoint me by stammering out excuses. I admire your carnal enthusiasm. However, we are not in the habit of constant, promiscuous, and public sex here at our headquarters. The focus must be on training for roles and performances."

"Of course," she said in apology.

"That is not to say we don't satisfy our sexual urges at other times, in other, more appropriate locales," he added. "But while you are here in the training facility, please refrain."

"Yes, sir." She tried to appear duly censured but couldn't help looking at him sideways with a flirtatious smile. For a moment he gazed at her, a probing, prolonged look that was not flirtatious in return. Then he shook himself and looked down at the folder on his desk.

"Anyway, about your file. You have probably realized by now that you've not been brought here to blend into the background of some existing cast. Like many who see you perform, I find myself compelled. Inspired." He leaned back in his chair and fixed her with an intent look. "Do you know what it means to inspire a man like me?"

Valentina wasn't one hundred percent sure she knew what it meant, but she acted on her best guess, rising to her feet and crossing to kneel before him. She could barely keep her excitement in check as she reached to unbuckle his belt.

"No." His hands came over hers, stilling them. "No, my dear. Not that."

"Oh."

"Oh, indeed. You begin to alarm me. Is there some...condition? If so, please be honest with me. We'll work with it as well as we can."

"A condition?" she asked, her cheeks flushing with embarrassment.

"A medical condition which requires you to have sex at least once an hour? As I said, please be honest. There will be no repercussions, and we will make allowances as we may."

"No, there's no medical condition." She straightened, wishing there was a way she could instantaneously be sitting back in her chair. "I'm sorry. I misunderstood what you were asking."

"That seems patently clear. When I want sex from my partners, I am very direct about it." He indicated that she should go sit down again. "If I am not demanding sex from you, you may rest assured it is not desired."

"I'm sorry," she said again, miserably. His cool tone wasn't mocking, but Valentina nonetheless felt mocked. "I do have a bit of a condition. I am too enthusiastic sometimes. Too impulsive and passionate, not just with sex, but everything."

"These are excellent problems to have, in my opinion. Before I knew you were called *La Vampa di Napoli*, I sensed you had a bit more fire than everyone else. I need your fire, Miss Sancia."

She stared at him, at his broad, classically handsome face, his generous mouth. What was there to say to such a man? "You can have my fire, *signore*. As much as you want."

He leaned forward, fixing her with the full weight of his stare. "What if I want all of it?"

Did he mean—? She leaned forward to go to him again.

"No." He held up a hand. "I do not mean that. I mean that we are to mount a new production here in Paris. New cast, new performances, new blood. I have conceived a show about the elements, but it needs a central symbol. A flame, a fire, an explosion of life to anchor the rest of the acts. You understand? The show needs a spirit to drive it. You have this spirit and I want to use it to delight Paris audiences. The production will be named *Cirque Élémental*."

"But..." She wasn't sure what he was asking of her. "I'm an acrobat, a banquine flyer. I don't have an act to last an entire show."

"Not an entire show. There will be other acts, but you'll be the show's figurehead, the vision on the poster. We'll create an entire production with ten or fifteen other acts. Dance, lights, costumes, humor and pathos, feats of strength and agility. You know...circus."

The steady tone of his voice never altered, but some deeper challenge in his gaze excited her almost beyond bearing. At the same time, he was making it clear he wanted her artistry, not her sexual advances. He hadn't wanted her on her knees before him. Very sad.

"I will do whatever you like, Mr. Lemaitre. Simply tell me." She gave him a look, one she hoped communicated that she was his vessel to use, artistically or otherwise. "Whatever you want from me, sir, I am yours."

Sign up for Annabel's Naughty Newsletter at annabeljoseph.com to learn more about upcoming releases and promotions.

About the Author

Annabel Joseph is a multi-published BDSM romance author. She writes mainly contemporary romance, although she has been known to dabble in the medieval and Regency eras. She is known for writing emotionally intense BDSM storylines, and strives to create characters that seem real—even flawed—so readers are better able to relate to them. Annabel also writes vanilla (non-BDSM) erotic romance under the pen name Molly Joseph.

Annabel loves to hear from her readers at annabeljosephnovels@gmail.com.

Made in the USA
Middletown, DE
04 February 2016